SOMETHING'S KNOT KOSHER

Lucy wrinkled her nose and sniffed. "What is that smell?"

I put up my hand. "You and Jazz better stay here, Birdie. Come on, Lucy."

I took my tall friend's arm and walked with her toward the back of the hearse. The rear door had popped open, allowing the coffin to fly out the back. The big casket now lay gaping open on the ground.

The good news was, that despite my worst fears, Towsley had not cheated Birdie. Russell's body had been perfectly preserved by the embalming fluids.

The bad news was, I now understood what Arthur tried to tell me when he jumped on the side of the hearse and barked.

Russell wasn't alone.

On top of his body lay the source of the awful smell—the decomposing body of a strange man with dark hair . . .

Books by Mary Marks

FORGET ME KNOT

KNOT IN MY BACKYARD

GONE BUT KNOT FORGOTTEN

SOMETHING'S KNOT KOSHER

Published by Kensington Publishing Corporation

SOMETHING'S KNOT KOSHER

MARY MARKS

KENSINGTON PUBLISHING CORP.
http://www.kensingtonbooks.com

KENSINGTON BOOKS are published by

Kensington Publishing Corp.
119 West 40th Street
New York, NY 10018

All Kensington Titles, Imprints, and Distributed Lines are
available at special quantity discounts for bulk purchases
for sales promotions, premiums, fund-raising, and educa-
tional or institutional use. Special book excerpts or cus-
tomized printings can also be created to fit specific needs.
For details, write or phone the office of the Kensington
special sales manager: Kensington Publishing Corp.,
119 West 40th Street, New York, NY 10018, attn: Special
Sales Department, Phone: 1-800-221-2647.

Kensington and the K logo Reg. U.S. Pat & TM Off.

ISBN-13: 978-1-4967-0180-0
ISBN-10: 1-4967-0180-1
First Kensington Mass Market Edition: July 2016

eISBN-13: 978-1-4967-0181-7
eISBN-10: 1-4967-0181-X
First Kensington Electronic Edition: July 2016

10 9 8 7 6 5 4 3 2 1

Printed in the United States of America

For John William Marks, Ruth Helen Marks,
and Lee Anthony Marks.
Why was I the only one who didn't get a middle name?

ACKNOWLEDGMENTS

My thanks go first to my mentor Jerrilyn Farmer, my critique partner Cyndra Gernet, and my reader Nancy Jane Isenhart Holmes. I couldn't write a decent book without your help, insight, and encouragement. Also, many thanks to Betty Brown for the story inspiration.

As always, I have some experts to thank for keeping me accurate. My gratitude goes to Yeghishe "Jerry" Ayvazyan for his insight into the world of high finance. Thanks go next to Linda Greenberg Loper, Deputy DA (retired) LA County, and Malcolm Taw, MD, for their professional expertise.

I also want to credit my awesome agent, Dawn Dowdle, at Blue Ridge Literary Agency for her help and guidance. And finally, I offer slavish gratitude to my editor, John Scognamiglio, and all the talented folks at Kensington.

CHAPTER 1

I looked at the caller ID and smiled. My best friend, Lucy, often rang in the middle of the afternoon to chat. I fully expected to hear that her youngest grandchild had made the honor roll at Encino Elementary. I certainly wasn't prepared for the shocking news.

"Turn on your TV, Martha. Channel seven."

"Why? What's up?"

"It's bad. I'll stay on the line."

Her voice held an urgent tone I didn't like. I dashed to the living room and grabbed the remote. A local newscaster stood on the sidewalk on Ventura Boulevard next to yellow police tape. "This brazen robbery occurred two hours ago in front of a half dozen customers and employees of First Encino Bank. Witnesses said a single masked gunman forced everyone to lie on the floor in a back room and then pushed a hostage to the vault.

"A minute later, witnesses reported hearing four gunshots. The robber escaped carrying a duffel bag. When the police arrived, they discovered the body of the hostage inside the vault. His name is being withheld pending notification of next of kin."

My pulse hammered in my throat. "Oh my God, Lucy. Does Birdie know? That's Russell's bank." Birdie's husband, Russell Watson, was the vice president and manager of First Encino, Louise Avenue branch. "Who got shot?"

"I'm here with Birdie. We were visiting in her kitchen when the FBI came to notify her."

"Notify?" My stomach turned a flip. "Russell?"

"Yes. He's dead, Martha."

"I'll be right over."

Russell Watson hadn't been one of my favorite people. I never saw him treat Birdie with anything but indifference. Still, his shortcomings didn't justify murder. I couldn't predict how long I'd be gone, so I made sure my orange cat, Bumper, had enough food and water to last for a while. Then I grabbed my keys and jumped in my new Honda Civic. Less than five minutes later, I pulled up in front of Birdie's house behind two other cars, one a familiar silver Camry.

Lucy Mondello and Birdie Watson lived right across the street from one another in a more upscale part of Encino. My name is Martha Rose, and the three of us had been quilting together every Tuesday for sixteen years. We were so comfortable with each other, we didn't bother to knock before entering. I rushed up the stairs of Birdie's front porch and pushed the door open.

A pair of cozy, overstuffed green chenille chairs faced a slip-covered sofa in the living room of the California bungalow. Dressed in matching yellow blouse and trousers, Lucy sat next to Birdie on the sofa, hugging the older woman's shoulders with a comforting arm. Birdie wore her signature blue denim overalls and white T-shirt.

Across from them, a woman in a blue FBI jacket with yellow letters sat in one of the easy chairs. LAPD homicide detective Arlo Beavers sat in the other. My ex-boyfriend. In his mid-fifties, with a shock of gray hair and a white mustache, he appeared fit and as handsome as ever. Just the sight of him made my toes tingle. We exchanged a brief glance and then I rushed to sit next to Birdie and grabbed her hand.

"I'm so sorry, Birdie. I can't believe Russell's gone. You know you're not alone, right? You've got Lucy and me."

Birdie sniffed and reached a shaking, blue-veined hand toward the tissue box on the coffee table. She nodded and blew her nose. My heart broke to see how the shock and grief transformed her normally cheerful face. Her mouth hung slack and her eyes brimmed. She looked all of her seventy-six years.

"I know, Martha dear. I'm glad you're here." Silent tears spilled down her cheeks as she twisted the end of her long, white braid. She introduced the woman sitting in the chair as Agent Kay Lancet.

I nodded at the agent but looked at Beavers. "Do you know who did this? Why did they have to kill Russell? Why couldn't they simply take the money and run?"

Beavers pursed his lips under his mustache and shook his head once.

Agent Lancet wore her brown hair pulled back

into a severe, no-nonsense bun. "We don't have much information at this point. It's still early." She stood slowly and handed her business card to Birdie. KAY B. LANCET, SPECIAL AGENT FBI. "We'll do everything in our power to catch the people who killed your husband, Mrs. Watson. Meanwhile, if you can think of anything to help our investigation, please call that number. I'm very sorry for your loss." The heavy rubber soles of her boots squeaked on her way to the front door.

Beavers also rose and turned to me. "Can I speak to you outside?"

I followed him out the front door, curious. Agent Lancet drove away in an unmarked black SUV. Beavers and I hadn't spoken since December, almost seven months ago. I babysat his dog while he took his new girlfriend to Hawaii.

He turned his face toward me and his eyes softened. "How have you been, Martha?"

Those dark eyes. Why did I still find them irresistible? "Fine, until now. I'm still in shock."

He nodded. "Yeah. Nobody's ever prepared for a thing like this. Listen. Since this is a federal crime, the LAPD is officially off the case. But I know Agent Lancet. We go way back. She allowed me to come here as a courtesy when I told her I knew the wife of the vic. Can you think of anyone who might've wanted Russell dead? Did he have financial problems?"

"I haven't a clue. Why do you ask?"

"Just trying to help out."

"Well, Russell wasn't the warmest human being on the planet. He probably managed to piss off a few people in his time, but don't we all? Shouldn't you be asking Birdie this?"

Beavers ran his fingers through his thick gray hair and blew a puff of air out of his mouth. "Kay did ask her, but Mrs. Watson couldn't think of anyone. Maybe when the shock wears off she'll remember more. I figured she might've mentioned something to you and Mrs. Mondello in passing."

I shook my head. "Sorry." I turned to go inside.

He put up a restraining hand and cleared his throat. "Are you still seeing Levy?" Beavers referred to Yossi Levy, aka *Crusher*. Crusher and I had gotten together—sort of—after my breakup with Beavers. Seven months ago, Crusher, who led an interesting double life, caught a bullet in a shootout and almost died. He spent two months recuperating at my house. After I turned down his latest offer of marriage, he left LA for a new adventure in parts unknown. I hadn't heard from him since, and I missed him. But I didn't want to admit that to Beavers.

I answered with a question of my own. "Are you still dating what's-her-name? Kerry? The veterinarian?" I loved Beavers's German shepherd, Arthur, and hated the man-stealing vet.

"No. I broke up with her a while back. She was too . . . possessive."

I jerked my head up and snorted right in his face. "Look who's talking!" When I dated Beavers a year ago, he'd become jealous and demanding. When I refused to be manipulated, he broke up with me.

Beavers had the grace to stare at the ground and

said, "I'd like to take you out to dinner sometime. Just to catch up. Maybe start over . . ."

Did I hear him right? He wants to pick up where we left off? "I can't think about that, Arlo. The only thing I want to do right now is go back inside and help my friend."

He nodded and backed away as I turned around and pushed through the front door.

Lucy studied my face as I closed the door noisily behind me. Her perfectly penciled red eyebrows raised in question marks. I kept walking and bit my lip. I'd discuss my love life at a more appropriate time. Like when pigs came to Passover.

I headed toward the kitchen. "I'll make us a pot of coffee."

The items Birdie used every day were conveniently displayed on open shelves or behind glass doors in her old-fashioned kitchen. The glass-and-steel coffee press occupied a permanent spot on a counter paved with colorful Mexican tiles. I started a fire under a kettle of water on her large cast-iron stove.

The aroma of cinnamon and molasses led me to a freshly baked ginger cake cooling in a square jadeite dish. Birdie loved to bake in the mornings. Surely the present crisis justified my indulging in a slice. I'd think about Weight Watchers later.

I returned to the living room with a tray of steaming mugs and plates of cake. Birdie gratefully accepted coffee but declined the food. "I couldn't possibly eat anything, Martha dear. But you girls help yourself."

Lucy stretched, arching her back like a tall,

orange-headed cat. "What did Arlo talk to you about?" she asked, forking a piece of cake into her mouth.

"He asked if anyone would want Russell dead." I avoided looking at Birdie. "He also asked if you were having financial problems."

Birdie wrinkled her forehead. "Yes, Agent Lancet asked me the same questions, but I couldn't think of anybody who'd wish Russell harm. I mean, I wouldn't have been privy to something like that, anyway. Russell rarely talked about his work." She sighed. "As for financial problems, I really have no idea. He never bothered me with such things."

I understood what Birdie meant. She and Russell lived in a sterile marriage. They coexisted in separate bedrooms and didn't share much of a life. Why she had settled for such a loveless arrangement had baffled Lucy and me. But Birdie always replied, "He has his good points."

"Still," I persisted, "did Russell seem worried lately? Did he act any differently? Show some signs something bothered him?"

Birdie thought for a moment. "Well, he did get a disturbing phone call a week ago. Afterward, he was more snappish than usual." A look of alarm clouded her face. "Do you think the call's connected to his death?"

"Who knows? I mean, when a crook kills someone in a bank robbery, it's usually not personal. Right? So why ask if anyone wanted Russell dead? It's almost as if he thinks Russell was a target."

Beavers's question suggested Russell Watson's killing was deliberate. If so, did Russell know the masked man? Did he have money problems? Did he scheme to rob his own bank? Did something go wrong at the last minute that got him killed? I hoped not, for Birdie's sake.

Birdie looked off into the distance, wrung her hands, and muttered something I couldn't hear. She looked more fragile than I had ever seen her. Poor thing would be mortified if she learned Russell planned some kind of heist. I didn't want the FBI's suspicions to add to her distress.

I wished I knew more, but getting Beavers to part with any facts wouldn't be easy. He'd always been superprofessional. Conscientious. He never once revealed confidential details about a case when we were dating. Could I convince him to make an exception now because of Birdie?

Persuading Beavers to reveal any information would take a lot of finesse on my part but, for Birdie's sake, I had to try. I'd start with his invitation to dinner.

CHAPTER 2

The next hour Lucy and I helped Birdie focus on funeral arrangements—a process I had already become familiar with. Last year, right before Hanukkah, an attorney contacted me with the news I'd been named executor of a friend's estate. I accepted the sad duty of arranging for my friend's burial, along with untangling her very complicated life. At least I could help guide Birdie through the same procedures of dealing with the coroner's office and the funeral home.

Lucy cleared the coffee cups while I telephoned the mortuary and made an appointment for the following morning.

Birdie disappeared into her sewing room and emerged with an appliqué project—a barnyard scene featuring roosters with fancy tail feathers in dozens of different prints. "I need something to keep my hands busy. It helps to focus on sewing while we talk."

Lucy waved her hand. "Whatever works, hon! I

know this must be an awful shock. You and Russell were married for such a long time."

Birdie threaded her needle and sighed. "We knew each other for more than fifty years. We met in the fifties when we were students at Reed College in Portland, Oregon."

Lucy and I had heard this story before. The older Birdie became, the more she seemed to reminisce. She loved to recount the story about how she met her husband.

"I came from Massachusetts, but Russell was local. Fourth generation. His people traveled over the Oregon Trail in a covered wagon."

Lucy picked up a spool from Birdie's sewing kit and untangled the thread. "Does he still have family there?"

"After Russell's parents died, we didn't really keep in touch. There were problems between Russell and his brother, Denver." We had heard this before, too, but Birdie never offered any details.

"Do you want us to notify Denver?" I asked.

She shook her head. "I don't know if he's still alive."

"Did he have children? Shall we notify them?"

"Denver had a son, but I wouldn't know how to contact him. All I know for sure is Russell's parents are buried in McMinnville. Russell said when his time came, he wanted to be buried there as well."

"I'm certain we can make that happen, Birdie. I've scheduled an appointment with the mortuary in the morning. We'll go with you and help finalize all the arrangements, including transporting

Russell to McMinnville. Does he have a space in the family's plot?"

Birdie stopped sewing and frowned. "I don't know for sure. I assume he does."

"Don't worry, hon." Lucy squeezed Birdie's shoulder. "I'm sure they're used to handling situations like this. Right, Martha?"

The phone rang. Birdie put down her needle. "I don't think I can handle any calls right now."

I jumped up and headed for the phone. "No problem."

"Mrs. Watson? This is Tisha Goodall from LA Cable News. Can you give us an interview?"

"Mrs. Watson has no comment. Please don't call again."

Tisha Goodall spoke quickly. "If she could just step outside, this would only take a minute."

I peeked out the front window. Vans from all the major stations crowded the quiet residential street. Their antennas scraped the branches of the sycamore trees on the parkway. A vehicle with LA CABLE NEWS printed in tall blue letters partially blocked Lucy's driveway directly across the street. I stepped away from the window, closed the drapes, and spoke into the phone. "Mrs. Watson has no comment. Leave her alone."

A number of feet shuffled on the wide front porch, and someone knocked loudly. "Mrs. Watson?" A male voice this time. "Mrs. Watson, can we please talk to you?"

Birdie buried her face in her hands. "I—I don't

want to talk to anybody. Can't you make them go away?"

Lucy stood—all five feet eleven inches—and put her hands on her hips. "I'll call Ray right now." She reached for her cell phone. "He'll get rid of them *toot sweet.*" She made an air quote with the fingers of her free hand.

Lucy's husband, Ray Mondello, was usually a gentle, good-natured man. But he'd been an MP in Vietnam. If anyone could disperse a crowd, he could. Fortunately, Ray's auto repair shop was close by on Ventura Boulevard.

The knocking continued off and on for another minute before I got fed up. "I can't wait for Ray. I'm going out there."

I opened the door and a dozen microphones, cell phones, and cameras were thrust in my direction. I stepped outside and closed the door behind me, waiting silently for the barrage of questions to stop.

Once I had the reporters' full attention, I spoke. "Mrs. Watson is in mourning right now. She will not make a statement no matter how long you pound on her door or how many times you call her phone. Right now, you're trespassing. Do the decent thing. Turn around. Leave quietly. Respect her privacy."

Across the street, Ray barely squeezed his green Range Rover around the vehicle blocking his driveway and jumped out of his car. His shirtsleeves were rolled up and his mouth drew a grim line across his face. In addition, two of his biggest car mechanics, still dressed in greasy blue overalls, jumped out of the car. The three of them waded like Schwarzenegger toward the back of the crowd.

The reporters were unaware of the angry posse coming their way at first and began shouting questions again. Journalists in LA generally respected private property, but an armed robbery and the murder of a bank official had become a major story.

I took a deep breath. "Step away immediately, or I'll have you thrown out."

Ray and his guys pushed their way through the media hounds. A bearded man holding an expensive camera stumbled sideways. A man in a baseball cap stopped taking pictures with his cell phone and turned to leave, briefly revealing a tattoo on the side of his neck. The other journalists had to be pushed back to the street. A blonde in tan makeup from a major network shrieked in protest as a burly mechanic pushed her backward toward the sidewalk. Tisha Goodall.

Ray's voice boomed, "LA Cable News has two seconds to remove your vehicle from in front of the driveway across the street."

The media got the message and began to disperse. Ray turned to me over his shoulder and nodded once. I went back inside.

The phone rang again, and I answered it. "Watson residence."

The female voice on the other end dripped with concern. "This is Sandra Prescott. I'd like to speak to Birdie."

"What is this regarding?"

Her voice took on a commanding edge. "Just tell her it's Rainbow."

I placed my hand over the mouthpiece so the caller couldn't hear me. "Birdie, do you know someone named Sandra Prescott? She said to tell you it's Rainbow."

Birdie immediately stretched her hand toward the phone. "Oh! Give it to me."

Lucy looked at me and silently mouthed, *Rainbow?*

Birdie eagerly grabbed the phone and pressed it to her ear. "You heard? All the way in New York? No, I haven't been watching TV. My quilting friends Martha and Lucy are with me. He'll be buried in McMinnville. Of course I'll let you know when. It'll be a comfort to see you again, dear. I love you too."

Birdie handed back the phone. "She's an old friend from when we lived in Oregon. Rainbow has a business that keeps her pretty busy, but she'll be at the funeral."

The next few calls were from the media, so for the rest of the afternoon we let the phone go to voice mail. The ringing finally stopped around five. Lucy volunteered to cook dinner and spend the night in Birdie's guest room, so I got up to leave. "I'll see you in the morning, and we'll drive to the mortuary together."

The moment I walked into my house, Bumper headed straight for my ankles and began rubbing his head and purring. I stopped to scratch him behind his ear. "How's my favorite guy?" He purred louder and trotted after me into the kitchen. I filled his bowl with his favorite star-shaped kibble. Then I took a deep breath and dialed Beavers's number.

"Hi, Arlo. This is Martha."

He sounded surprised. "Oh! I guess I didn't expect you to call."

"Well, I got to thinking about your offer and decided I'd been a little hasty with my reaction. Sorry. Catching up sounds like a good idea. For one thing, I really miss Arthur."

Beavers chuckled. "Well, one out of two isn't so bad. When are you free?"

"Tonight, actually."

"Okay. I'm still tied up for a while, but I can pick you up at seven."

"Sure. Sounds good."

I hoped I hadn't just made a big mistake.

CHAPTER 3

Choosing an outfit to wear on a date with Beavers required some serious thought. I wanted to look my best but didn't want to give him the wrong idea. As far as I was concerned, we were just friends. I settled on my size sixteen black linen trousers and a pink short-sleeved blouse loose enough to button over my bosom, without gaping apart. My hair had grown long enough in the last year for me to sweep my salt and pepper curls up on the top of my head. A spritz of Marc Jacobs on my bare neck and arms, and I was ready.

Beavers knocked on my door at 7:05. I didn't know how he managed, but he always looked fresh, even after a long day's work. His white shirt was smooth and his tie hung perfectly straight. I think it must be easier for thin people not to wrinkle their clothes.

"I'm glad you changed your mind about dinner." The skin around his dark eyes crinkled with his smile. "Are you as hungry as I am?"

I grabbed my purse and locked the door behind us. "Starved."

In his typical courtly style, Beavers put his hand under my elbow and guided me to the car. "How about Jethro's?" When we first met, he had introduced me to a great barbeque joint on Sepulveda Boulevard. We ate there many times while we were dating.

Fifteen minutes later we sat at a small wooden table covered with a fresh cut of white butcher paper and two frosty glasses of beer. I wondered, as I studied the menu, if Beavers had ever taken his newest ex-girlfriend here. I pushed the thought out of my mind. *What do I care? This isn't a real date, and he's no longer my boyfriend.* I closed the menu and leaned back in the sturdy oak chair. "I'll have the tri-tip with coleslaw."

Beavers smiled. "That's what you always order."

"Well, if you remember, I don't eat pork, and I don't like getting strings of rib beef stuck in my teeth. Therefore, I'm left with only one other option—the tri-tip."

The smile left his face, and he looked at me intently. "I remember everything about you."

I swallowed some cold Heineken. *Uh-oh.*

About midway through dinner, I managed to steer the conversation toward Russell. "You know, Arlo, after you left this afternoon I asked Birdie whether she could think of anyone who wanted to harm Russell. She did recall he received a telephone call a week ago that seemed to upset him. She didn't remember anything else. As for financial problems, she had no clue because Russell always handled their money. I always thought he was pretty tight-fisted, because they seemed to live well below their means."

"Hmm." He rubbed his mustache. "Interesting. About the phone call, I mean."

Here's my opening. Might as well plunge right in. "Arlo, it seems odd you'd be asking about someone targeting Russell in a bank robbery. Do you have a reason to suspect his shooting was deliberate?" I held my breath, fully expecting Beavers to tell me to mind my own business.

He drained his second beer and ran a paper napkin over his wet mustache. "One of the witnesses claimed the shooter said something about a 'payback.'"

"Payback? Do you think Russell knew the masked man?"

"Maybe."

"Do you think someone wanted to settle an old score?"

"Something like that."

A dagger of fear pierced my heart. "Oh my God. If this was personal, could Birdie be in danger?"

He bit his cheek and frowned. "Too soon to tell."

Poor Birdie! She seemed so vulnerable and frail right now. What if someone wanted to harm her too? "Don't you think she should have police protection until you know for sure?"

He shook his head. "This is an FBI matter. You'd have to ask them. But if you're concerned, maybe you could persuade her to leave LA for a while."

Beavers had a point. Lucy and I would have to come up with a plan to get her out of town. But even if Russell had been a target, why would anyone be after Birdie too? "I really appreciate your frankness. Meanwhile, do you know when the coroner will release Russell's body?"

"The FBI is in charge of this one. I suspect the autopsy won't take more than a few days."

Thank goodness the feds were in control. I remembered how the LA County Coroner had botched the investigation last year into the death of my friend.

We finished our meal with slices of sweet potato pie. I settled my fork neatly across the empty plate. "How's Arthur? I miss him." Arthur, a retired police canine adopted by Beavers, had saved my life twice. I loved the dog, and so did my cat, Bumper.

"He's doing great. He misses you too. I can tell. Want to come over tonight and say hello?"

I looked at my watch. "It's almost nine. I've got a long day ahead of me tomorrow. Can I have a rain check?"

"Anytime."

Ten minutes later we pulled into my driveway. He turned off the engine and insisted on walking me to my front door.

The fragrance of night-blooming jasmine filled the air on that warm July night. Beavers reached over and held my shoulders. He pulled me gently toward him and said in a low voice, "I've missed you, Martha."

My body began to relax in his embrace, and all the old feelings of love and desire rippled through me. I stiffened and pulled back. A year ago, when I first dated Crusher, aka Yossi Levy, I felt disloyal to

Beavers, even though he had just dumped me. Now the reverse was true. Even though I hadn't heard from Crusher in the last five months, and five months was a long time, kissing Beavers would be cheating. I put a hand on his chest to stop him. "I'm sorry, Arlo. I don't think this is a good idea."

"Why? Are you still seeing Levy?"

"I simply think you and I are better as friends." I turned the key into the lock and opened the door. "Good night. Thank you for dinner, and thanks again for the information."

"Can I call you again?"

What should I say? I wanted to protect Birdie, and Beavers seemed willing to give me the help I needed. On the other hand, I didn't want to send him the wrong message. I finally said, "Of course. Let's keep in touch."

A corner of his mouth turned up. "Touching is good."

CHAPTER 4

The next morning was Quilty Tuesday—the day Lucy, Birdie, and I always spent sewing together, no matter what. I packed my red tote bag with my newest project, a hand-pieced Double Wedding Ring quilt for my daughter. Quincy worked in Boston and lived with a professor of theoretical physics at MIT.

I had hopes.

Before I left, I called Lucy and told her Russell's killing might have been personal. "Arlo doesn't know if Birdie's also in danger, but he suggested we get her out of town for the time being, just in case."

Lucy drew in a sharp breath. "Does Birdie know?"

"No, and I don't want to worry her unnecessarily. She has enough on her plate. We just have to figure out a way of getting her out of LA without alarming her."

"Right. Maybe we can take her on a cruise."

"Good idea. I'll see you in a little while."

Instead of my usual stretch denim jeans, I wore a blue linen dress more appropriate to the sad business the three of us would be conducting this morning. When I arrived at Birdie's house, I headed straight to the kitchen, where I heard my friends talking.

Lucy sat with a cup of coffee at an old farm table painted green. Famous for always dressing with a theme, she wore peach-colored slacks with matching sandals. A long strand of white pearls rested luxuriously against an orange silk blouse. She looked as cool as a mango smoothie.

Birdie pulled a sheet of fragrant coconut ginger cookies out of the oven. White flour dusted the bib of her denim overalls. She transferred the hot cookies onto a cooling rack and we hugged. She smelled like vanilla extract and cinnamon. "Hello, Martha dear. There's fresh coffee on the counter."

I grabbed a cookie. "My favorite. It's almost time to leave, Birdie. Are you going to change?"

She glanced at her clothes and brushed off the flour. "No. Let's get this over with." Birdie grabbed her house keys and hobbled toward the front door. I could tell her arthritic knees gave her grief today.

My seventy-six-year-old friend was one of a kind. Lucy and I suspected she had once been a beatnik or a hippie, because she refused to play the part of a snooty banker's wife. Her only interests were her garden, her kitchen, and her quilts. You got what you saw with Birdie—long white braid, denim overalls, Birkenstock sandals, and a heart as big as the earth. How she ended up in a loveless marriage with a fussy old banker for a husband baffled me. Equally mysterious was why Russell Watson chose such a free spirit to spend his well-ordered life with.

Lucy's eyes widened at Birdie's refusal to wear something more appropriate to her appointment at the mortuary. She threw me a quizzical look behind Birdie's back.

I shrugged and whispered, "Cut her some slack. She's grieving."

A half hour later we arrived at Pearly Gates Presbyterian Mortuary. The tan brick and stucco building sat on a quiet corner in Burbank and blended in with the pre-World War II neighborhood. A discreet sign on the wide front lawn directed us to a parking lot in the rear. Lucy maneuvered her vintage black Caddy with the shark fins down the long driveway and pulled into a handicapped space nearest the entrance.

I slid out of the backseat, opened the front passenger door for Birdie, and helped her stand. "You okay?"

She stood in the warm July morning and eyed the door without moving. Jaw set in determination, she swallowed once and nodded. Then she grabbed my arm for support and walked slowly toward the entrance. My heart ached for her.

A blast of cool air hit our faces when we pushed open the door. Soothing elevator music wafted into the reception area through speakers in the ceiling.

The walls were painted a muted teal, and a gray carpet muffled our steps.

A dark-haired woman sat texting on her cell phone. As soon as she saw us, she quickly put down the phone and lifted her pleasant round face. "How may I help you today?"

"We called yesterday for an appointment regarding Russell Watson." I gestured toward Birdie. "This is Mrs. Watson."

The woman directed us to comfortable chairs upholstered in pumpkin-colored velvet and brought us each a bottle of cold water.

Five minutes later, the door opened to an office directly behind the reception desk, and a man in a dark suit emerged. He stood about five feet ten with a receding hairline and a chin to match. He clasped his hands and glided toward us. "I'm Chester Towsley, owner of Pearly Gates. May I say how sorry I am for your loss." His left eye winked in a nervous tic as he examined our faces. "Which one of you ladies is Mrs. Watson?"

"I am."

Towsley's eye fluttered wildly as he scanned Birdie's overalls. "You're Mrs. Watson? The banker's wife?"

When Birdie didn't respond, Towsley recovered his composure and grasped her hand in both of his. "Of course, dear lady. No need to fret. I will make this process simple and easy. Just come with me to my office and we'll get started."

Lucy's eyebrow arched at the exchange, and she glanced at me with silent disapproval. I rolled my eyes and grabbed one of Birdie's arms. Lucy took the other, and we marched behind Chester Towsley into a dark paneled office.

The mortician arranged three chairs in front of his broad desk and took a seat behind it. "I understand Mr. Watson is still with the coroner?"

Birdie nodded.

His slender fingers slid two documents and a pen across the desk toward Birdie. "Well, the first thing we need to do is sign these papers. The first tells the coroner Pearly Gates has permission to retrieve Mr. Watson's remains once they are released. The second is a contract authorizing Pearly Gates to handle Mr. Watson's funeral and burial. I'll fill in the details as we go along." He sat back and folded his hands. "Do we have any questions so far?"

Birdie slid the papers back across the desk and glared. "You just told me what you want, Mr. Towsley. Now I'm going to tell you what I need."

Lucy looked at me and a smile curled the corner of her mouth. Our friend Birdie usually treated everyone with kindness, but she hated being patronized. Towsley had made a big mistake when he addressed her as if she were simple and helpless.

His left eye quivered. "Of course, dear lady . . . Mrs. Watson. I meant no offense."

Birdie leaned forward. "My husband wished to be buried with his relatives in McMinnville. I want you to prepare his remains and take him there."

"Mcwhere?"

"McMinnville, Oregon. Just south of Portland. In the Willamette Valley."

"Ah. Portland shouldn't be a problem. We've handled similar requests."

"And, of course, I want to accompany my husband's body."

Great! This is the perfect opportunity to get Birdie safely out of town, as Beavers suggested last night. Lucy and I exchanged a knowing glance.

"Of course." Towsley smiled. "We'll arrange transportation for both you and Mr. Watson on the same flight."

Birdie bit her bottom lip. "Oh, dear. That's the thing. I don't fly."

Towsley briefly closed his eyes and took a deep breath. "Well, I haven't done this before, but I'll look into booking passage on the train."

Birdie's hand flew to her mouth. "Oh, no! I could never go on another train. Not after what happened the last time."

"I'm sorry?" Towsley peered at her.

"I rode on a train that derailed back in the sixties. Hundreds of poor souls were killed and injured. I'm still haunted by nightmares. I swore I'd never get on another train again. And I haven't."

Never in our sixteen years of friendship had Birdie ever told us about a train accident. I leaned toward her. "Really? You never mentioned any of this before. Where did it happen?"

"India."

Whoa! This was a whole side of Birdie Watson I never suspected. What was the story behind that little detail? "India! Really? How come you never told us you traveled to India?"

Birdie waved her hand. "I don't know. I don't like to think about the past." She turned to Towsley. "We'll have to drive Russell to Oregon."

Towsley shifted in his chair and cleared his throat. "Very well. We could arrange to have someone transport Mr. Watson in a decedent vehicle, but the trip will take two to three days and be very costly. Are you sure you don't want to fly him to his eternal rest?" He eyed her overalls. "It would be more, uh, economical."

Birdie leaned forward. "If by decedent vehicle you mean a hearse, I could ride in front with the driver." Birdie couldn't drive to Oregon on her own. Her license had been confiscated a few years ago. She failed the driving test when she bashed a police car while attempting to parallel park.

Towsley coughed into his hand. "I'm sorry, dear lady, but only Pearly Gates employees are allowed inside the decedent vehicle. Insurance, and all that. But I could—for an extra fee, of course—arrange for you to ride in style in a limousine right behind your husband. In a sort of solemn and dignified cortège. Does this appeal?"

She wrinkled her forehead. "How much would it cost?"

"Portland, Oregon, did you say? Let me see." Towsley turned his cell phone into a calculator and punched in numbers. "Rental of two vehicles, gas, mileage, meals, overnight accommodations, and salaries for two drivers, I'd say you were looking at roughly twenty-five hundred dollars a day."

He turned off his cell phone and smiled at Birdie.

"Assuming the trip takes three days up and three days back, fifteen thousand dollars."

In a trembling voice, Birdie said, "Mercy! Fifteen thousand's an awful lot of money!" Her eyes filled with tears.

We couldn't let money stop Birdie from leaving town.

I put my arm around her shoulder. "We could cut the expense in half, Birdie. Lucy and I will drive you to Oregon. Right, Lucy?"

"Absolutely. We'll take my car. It has plenty of room. We'll follow the hearse, just the same as if you were in a limousine. We won't leave your side until Russell has been safely laid to rest."

Towsley's face fell. "Are you sure you won't opt for the limousine? All three of you ladies could ride in comfort."

I squeezed Birdie's hand. "We're quite sure."

We followed him to the casket room, where coffins were strategically placed. A plain, unlined pine box sat closest to the entrance. The farther we walked into the room, the greater the prices grew.

Halfway across the area, Lucy nudged me in the ribs with her elbow and whispered, "Get a load of that little number!" She pointed to a purple casket with a gold LA Lakers logo painted on the side. A part of the lid was propped open above where the head would be positioned. Pasted on the inside, for the deceased to admire for eternity, were smiling photos of Magic Johnson, Shaquille O'Neal, and Kobe Bryant.

Birdie stopped in front of a large mahogany casket with brass handles. "This looks like something Russell would like." She touched the white velvet lining. "Distinguished, but not too lavish."

A half hour later, she finalized the details, signed a contract, and wrote a check. Towsley promised to coordinate everything with the McMinnville cemetery.

We headed west on the 101 Freeway toward Encino. When we got to the 405 interchange, Lucy said, "Dang it, I hate driving this part of the freeway. You have to move over two lanes so you don't accidentally head toward Sacramento."

Birdie clutched the grab bar above the passenger door. "Well, how are you going to drive all the way to McMinnville, dear? We're going to travel a thousand miles of freeway. What if we take a wrong turn?"

I reached forward from the rear seat and patted Birdie's shoulder. "Don't worry. We'll be following the hearse, remember? What could possibly go wrong?"

CHAPTER 5

Once we got back to Birdie's house, she insisted on making lunch. "I'm not sick, Martha dear. I'm perfectly capable of making a couple of cheese sandwiches. Besides, I need to use up this bread before it goes stale."

Lucy and I sat at the green table in her kitchen while Birdie vigorously sawed slices from a loaf of homemade bread with a long, serrated knife. The message light blinked wildly on her cordless phone.

"Do you want me to play your voice mail?" I asked.

"Just delete them. They're probably from those reporters."

"But what if the coroner's office called? Or the FBI?"

She put down the knife and wrapped the remainder of the loaf in a plastic bag. "I didn't think of that. I guess you might as well. There's a pencil and pad next to the phone to write down anything important."

Only two messages were from the media. Several quilting friends phoned offering condolences and help. "Let me know if I can do anything," and "I'm here for you if you need something." Two quilters said they'd be over in the afternoon with food.

Birdie handed us each a plate, with a cheese and pickle sandwich, and poured three glasses of iced tea. Her eyes brimmed with tears. "I'm going to have to get used to cooking for one now."

"Oh, hon, I know this is hard." Lucy reached a comforting hand across the table as Birdie dabbed at her eyes with a napkin. "Remember, you're not alone. You have Martha and me."

I finished my sandwich and leaned back in the chair. "Okay, Birdie, I'm dying to ask about the train wreck you mentioned in Pearly Gates Mortuary. What were you doing in India?"

A faint smile curved her lips. "Don't you remember how the sixties were? Everyone tried out new things and enjoyed breaking the rules."

"Weren't you and Russell married at the time?"

She looked at her hands and played with the hem of her napkin. "Sort of."

When she remained silent, Lucy said, "Come on, girlfriend. You can't just leave us hanging."

Birdie took a deep breath, and her cheeks flushed pink. "We lived on a communal farm near Ashland, Oregon, started by a group of our friends. We grew our own vegetables. Raised goats. We called our place Aquarius."

Now I understood why Birdie preferred to wear overalls. She must have gotten into the habit of wearing them during her days on the farm. "I can just picture you growing vegetables and feeding goats. But I have a tough time seeing Russell getting his hands dirty."

Birdie disappeared into the living room and came back with an old photo album. "Here. If you don't believe me, take a look at this." She opened the album and extracted a group photo. Lucy and I crowded around her to get a better look. Standing in the middle of the photo, a shapely and gorgeous younger Birdie wore a pair of cut-off shorts and a white tank top. Thick auburn hair cascaded over her shoulders to her waist.

Lucy tapped the image. "Look at those fabulous legs. You were one hot tomato, girlfriend. But which one is Russell?"

Birdie pointed to an eager-looking man standing on her right, wearing jeans and a denim shirt, with mutton chop sideburns and straight brown hair in a Beatles' haircut.

I had to squint hard to see the resemblance to the prim, white-haired old banker I knew. Nowadays, when Russell wasn't wearing a tie, he wore Ralph Lauren Polo shirts and slacks. "Get out! This was Russell? He looks so . . . relaxed."

Lucy tapped the photo again. "Who's the good-looking guy with the long hair and mustache standing on the other side of you? He reminds me of a young Richard Gere."

"Russell's brother, Denver."

Standing next to Denver was a blonde in a pink halter top and long cotton skirt.

"Who's that?" I asked.

Birdie knit her brows. "That's Feather. She and Denver had a son a few years after we took this photo. Standing on the end is Rainbow, my friend who called yesterday from New York." She pointed to a girl in her late teens with long braids.

I finished the last of my iced tea. "So when you said you were 'sort of' married, did you mean you and Russell just lived together? These days, shacking up is no big deal. But back then the two of you must have felt pretty daring."

Birdie took a deep breath. "Not exactly. We called our farm Aquarius because we thought we were ushering in a new age." She paused. "Everyone was married to everyone else."

Lucy held up her hand like a stop sign. "Wait. Did you say *everyone* was married to *everyone* else? As in sex?"

Birdie blushed. "Those were experimental times, Lucy dear. People tried lots of alternative lifestyles."

"Not where I come from. You only had two alternative lifestyles in Moorcroft, Wyoming. Live on a ranch or live in town. Maybe a third if you count old Weezer, who spent half his nights sleeping it off in jail."

I smiled at Lucy's description of her hometown. "Why India?"

"Some of us were into TM and wanted to make a pilgrimage to the ashram of the Maharishi."

Lucy raised her hand again. "I forgot. What is TM again?"

"Transcendental Meditation."

"Right."

I had a hard time picturing Russell Watson living on a commune raising goats, let alone sitting cross-legged in the dirt and meditating. "So you and Russell went to India?"

Birdie bit her lip. "Not exactly. Russell had just landed a good job in Portland. He wanted us to move away from the commune, get married, and live a straight life. That wasn't what I wanted, so Russell left for Portland without me, and I took off with one of the other men."

Lucy gasped. "Who are you and what did you do to my old friend Birdie?"

Birdie cleared her throat and looked at her napkin again. "I went to India for six months with Russell's younger brother, Denver."

Lucy's eyes got wider with each revelation. "Dang it, Birdie. Just when I thought I knew everything about you."

"How did you get into a train accident?" I asked.

"Denny and I were traveling from Madhya Pradesh to Mumbai when the train derailed. So many died. The screams were horrible. I couldn't leave India fast enough. I just wanted to go home. They took us in buses all the way back to Mumbai. It was called Bombay then. From there we made our way back to the States on a merchant ship."

"So, if you ran away with Denver, how did you end up with Russell?" Lucy asked.

Birdie briefly raised her shoulder. "I guess the accident changed me. I kept having nightmares. Nowadays they call it PTSD. Anyway, I just needed to feel safe. Denver was a lot of fun, but not very reliable. When we got back, he wanted to hitchhike around the country. Hop on freight trains just for the adventure. I was too frightened. One morning Russell showed up at Aquarius. He wore a suit and tie. Everyone made fun of him and called him a 'sellout.' But after spending six months with Denver, I could see what I had missed before. Russell represented security. Safety. He took me aside and asked me to reconsider. I packed my things, and we left for Portland the same afternoon."

Lucy began to gather the empty dishes on the table. "How did Denver react?"

"He was angry. And hurt. He tried several times to persuade me to return to Aquarius, but I was done with that life."

"So the 'problem' between the brothers was you?" Lucy bent her fingers in the air quotes she loved so much.

Birdie closed her eyes. "That's what started it, yes."

Did Denver have anything to do with the "payback" that got Russell killed? What were the chances of a man on Medicare carrying such a profound grudge after nearly fifty years?

We moved from the kitchen table to the living room. I settled in my favorite green chenille chair and spread my quilting supplies on the broad arms. Adjusting the Double Wedding Ring quilt in the hoop, I began to carefully stitch the white background fabric around the intersecting loops. The Double Wedding Ring design resembled the Olympic flag, with rows of linking circles. I had pieced each circle with dozens of wedges of fabric, using one color family for each circle. The one I currently outlined consisted of different yellow fabrics.

In the afternoon, two quilty ladies showed up with a foil-covered pan of lasagna, a tuna noodle casserole topped with cheese, lemon pound cake, cornbread muffins, and a pan of double chocolate brownies—everything homemade. Lucy pulled over chairs from the dining room and served coffee with some of the brownies on a plate. I couldn't wait for them to leave so I could ask Birdie about the mysterious phone call Russell received before his death.

Once we were alone again, I asked, "Birdie, do you remember telling us Russell got an upsetting phone call before he was killed?"

She got very quiet and studied my face. "I can tell you think the two things are connected."

"Well, we did briefly talk about the possibility yesterday."

"Yes, we did. I've also been thinking about the same thing off and on since then. What if Russell's murder wasn't random? What if he knew the man who shot him? Otherwise, why would both Arlo and Agent Lancet ask if anyone wanted to harm my husband?"

I should have known better than to suppose Birdie wouldn't figure it out. She was a fan of every cop show on TV and spoke forensics as a second language.

"What exactly do you remember about that day?

Did you hear whether the caller was a man or a woman?"

"I didn't answer the phone, so I can't say for sure. But from the tone of Russell's voice, I had the impression he spoke to a man."

"What did he say?"

"He said, 'What do *you* want?' like he knew the person. He listened for a minute and then he said, 'When hell freezes over!' and hung up."

Lucy gasped. "You don't think the caller was his brother, Denver, do you? Could he be trying to get even after all this time?"

"For pity's sake!" Birdie closed her eyes. "You're asking about ancient history. Denver moved on with his life years ago. Just like we did."

I continued to prod. "Did the call come in on your home phone or a cell phone?"

"I think . . . yes. Our home phone."

"Did you ask Russell about the call, or why he was angry?"

She sighed. "No. He wouldn't have told me even if I asked. We seldom discussed his business at the bank."

"How did you know this wasn't personal? After all, the call came to your home phone, not his business phone."

She pulled her head back slightly. "I guess I don't know for sure. I just assumed the call was business. It's not like he had a lot of friends who called the house."

"I think you should tell the FBI everything. Give them permission to examine your phone records.

Maybe they'll be able to discover the identity of the caller."

Lucy helped herself to another brownie and pursued another line of questioning. "How old was Russell, anyway?"

"The same as me. Seventy-six."

"Yet he went to the bank every day? Why wouldn't he retire and enjoy life? He didn't really have to work, did he?"

Birdie rubbed her eyes. "You know Russell. He loved his job. Work was his main interest. He could no more stay home doing nothing than he could sew a quilt."

"Did the bank ever push him to retire?" Lucy asked.

"No. Russell may have been in his seventies, but he excelled at his job. As branch manager, he focused on bringing in new business. Over the years, he acquired their biggest accounts. Multimillion-dollar companies. And he maintained relationships with all of them. If Russell retired, the accounts might've gone elsewhere."

Lucy examined her fingernails. "What about you? Did you ever ask him to retire?"

"Lord, no!" Birdie shook her head. "He would've been miserable. And he would've made me miserable hanging around the house all day. We always had an understanding. He did his thing and I did mine."

I learned significantly more about Birdie that day than I had learned in the previous sixteen years. She'd been a hippie, lived on a commune, and ran away to an ashram with Russell Watson's brother,

Denver. Yet in the end, the free spirit chose to be with Russell, a conservative banker.

And I learned so much more about Russell. He hadn't always been so conventional. Even though Birdie ran off with his brother, he took her back when she wanted to settle down. Perhaps I had judged him too harshly over the years.

What I perceived as indifference toward his wife might have merely been a willingness to give the peripatetic Birdie some space. Maybe Birdie's agreement with Russell to each do their own thing hadn't been his choice. Maybe it was the only way he could be sure she'd stick around.

CHAPTER 6

Birdie sent me home with the rest of the pan of double chocolate brownies and a generous serving of lasagna wrapped in foil. I pulled off a tiny piece of the mozzarella for Bumper and warmed the pasta in the microwave.

The phone rang. "How'd you like a visit from Arthur tonight?"

Arlo Beavers never announced himself when he called. He had an annoying habit of plunging right into the conversation without so much as a preamble.

"Good evening to you, too, Arlo."

"Well? We could be there around eight. I promise we won't stay long. Unless you want us to. . . ."

Oh my God. He's flirting again. "I'd love to see Arthur. You, I'm not so sure about."

He chuckled. "How's Mrs. Watson? Is she feeling any better?"

"She's had a rough day. I'll tell you about it when I see you."

"So that's a yes? About tonight?"

"Only because it's Arthur."

The microwave dinged, and I removed a steaming plate of lasagna and poured a glass of Ruffino Chianti Classico into my favorite red Moroccan tea glass with gold curlicues. Thanks to the generosity of quilters, Birdie was going to eat well for the next few days, and she wanted to make sure I did too.

After dinner, I changed from the blue linen dress I'd worn earlier into my comfortable jeans, T-shirt, and fuzzy pink slippers. I purposely didn't dress up for Arlo Beavers. No sense in sending him the wrong message.

At eight, a smiling, tail-wagging, German shepherd greeted me as I opened the door.

I bent down and hugged the dog who had twice saved my life. "How's my Arthur? How's my boy?"

He barked once and licked my face.

With a pang of sadness, I noticed his black muzzle had turned gray in the last year, a sign of aging. I ran my fingers over the scar in his shoulder where he had been knifed while protecting me from a very bad guy; a visible reminder of the reason Beavers broke up with me.

I buried my face in his fur and whispered, "I've missed you, boy."

I stood and Arthur immediately turned his attention to my orange cat, Bumper, who had been waiting patiently to say hello. After some nose touching and butt sniffing, the two of them headed through the kitchen toward the laundry room, wanting to go outside and play.

Beavers stood tall and lean with dark Native American eyes and a raptor's profile. He had changed into casual clothes—cowboy boots, a white western shirt with pearl snaps, and a pair of snug jeans that should have been illegal. Only his white mustache and gray hair suggested he was over fifty.

I opened the back door to let the animals out and joined Beavers in the kitchen. We sat at the table where I placed the brownies.

He reached for the plate. "So, tell me about Mrs. Watson." He took a huge bite and chocolate crumbs fell on his white shirt.

I told him about the visit to the mortuary and our plans to drive Birdie to McMinnville, Oregon, as soon as the coroner released the body. "Have you spoken to Agent Lancet? Do you know how the investigation is going?" I fully expected him not to share. In the past, he had done everything in his power to stop me from poking my nose in police business. But this time he surprised me.

Beavers pulled his cell phone out of his pocket and swiped the screen. "As a courtesy, Kay Lancet sent me a copy of the bank surveillance video. She plans to release part of it to the press. Even though the shooter wore a ski mask, we still got some details. White male. Around five feet ten, one hundred eighty pounds."

"I've always been puzzled about how you can be so sure of the height and weight of someone from just a picture."

"I'll show you."

He angled the screen of his iPhone toward me and pressed *play*. The camera, located up high, showed a panoramic view of the inside of First Encino Bank. Terrazzo tiles paved the floor, and two female tellers sat behind the dark wooden counter. Two male customers and an elderly couple stood in line. A man with an automatic weapon stormed through the front doors, covered from head to toe in black, including the ski mask.

Beavers paused the video at the point where the gunman first entered the lobby. He zoomed in for a close-up of the door. "See there?" He pointed to a strip on the side of the door.

"What am I looking at?"

"A height scale." Taped unobtrusively to the door frame was a vertical strip labeled with horizontal lines and numbers. The robber stood just under the six-foot mark. "We can estimate the weight by knowing the height."

I immediately flashed back to a similar doorway in my own home growing up. Every six months my bubbie and Uncle Isaac would stand me up against the wall and mark where the top of my head landed. Then they'd write my new height next to the line. "Look how tall you're growing, *faigela*. Mazel Tov!" We always celebrated with a cookie.

Beavers restarted the video. There was no sound, but you didn't need audio to understand what was going on. The robber swept his weapon in menacing arcs and shouted. The two tellers came out from behind the counters and the gunman herded everyone into a back room.

A door opened in the background and Russell emerged. I gasped and put my hand over my mouth in an involuntary gesture.

Beavers pressed *pause.* "You don't have to watch

this. But you can't see any gory details. Another camera in the vault recorded the actual shooting."

Arthur barked once, and I got up to let the animals back inside.

I sat back down at the table. "I'm okay. Keep going, I want to see the rest."

Beavers tapped the *play* arrow. At first Russell looked confused, then angry. He waved his arms and shouted something.

"How odd. What did Russell think he could do against a heavily armed man? Why didn't he just give him what they wanted?"

Beavers paused the video. "I wondered the same thing. Under the Bank Protection Act, all bank employees are required to be periodically trained in how to respond during an armed robbery. Mr. Watson knew the drill backward and forward. No confrontation. Full compliance with the robber's demands. No heroics. Why did he deviate from the protocol?"

Beavers hit *play* again. The gunman turned his head toward Russell, and the video stopped. The next frame showed a close-up of the robber's neck.

"This is where we got lucky."

Several dark lines wrapped around the man's neck in a spiderweb tattoo.

Where have I seen one of those before?

The video continued. The robber approached Russell, and the two of them argued.

I pointed to the screen. "The conversation seems personal. Almost like they know each other."

"You're right. This is the part where the witness heard the shooter say something about *payback*."

The gunman forced Russell to carry the bag, grabbed his arm, and shoved him toward the back of the lobby and out of camera range.

A minute later the robber emerged from the back of the bank carrying the duffel bag sagging with weight. He disappeared through the front door, and the video ended.

Then the truth hit me. "Arlo! I think the same man might have come around Birdie's place yesterday when all the reporters were there. I saw a guy with a spiderweb tattoo on his neck. He hung in back of the crowd, taking pictures with his cell phone. I just assumed he was a reporter. When Ray Mondello showed up to disperse the crowd, he left."

"So, how could you see the tattoo?"

"When he turned to go, I saw the side of the guy's neck."

"Lancet needs to hear this. Could you work with a sketch artist?"

"I don't think so. All I remember is he was white, average height, and wore a baseball cap and sunglasses. He held his cell phone in front of his face, so I didn't make out any features."

"Can you remember anything else? Clothes? Age? What kind of car did he drive? Did you get plate numbers?"

I squeezed my eyes shut and tried to picture the figure standing on the edge of the crowd. Only the vaguest impression came through. "Dark clothes. That's all I remember. What if he's the same guy? What if he scoped out the house so he can come back later? Birdie could be in danger."

"Let's not jump to conclusions. Ten million people live in LA. Spiderweb tattoos aren't as rare as you might think. They're popular in the Goth community and among certain gangs."

"Just the same, I think Birdie needs protection."

"Okay, let's look at the time line. The robbery and shooting happened around one. When did you have your confrontation with the media?"

"Gosh, it must have been around three-thirty."

Beavers frowned. "About two and a half hours from the time of the robbery to the time you spotted the guy with the tattoo. I suppose it's possible he could have stashed the money, changed clothes, and driven to the Watson residence, but that would have been pretty risky behavior."

He reached for a third brownie. Some people had all the luck. Beavers could pack in the calories and still stay trim and fit. If I ate three brownies tonight, I'd have to buy larger jeans in the morning.

"She's probably okay," he said. "But it wouldn't hurt to get her out of town as soon as possible." He pulled out his cell phone. "I'm calling Kay."

While Beavers gave the FBI agent the details over the phone, I began to pace. I pictured Russell's killer breaking into Birdie's house at night when she was all alone and defenseless.

Beavers closed his cell phone. "Kay's going to contact you tomorrow. She'll have some questions, I'm sure."

"That's not good enough. I'm going back to Birdie's house and stay with her tonight."

"Suit yourself, but you should be careful too." His dark eyes swam with concern. "The killer may not know what Mrs. Watson looks like, Martha. The guy who showed up at her house yesterday took pictures of you. He might assume you're Birdie Watson."

My face went numb. "But I told the reporters Mrs. Watson wouldn't make a statement. Surely no one could mistake me for Birdie."

"You said he hung in back of the crowd?"

I nodded.

"Are you certain he could hear you?"

The shepherd's toenails clicked across the hardwood floor. He stopped at my chair, looked at me, tilted his head, and sent me a telepathic message. I knew what I had to do. I took a deep breath. "Arlo, can I borrow Arthur for the next few days?"

CHAPTER 7

The following morning Birdie woke me up with a cup of hot coffee and cream. The aroma of cinnamon and yeast baking in the oven filled her house. She seemed to be full of surprises lately. Her husband had just been murdered, yet she stuck to her routine of baking every morning. Maybe she found comfort in sticking to a familiar schedule. "It's six, Martha dear. Arthur needs to go outside."

She'd been surprised last night to find me on her front porch with the German shepherd in tow but agreed to let us stay—especially after I told her about the man with the spiderweb tattoo.

A half hour later, we sat at the green farm table in her kitchen eating cinnamon rolls. I dunked a piece, still warm from the oven, in my coffee. Arthur sat staring at my hand and drooled. Last night before I left my house, I arranged for my neighbor Sonia to take care of Bumper. Then I drove to Beavers's house, where he supplied me with kibble and strict instructions not to feed the dog "junk." But these rolls were made with organic flour. I broke off a small piece, picked out the raisins, which were toxic to dogs, and fed the rest to the shepherd.

Birdie picked up the telephone when it rang. A smile creased her face as she spoke. "Good morning, Rainbow." She walked into the other room for a private conversation.

After five minutes, she returned to the kitchen. "That was my friend Rainbow checking up on me."

"The one from the commune?"

"Yes. We used to work together raising vegetables in the garden and preparing meals for everyone. She was young when she came to Aquarius, but very capable, and a terrific cook. Much better than me. When I left, she took over the complete management of the garden and kitchen, despite only being in her late teens. She did a terrific job."

"And you're still in touch? I don't believe I've ever heard you mention her before."

Birdie got a faraway look in her eyes. "We became very close at Aquarius. She's always looked to me as a kind of mother figure. Rainbow's been a devoted friend over the years. She even chose Russell to be her banker."

I poured myself a fresh cup of coffee and regarded my friend. "I'm worried about the man with the spiderweb tattoo, Birdie. The sooner we get you out of LA, the better."

She furrowed her forehead. "If the robber was outside my house, what could he possibly want with me? Even if Russell had enemies, I've never done anything to harm anyone."

"Maybe he's not interested in you. Maybe he's

after something in this house. Something belonging to Russell. Is that possible?"

"We weren't interested in collecting valuables, like art or jewelry. And we didn't really go on elaborate vacations. I hate to travel. Russell always gave me money for whatever I wanted, but my needs have always been modest. Quilts, gardening, cooking, nothing elaborate."

"Well, as bank manager, he must have earned a decent salary. Did he have a gambling habit? Where did the money go?"

"Russell liked to invest. I left the details up to him, but I know he did rather well, because he bragged about his success more than once."

If Russell boasted about his net worth, he'd have no reason to rob his own bank as Beavers had suggested early on.

"Did he keep any cash in the house?"

"There may be a little in the safe. He liked to have some cash in case of emergencies—like after the Northridge earthquake in ninety-four."

I stood. "Why don't we look and see?"

Birdie led me down the hall to Russell's bedroom. Lucy and I knew the Watsons hadn't slept together for a long time, but in all the years we had known them, neither of us had been in their private spaces. Russell's sky blue drapes were drawn, making his room dark and gloomy. One sliding closet door sat partially open to reveal precise rows of dress shirts hanging on two horizontal poles, one above the other. Several pairs of wing tip shoes in black and brown rested in a military line on the closet floor.

A walnut bed with turned posts had been stripped down to the mattress, standing as an empty testament to the fate of the man who once slept there. Folded across the foot of the bed lay an elaborate Baltimore Album quilt in reds and greens on a cream-colored background. The quilt had earned Birdie first prize in our quilt show years ago.

Baltimore Albums became popular in the beginning of the nineteenth century and showcased the skilled needlework of the women who sewed them. The quilts consisted of individual blocks appliquéd with symmetrical designs of wreaths, flowers, birds, and animals. When several of those blocks were joined to make a quilt top, the result looked like the pages of a picture album.

She walked over to the bed and gently straightened the edges of the quilt. Her shoulders sagged as she briefly ran her fingertips over the design.

What must she be thinking? A wave of pity swept over me.

She took a deep breath and turned toward a dresser with a print of a watery Turner landscape hanging on the wall behind it. She reached up and swung the picture frame like a door away from the wall to reveal a safe. The digital lock had space for six numbers. She slowly turned to me. "The problem is, Russell never told me the combination. He only gave me a hint."

"A hint?"

"He told me to 'look in the fruit' if anything happened to him."

"The *fruit?*"

She spread her hands. "When I asked what he meant, he laughed and said I'd enjoy figuring it out."

I thought I understood what Russell intended. Birdie loved brainteasers. She worked all the daily puzzles in the newspaper and subscribed to a monthly crossword magazine. "Well, let's start with the obvious."

We returned to the kitchen and Birdie opened one of the clear plastic refrigerator drawers. Fresh apples, oranges, and nectarines rested in the bottom. Nothing else. I wasn't surprised. She would have found a clue long ago whenever she cleaned the refrigerator.

We turned our attention toward the cupboards and spied a vintage cookie jar with two bright red apples painted on the crockery. Birdie lifted the lid and looked inside. Empty. "Look on the bottom," I said.

She turned the jar upside down. "Nothing."

We moved to the dining room. "There!" I pointed to four framed botanical prints hanging on the dining room wall. One featured lilies, one pomegranates, one oranges, and one lemons. We took the pictures off the wall and laid them facedown on the dining room table. The backs were covered with blank paper glued to the frames. Birdie brought a sharp knife from the kitchen and slit open the paper along the edges. The inside of the pictures were empty.

A futile walk through the rest of the house yielded nothing else having to do with fruit. We ended up back in Russell's bedroom, staring at the safe.

Birdie crossed her arms. "I'm stumped, Martha. I don't know where else to look."

I scanned the bedroom and stopped at the bed. "Birdie! The bedposts. Look at the tops." Crowning the walnut bedposts were finials carved in the shape of pineapples.

We rushed over to the bed and reached up. One of the pineapples wiggled and easily came off the post in my hands. I could just squeeze two of my fingers in the hole beneath. After some coaxing, I extracted a tiny slip of folded paper. Six numbers were written in a precise hand.

"Here it is!"

She reached for the paper and her eyes turned smoky. "In some ways, Russell was so predictable, but he did like his little secrets. He must have had a lot of fun devising this surprise."

Did I detect a note of anger in her voice?

The green light flashed after she punched in the six digits, and the door to the safe clicked open. "Mercy! What is all this?" She reached inside and pulled out five stacks of currency, all neatly bundled, and placed them on top of the dresser. Underneath the bills lay a small red leather diary. Underneath that lay a manila envelope full of loose certificates. And underneath that was a key.

Birdie's jaw dropped and she looked at me. "I had no idea."

CHAPTER 8

I suggested we take the contents of the safe into the kitchen and examine everything in the light. Back at the farm table, we counted the cash. Each of the five stacks contained one hundred Benjamins, ten thousand dollars. I lined them in a neat row. "Fifty thousand dollars seems like an awful lot of emergency money."

Birdie nodded. "I agree. But Russell feared natural disasters. He always said if the city were destroyed by an earthquake or a dirty terrorist bomb, we'd have to pay dearly for any supplies." She inspected the contents of the envelope then handed me the stack of papers. "Are these what I think they are?"

I examined them twice to be sure. "I'm pretty sure these are bearer bonds, each issued for ten thousand dollars. Some of them date back to the 1940s. There are twenty of them, and they all have interest coupons attached. They're worth two hundred thousand plus interest."

Birdie wagged her head. "Heavens! To think he kept them in this house."

Bearer bonds were as good as cash. Because they didn't require verification of ownership, anyone possessing the certificates—the bearer—could redeem them. "Maybe this is what the tattoo guy was after." I handed them back to Birdie. "Who else knew Russell had these?"

She raised her eyebrows. "Even I didn't know."

We opened the red diary. Inside were pages of handwritten letters and numbers divided into three columns. The first column contained letters, the second was a mixture of letters and numbers, and the third contained all numbers. "Birdie, you're good with puzzles and codes. What do you make of these?"

"Russell and his blasted secrets." She turned the pages slowly. "The middle column looks like it might be dates. Beyond that I haven't a clue."

I rotated the key in my fingers. "This isn't a door key. There's a number engraved on top. I'm sure this opens a safe deposit box. Do you have one?"

"I recall Russell brought home a bunch of signature cards for me to fill out a few years ago. The box is probably at First Encino Bank."

"If you're on the card, you'll have access to the box. We can go there today if you think you're up to it."

She frowned and twisted the end of her braid. "I am curious, of course. But that's the spot where Russell was murdered." Her eyes filled with tears.

I tried to make sense out of my friend's reaction. One moment she became wistful and teary, clearly grieving over her husband's death. The next moment she sounded bitter and annoyed about the secrets he kept. Maybe mixed-up feelings were all part of the grief process. And maybe in the midst of her emotional roller coaster she found comfort in sticking to the structure of her usual routines, like baking first thing in the morning.

The doorbell rang and Arthur barked once, tail wagging. I stood. "Stay here. I'll go. Be ready to hide this stuff in a hurry if you have to. I looked around and pointed to the huge bag of dog food. "In there."

Birdie nodded, still stunned by the valuable items lying in front of her on the kitchen table.

I spied Lucy waiting on the front porch and unlocked the door. She wore a blue V-neck T-shirt and jeans with a crease pressed down the front. Small lapis discs hung from her ears. Blue was her best color; it made her orange hair look more authentic. She breezed into the room with her long-legged stride, gold bangles jingling on her wrist. "I thought I recognized your car parked in front. You've been there since last night." She spotted Arthur. "What's he doing here?"

I told her about the man with the spiderweb tattoo in the surveillance video and in front of Birdie's house.

"You should've told me. I'd have brought over your favorite Browning semiautomatic." Lucy teased me about the time she lent me a gun to protect myself and I had to use it against someone who tried to kill me.

I stroked the dog's head. "Who needs a gun when they have Arthur?"

We joined Birdie in the kitchen. Lucy stared at

the cash and papers on the table. "What in the name of Mother Teresa?"

I told her what we discovered in Russell's safe. She gestured toward the table. "So you think Spider Man is after this loot?"

Despite the horror of the situation, I smiled at her nickname for the killer. "It's a possibility. We need to get this money out of the house."

Lucy helped herself to a cinnamon roll. "No problem. This stuff will be more than secure in our gun safe. The thing weighs a half ton. Plus you'd have to know the combination to get inside—if you can get past Ray."

I knew that safe. More than a year ago, we hid some valuable quilts inside while investigating the murder of the quilt maker friend.

Twenty minutes later, we returned to Birdie's kitchen, minus the cash and bearer bonds. "Thank you so much, Lucy dear. I feel much better knowing all the money is out of the house."

Lucy opened the little red book and frowned. "I don't get it. What's this?"

"Some kind of code." I shrugged. "We need a lot more information to figure it out."

She examined the key. "Don't you want to see what's in the safe deposit box?"

"Yes, but I don't know if I'm ready to step foot inside the bank." Birdie shuddered.

"We'll go with you. You're going to have to go sooner or later, hon."

Birdie sighed. "You're right, Lucy dear. The president of First Encino has called me every day. I'll ask him to gather Russell's things and meet us there."

"Great idea," I said. "Why don't you also ask him to make copies of your bank records while he's at it? You'll need them for probate."

Three hours later, we walked through the front door of First Encino. Birdie leaned heavily on Lucy's arm. I spied the strip on the doorjamb that measured the killer's height. In the ceiling, I also spotted the camera that recorded the video now being broadcast on every news station. A man in a yellow golf shirt stood in front of one of the teller windows.

We walked across the terrazzo floor to an attractive dark-haired woman sitting at a desk.

She looked up from her computer. "May I help you?"

Birdie's voice came out in a whisper. "I have an appointment with Ivo Van Otten."

The woman's eyes widened with comprehension. "You're Mrs. Watson?" She jumped up. "My name is Gail. I'm so sorry about your husband. Mr. Van Otten is expecting you. I'll tell him you're here." She disappeared into the office I recognized from the video as Russell's and quickly emerged with a tall man in an expensive blue suit, with silver hair cut military style.

He marched up to us with a look of deep concern and extended his hand. "Hello, Birdie. It's been a long time. I can't tell you how devastated we all are. I don't know what we'll do without him. What a terrible loss."

Lucy and I introduced ourselves, and he whisked

us away to Russell's office, where we sat in prim wooden armchairs upholstered in black vinyl. "May I bring you a cup of coffee, or maybe some water?"

When we declined, he looked down and slowly rubbed his hands together. His voice cracked when he finally spoke. "As you know, Russell was more than a friend to me. He was my mentor. If not for him, I'd never have become president of this bank. His loss is deeply personal." Van Otten worked the muscles in his jaw.

Birdie studied the man in front of her and said in a soft voice, "I know, dear. Russell spoke fondly of you. We shall both miss him, won't we?"

I smiled at the tall bank president. "Actually, Mr. Van Otten, the sooner we can conduct our business and leave, the better. As you might imagine, Birdie isn't really comfortable being here so soon after . . . so soon after the incident."

He nodded gravely. "Of course." Van Otten pointed to the top of the desk, where a banker's box sat, a white carton the size of a file drawer with a lid. "Inside are all of your husband's personal effects and copies of the bank records you asked for. I can carry this out for you when you leave. Would you like to access the safe deposit box now?"

"If you don't mind."

Van Otten gave Birdie a log to sign then led us to a small room, which he unlocked with a key. The walls were lined floor to ceiling with little steel doors. The tallest were about twenty inches high and located on the bottom level. They grew smaller in size with each ascending row.

Birdie handed Van Otten her key. He checked the number, stopped in front of a door in the middle row, about twelve inches wide and six inches tall. He selected a similar key from half a dozen others on a ring and inserted them both in the twin keyholes on the top of the door. One key turned clockwise, the other counterclockwise, and the door swung open.

Behind the door sat a red metal container. Van Otten reached in, grabbed the wire handle, and pulled. A lid concealed the contents. He carried the box to a wooden table and chair in a cubicle with a privacy door. "I put another carton in there in case you want to remove anything. I'll wait out here."

Birdie smiled. "Thank you, Ivo. I don't think this will take long." I closed the door to the cubicle, anxious to see what other secrets Russell Watson hid from his wife. She lifted the lid and we looked inside. I stopped breathing.

Holy crap!

CHAPTER 9

A small crystal ring box with gold hinges on the lid sat on top of a stack of manila envelopes and file folders. Something sparkled inside. Birdie lifted the lid, and we stared at a dazzling gold band encrusted with at least three carats' worth of diamond baguettes.

Lucy gasped and raised her hands to her cheeks. "Birdie, I didn't know you owned such a beautiful piece of jewelry."

Birdie's eyebrows plunged toward each other, creating deep creases. "Neither did I."

Lucy and I glanced at each other.

"So this isn't your ring?" I asked.

"I've never seen it before."

Birdie reached for a card-sized envelope resting under the crystal box with the word *Jazz* written on the front, and opened it. Lucy and I crowded closer to get a better look.

Happy twenty-fifth anniversary
to my darling Jazz.
All my love, Russell.

Still gaping at the note, Lucy flung her arm around Birdie's shoulders in a supportive gesture. "No!"

Poor Birdie. We had just discovered another bombshell secret—Russell Watson had carried on a twenty-five-year affair with a woman named Jazz. The note read "anniversary." Did this mean he'd married the woman? Was he a bigamist?

I had serious trust issues with men because of my own cheating ex-husband, and this discovery only fueled my cynicism. Bright red anger blossomed in my brain on behalf of my friend. "I'm so sorry."

Lucy held the ring up to the light. "Don't you think this looks like a wedding band? Something's engraved inside, and I forgot my glasses. What does it say, Martha?"

I read aloud the script written inside. *Russell and Jazz Fletcher-Watson.* "There's also a date. It's for two weeks from now. He must have been planning to give the ring as a surprise in the near future."

"What kind of name is Jazz, anyway?" Lucy's lip curled in contempt.

I shrugged. "Maybe her father played the saxophone."

Birdie reached out for the ring and slid into the only chair in the small room. She stared at the glittering band. "I had no idea he'd taken things this far."

So she knew about the woman? I studied her face

and concluded she must be in shock. For a woman who'd just found out her husband had been cheating on her for twenty-five years and had possibly even married the woman, she displayed a remarkable lack of outrage.

I spoke gently. "It sounds like you were already aware of this situation."

"Is Martha right, hon?" Lucy asked. "Did you know about the affair?"

Birdie took a deep breath. "It's a little more complicated than that."

Lucy put her fists on her hips. "How much more complicated can it be? That little weasel betrayed you. For twenty-five years. If I ever found out Ray cheated on me, I'd throw his rear out so fast, he'd break the land speed record."

Birdie stood and began transferring the contents of the safe deposit box into the carton Van Otten had supplied. "Let's take all this back to the house and I'll explain everything."

With the bank president's help, we transferred both cartons to the trunk of my Civic and then drove to Birdie's place.

Back inside her kitchen, we settled around the farm table with fresh cups of coffee and slices of lemon pound cake the quilty ladies had brought the day before.

Birdie relaxed in her chair. "I never thought I'd have a chance to say this to the both of you, but I'm so relieved I don't have to keep Russell's secret anymore."

Lucy rummaged around in the cartons until she found the crystal box. "What I don't understand is how you could put up with his unfaithfulness." She easily slipped the ring on her finger. "I'm a tall person, and I have rather large hands. But this ring is big even on me. Either Russell misjudged her size, or Jazz Fletcher is an awfully big woman."

Birdie smiled faintly. "His secrets were always safe with me, but he's dead now, so there's no more reason to protect him."

Lucy stopped twisting the ring and leaned forward. "You have my full attention, girlfriend. Dish."

"Our marriage has always been more of an arrangement between two friends rather than lovers. We loved each other, but not in the way you and Ray do."

Birdie's disclosure confirmed my earlier suspicions and so many other things—like separate bedrooms and separate lives.

Lucy stared at the ring hanging loosely on her finger. "This ring would fit a man's hand." Suddenly she looked at Birdie. "Oh my God! Is Jazz Fletcher a man?"

Birdie nodded.

"Russell was *gay?*" Lucy considered her gaydar to be well-developed since her son, Richie, had a boyfriend. But Birdie's revelation had clearly blindsided her.

"How long have you known?" I asked.

"I've always known. Russell and I dated in college. After graduation, we got caught up in the whole idealism of the sixties and joined the group that started Aquarius right outside of Ashland."

"You mean the commune where *everyone was*

married to everyone else?" Lucy curled her fingers in air quotes.

Birdie smiled. "Like I explained before, the sixties was a time of breaking rules and experimenting. That's when Russell finally admitted he preferred men. In those days, society didn't make it easy for people to acknowledge to themselves— let alone the world in general—they were gay. Remember, until recently, the law in most states considered homosexuality a crime you could go to prison for. Russell had successfully buried those feelings until we got to Aquarius."

"How did his being gay make you feel?" I asked.

"I was happy for him because I went through a liberating experience of my own."

Lucy raised her eyebrows. "No! You're gay too?"

Birdie laughed. "The word is *lesbian,* and no, I'm not. But I found a passion with his brother, Denver, I never experienced with Russell."

Lucy curled her fingers in air quotes again. "You mean the big 'O'?"

Dear God.

I reached for another slice of pound cake; to heck with Weight Watchers. "So we know you went to India with Denver for six months, and yet you came back, left the commune, and married Russell. Why?"

"Russell wanted to work in the world of finance but knew he'd never have a chance if he stayed at Aquarius. So he cut his hair, put on a suit, and landed a great job in Portland. He had a real opportunity to move up the corporate ladder, but only if he fit the image of a happily married straight man. He knew I'd keep his secret, so he begged me to marry him."

"But you loved Denver?" I asked.

"Yes. However, the whole experience in India changed me. I needed stability. Denver was too restless and wild. In the beginning, I found that quality so attractive. But I couldn't live with the anxiety that went along with his lifestyle. When Russell heard we were back at Aquarius, he drove down and proposed to me again. He said I could have the best of both worlds and promised to always take care of me. I could continue to see Denver—or anyone else—as long as I was discreet. And he could do his thing and still remain in the closet."

I wondered how angry Denver might have been when Birdie moved to Portland with Russell. Angry enough to want payback fifty years later? "Didn't you already tell Lucy and me Denver tried to talk you out of marrying Russell?"

"Yes. He thought I'd be throwing my life away. But he calmed down when he realized we could still be together. Denver stayed at Aquarius, making regular trips to visit me in Portland. At the same time we had our thing, he also fathered a child with Feather."

"Weren't you angry?" I asked.

"I wasn't surprised. Rainbow knew about my arrangement with the Watson brothers. She used to call me regularly with the latest gossip on Denver and Feather. Rainbow hated her. Feather once boasted she was going to deliberately get pregnant and make Denver leave the commune with her."

I recalled the photo Birdie had shown us. "You

mentioned before that Denver had a son with Feather."

Birdie sighed. "Yes. Her plan worked. Once the boy was born, Denver felt obligated to go along with her. He wanted to give his son a stable environment, like the one he had growing up. So they got married and moved back to McMinnville. I never saw him again." Tears escaped and ran down her cheeks.

Lucy asked, "So how did things sour between the two brothers?"

Birdie shook her head. "I'm not sure of the details. It happened around the time their mother died. The father had been dead for years, and Russell and I had already moved to Encino. I remember Russell argued with Denver over the phone. As far as I know, we never heard from him again."

Russell's brother must also be elderly. Clearly, a man in his seventies didn't rob the bank and shoot Russell. But he could have hired someone to even an old score. "Is there some way to contact Denver?"

"Actually, he phoned last night before you showed up, Martha."

"What?" Lucy and I both spoke at the same time.

"He heard about the shooting on the nightly news. He wants to see me."

So Denver is alive! What could he want with Birdie? "Did he say why?"

"He just said we have to talk about something Russell had that didn't belong to him. Something he wants back, but he wasn't specific. I told him I'd see him at the funeral." She stood stiffly and excused herself to visit the restroom.

Why did Birdie seem so reluctant to talk about Denver?

As soon as she left the kitchen, Lucy whispered, "I wonder if she's still in love with him."

I lowered my voice and leaned toward Lucy. "What I'd like to know even more is how far he'd go to get something back from Russell. Until we know if he was involved in the murder, we've got to protect Birdie."

"Denver's too old to be the killer."

"That doesn't mean he wasn't involved in some way. Meanwhile, a guy fitting the description of the bank robber skulked outside Birdie's house the same day of Russell's murder. She's not safe here."

CHAPTER 10

Arthur and I stayed at Birdie's another day, waiting for the coroner to release Russell's body. That night she received another phone call from her friend Rainbow. While she talked, I went to my room and changed into my pajamas. When I returned to the living room, Birdie was poring over her photo album.

"Taking a trip down memory lane?"

She looked up; a wistful smile painted her face. "Yes. Rainbow reminded me about the time the goats got loose in our vegetable garden. We screamed for help as we tried to chase them away. Denver came running and slipped in a huge mud puddle. He was covered in goo. I laughed at him so hard, he picked me up in his arms and set me down in the puddle. By the time more help arrived, the three of us were slinging fists full of the stuff at each other. Everyone else joined in the mud fight. When we were done, it dripped from our clothes, our hair, everything. Afterward, we all went skinny dipping."

"What happened to the goats?"

She laughed. "They got disgusted and returned to their corral all by themselves."

Around ten that evening we said good night and Birdie went to her bedroom. I turned off all the lights and retired to the guest room. Arthur settled on the floor next to my bed. Fifteen minutes later, he suddenly lifted his head, looked at the window, and began growling deep in his throat.

I propped myself on my elbow and listened. Footsteps crunched through the gravel path leading to the backyard.

Heart pounding, I reached for my cell phone and called Beavers. "Someone's creeping outside Birdie's house!"

The dog began to bark and snarl.

"I can hear Arthur in the background," he said. "I'll call it in. I'm on my way."

I headed toward Birdie's bedroom, and she met me in the hallway. "What's going on?"

"Someone's outside my window. I just called Arlo."

She looked around anxiously. "What'll we do?"

Arthur ran past us and positioned himself at the back door, barking and growling a warning. I pushed Birdie into the hall closet. "You hide behind the coats until the police get here."

"What about you?" A dozen woolen sleeves muffled her voice.

"Don't worry about me. I've got Arthur."

My heart pounded as I ran into the kitchen. I looked around frantically and grabbed a small cast-iron skillet off the stove. Weapon poised in my hand above my head, I stood to the side of the back door. *I should have taken Lucy's offer of a gun more seriously.*

The knob rattled. Metal scraped against metal.

Arthur stopped barking and leaned slightly backward—every muscle in his body poised to spring forward.

Good dog. When Arthur attacked, I'd clock the guy on the skull with the frying pan.

The knob clicked. My mouth felt like the surface of Mars.

The door opened a crack.

Where are the police? My vision narrowed and my heart raced like a bullet train.

Arthur bared his fangs.

Over the pounding in my ears, I heard several sirens approaching. *Please God! Get here in time.*

The sirens grew louder and brakes screeched.

A man's voice cursed, "*Merde!*" Then footsteps ran away.

I let out the breath I'd been holding. *Thank God!*

The dog barked and tried to open the door wider with his paws. I grabbed his collar to keep him from going outside and slammed the door shut again. "Stay! We don't know if he's armed, and I don't want you to get hurt."

The well-trained police canine reluctantly obeyed.

I hurried toward the closet and shouted, "He's gone, Birdie."

She came out from behind the coats, sweating and clutching an umbrella with a pointed end. "This is the only thing I could find to defend myself with."

A heavy fist pounded on the front door. "FBI!" As I rushed to open the door, I saw a number of flashlights sweeping the darkness outside.

Agent Kay Lancet from the FBI and two LAPD uniformed officers stood with their guns drawn.

I pointed toward the laundry room in the rear of the kitchen. "Back there! A man tried to break in just now."

They rushed to the back door, looked outside, then walked back to where Birdie and I stood hugging each other. Agent Lancet holstered her gun. "Nobody's there, but we've got agents and police officers searching the area. Did you see what he looked like? Which direction he went?"

I shook my head. "I didn't see him. My dog heard him, though, and alerted me."

Just then Beavers hurried through the front door. When he saw we were safe, he let out a breath and put his gun away. He turned to the FBI agent. "Can you tell me what you've got, Kay?"

"Nothing yet, Arlo. The guy's gone. The vics never got a look at him."

Beavers turned to me. "You okay?"

I reached down and stroked the dog's head. "Yeah, thanks to Arthur." I described our ordeal, stopping to answer an occasional question. "You know, just before the guy left, he said something odd."

"What?"

"He swore in French."

Lancet regarded me for a moment and wrote something in her notepad. "This confirms one of the witness statements. He said the robber spoke with a foreign accent."

As my pulse returned to normal, the sharp fingers of a migraine dug into the right side of my brain, and my whole body throbbed with a fibromyalgia flare-up. "Excuse me. I've got to take something for this headache." I found my pain meds in my purse and stumbled into the kitchen for a glass of water.

When I returned to the living room, Lancet snapped her cell phone shut. "The crime scene techs are on their way over to dust for prints." She focused on Birdie. "They're the best in the world, Mrs. Watson. If the burglar left behind any evidence, they'll find it. Meanwhile, you might want to leave the house for your own safety. We can offer you protection."

Birdie pressed her lips together. "I won't be forced out of my own home. Anyway, he won't be coming back tonight."

Beavers grunted and walked with Lancet toward the back door, talking in a hushed voice. Arthur followed behind.

Birdie's phone rang, and she looked at the caller ID. "It's Lucy." She switched on the speaker. "Hello, dear."

"Thank God you're alive! As soon as Ray and I heard the sirens, we rushed over, but the police won't let us in. We're standing in front of your house. What happened?"

I got up and opened the front door. Police and FBI agents mingled on the lawn. I waved for Lucy and Ray to come inside.

They sat on the sofa and Birdie told them about the prowler. Then she yawned. "As soon as the police leave, I'm going back to bed."

Lucy jerked her thumb toward her husband and whispered, "Ray brought a gun with him. He's gonna spend the night on your sofa."

The sixty-five-year-old veteran of Vietnam and gun collector patted the bathrobe covering the very obvious bulge on his chest and whispered, "Mag. Shoulder holster."

Birdie waved her hand. "For pity's sake. The perp isn't going to return tonight."

Lucy's voice rasped. "How can you be so sure?"

"I watched an episode like this on *Rizzoli & Isles.*"

Eventually Lucy went back home, leaving Ray to sleep on Birdie's sofa. At one in the morning, the last of law enforcement and the crime scene techs left. Birdie covered the snoring Ray with a quilt, and we finally crawled into bed.

My headache had subsided, the adrenaline wore off, and I fell into an exhausted sleep.

Ray left early the next morning before I woke up. At nine I called my uncle Isaac. We usually spent Friday evening together. But because I'd be staying with Birdie, I had to cancel our Shabbat dinner.

"You're doing the right thing, *faigela.* Your friend needs you now. Comforting the mourners is not only a mitzvah, it's your duty. Have a good *Shabbos.*"

"Shabbat Shalom, Uncle. Thanks for understanding."

I had just hung up the phone when Lucy appeared in Birdie's kitchen. She resembled a Dalmatian sitting in a fire engine. She wore red cotton trousers, red leather sandals, and a black and white polka dot blouse. Ruby studs sparkled in her ears.

By the way she marched in and sat down, I could tell she meant business.

She reached into her quilting bag and pulled out a Browning .22 caliber semiautomatic, then handed the pistol to me. "No arguments. You know how this works. You've used it before."

I held the gun in the palms of my hands. She had a point. Last night I would have felt a whole lot safer if I'd had the Browning. "Is it chambered?" I remembered from my shooting lessons: if a bullet was already loaded in the chamber, I'd merely have to open the safety switch and the gun would fire with the slightest pressure on the trigger.

Lucy regarded me with a raised eyebrow. "No. Transporting a gun that way isn't safe." Both she and Ray grew up in Wyoming. They knew their way around guns and gun safety.

We settled at the farm table with fresh coffee and slices of applesauce cake, still warm from Birdie's oven.

At nine-thirty, Birdie received a call from Pearly Gates Presbyterian Mortuary. She put Chester Towsley, the mortician, on speakerphone so we could all hear him. "I don't wish to alarm you, Mrs. Watson, but the obituary we published in today's paper has caused a tiny little problem."

"Oh?" Birdie frowned.

"There's a gentleman in my office insisting he has an equal claim to the deceased."

Someone cried hoarsely in the background.

Lucy quickly drew in a breath. "It's gotta be Jazz Fletcher!"

"What do you want to do?" I leaned toward Birdie.

She folded her hands in her lap and relaxed into the back of the chair. "Let me speak to him, Mr. Towsley."

"Are you certain? You don't have to."

"Quite certain."

After some shuffling sounds, a man's voice sniffed and hiccupped. "Is this Birdie Watson?"

"Yes. You must be Jazz."

A brief silence followed, and then a calmer voice said, "You know?"

Birdie took on the gentle, motherly tone she so often used to put people at ease. "Yes, dear. I do."

Lucy and I exchanged a knowing look. Birdie had such a big heart; she even had room enough to comfort her dead husband's lover.

Jazz began to cry. "I miss him so much. I have a right to say what happens to him."

"Would you like to come over now and discuss it?"

Lucy sent me a puzzled *Can you believe this?* look.

Another silence. "You'd do that?"

Thirty minutes later, Arthur barked at someone approaching Birdie's front porch. I got up and opened the door. Jazz Fletcher was not at all what I expected.

CHAPTER 11

The man at the door loomed at six feet. He looked as if he'd just come from an upscale country club in Palm Springs—tanned, athletic, and handsome. His thick brown hair, combed straight back behind his ears, revealed a slight bit of gray at the roots. Diamond studs sparkled in his earlobes. I estimated his age to be mid- to late fifties, at least twenty years younger than his lover.

Could this really be Russell Watson's partner of twenty-five years? Russell only stood at five foot six on a good day. *Birdie's going to plotz when she sees this guy!*

"I'm Jazz." His teeth dazzled pure white against the sun-kissed brown of his face.

The name certainly suited him. He wore white espadrilles without socks and white linen pants rolled up on the bottom, exposing slender ankles. Tucked into his trousers was an exquisitely tailored shirt in a wild pink and yellow floral print with a banded collar. A yellow canvas tote bag hung over his left arm.

I smiled and offered him my hand. "I'm Martha Rose, Birdie's friend."

He bowed slightly and kissed the air above it. "*Enchanté.*"

French!

A sudden chill of fear surged up my spine. Arthur, however, seemed more curious than alarmed. Surely if this were the prowler from last night, he'd know. When the dog showed no signs of recognition, I stepped aside and motioned for Jazz to enter. The shepherd immediately walked up to him and sniffed, beginning at his ankles and heading for the man's crotch. He reached the tote hanging from Jazz's arm and glued his nose to the fabric, tail wagging furiously.

Although Arthur didn't seem particularly troubled by the stranger, as a police canine, he'd been trained to sniff out all kinds of things. What if Jazz carried a weapon?

I gestured for him to sit in a chair and whispered, "Birdie's been incredibly generous to invite you over. Russell did his best to shield her from his other life. So if you say anything to upset her, you're going to have to leave."

Jazz sat with his knees pressed together, the tote bag resting on his lap. "God forbid."

I hurried to the kitchen. "Oh my God, Birdie. Are you sure you want to do this?"

"Of course."

"Well, then, prepare yourself for a shock. Let me go first." I grabbed the pistol off the table and slipped it into my purse.

"Is the gun really necessary, dear?"

"I hope not."

They followed me into the living room. Jazz jiggled his right foot against the floor.

Birdie stepped out from behind me and said, "I'm Birdie Watson."

Jazz stood. "Well, this is awkward, isn't it?" He fingered the handle of the tote bag.

Birdie smiled. "I think Russell would have a heart attack if he knew."

He let out a sigh of relief. "Tell me about it! I've wanted to meet you for the longest time, but he always refused."

Arthur fixed his eyes on the bag. *Something is in there.* I reached in my purse and wrapped my fingers around the pistol grip. Between the dog and me, we ought to be able to subdue the guy if necessary.

Birdie introduced Lucy. "Why don't we all have a nice little chat?"

The two women sat on the sofa, while Jazz and I each took a chair. I kept my hand on the gun. Just in case.

Jazz shifted the yellow bag. He pressed his lips together in a tight little smile and started to reach inside. Arthur tilted his head and his ears swiveled forward like two pointed radar dishes.

I just knew something was fishy! I jumped up, whipped out the gun, and pointed it straight at his chest. "Freeze right there!"

Lucy watched me slip off the safety and threw her body in front of Birdie.

I gulped for enough courage to pull the trigger if I had to.

The color drained from Jazz's face. He threw

both arms above his head, squeezed his eyes shut, and wailed. "Go ahead and kill me. My life's over anyway."

Arthur looked at me and whined but didn't move.

"Lucy! Grab the bag. Arthur's been suspicious of it ever since this man walked in."

My orange-haired friend lunged toward Jazz and snatched the bag with one hand.

Jazz opened his eyes in horror. He lowered his arms and stretched them toward Lucy. "No! Torture me. Kill me. But please don't hurt my baby."

Lucy frowned and gave me a *What's he talking about?* look.

I gestured with my chin toward the bag. Lucy opened it, peeked inside, and snorted. "You're going to feel so stupid, girlfriend."

She handed the bag back to Jazz, who removed a fluffy Maltese dog. She wore a yellow bow tied around a topknot of long white hair with bright pink polish on her tiny toenails. She yawned and blinked the sleep out of her glittering black eyes.

Jazz cuddled and kissed her, murmuring in a baby voice, "My precious little girl. Daddy will protect you." The Maltese rewarded him with several enthusiastic licks on the face, curly tail swinging rapidly from side to side.

I slipped the safety back on the Browning with shaking hands, put it back in my purse, and slumped down in the chair. "I'm sorry, Jazz. We can't be too careful."

He threw a dirty look in my direction.

Birdie raised a conciliatory hand. "My friends are

only trying to protect me, dear. The same person who killed Russell may have tried to break into my house last night."

Jazz hugged the pint-sized dog to his chest. "Why?"

I sighed. "That's the big question, isn't it?"

He lifted his chin and glared at me. "I've never had a gun pointed at me before."

Lucy crossed her arms. "Well, now you have. Let's cut to the chase. What do you want from Birdie?"

"I want to have a say in whatever happens to him. We were together for twenty-five years." His lips trembled. "I loved Rusty deeply."

Birdie scrunched her forehead. "Rusty?"

"That's what I called him."

Lucy rattled her head from side to side and spoke with the authority of a woman who had raised five sons. "Well, here's what's going to happen, Jazz. We're going to bury Russell in the family plot in McMinnville according to his wishes."

"Perfect! He told me about McMinnville, and I wanted to make sure his wishes were honored. When is the funeral?"

Lucy relaxed a little. "As soon as the coroner releases his body, Birdie has arranged for him to be driven all the way, and she wants to accompany the body. The three of us plan to follow right behind the hearse in my car."

"Don't forget about Arthur," I said. "Until we know Birdie is safe, I'm convinced Arthur should come with us."

Jazz patted his chest with the palm of his hand.

"But what about me? I deserve to escort his body as much as any of you."

Birdie was silent for a moment. "Even though Russell would be horrified, I believe you're right. He grew up in the forties and fifties. God help you if anyone suspected you were gay back then. Especially if you lived in a small community like he did. But in spite of changing attitudes over the years, I don't think he ever felt quite safe enough to come out of the closet. Do you?"

Jazz pointed a finger at her. "You are so perceptive! I kept telling him being gay's no big deal anymore, but he could be such a little diva, right?"

Birdie rested her hand on Lucy's arm. "You know, your Cadillac is plenty big. I'm sure, even with the German shepherd, the four of us could comfortably fit inside."

"You are one fabulous woman." He rapidly blinked back tears. "I appreciate this more than I can say. Quite honestly, I wasn't prepared for you to be so nice." He pointed to my purse where the gun rested and his voice hardened. "Except for that."

Lucy waved her hand in the air. "Get over it. We'll be traveling a thousand miles in close quarters. Everyone needs to get along. You're gonna have to adjust your attitude."

"Sorry." Jazz glanced at me. "We won't cause any problems."

"*We?*" I asked.

"Me and Zsa Zsa."

"Who?"

Jazz grinned. "Where are my manners?" He held up the little white Maltese, who tried to wiggle out of his hands and join Arthur on the floor. "Meet Miss Zsa Zsa Galore."

Lucy rolled her eyes.

Oy vey!

The Maltese squirmed onto the floor. She ran around Arthur's legs, barking and jumping and trying to reach his face. The shepherd lay down on the floor and rested his head on his paws. The little dog measured the same size as Arthur's head. She let out a playful growl and chewed his ear.

"I have something Russell meant for you." Birdie stood and headed for her bedroom.

The ring!

Jazz gazed at her back disappearing down the hallway. "She is one of the nicest people I've ever met. No wonder Rusty stayed so loyal to her."

"Loyal?" Lucy scoffed. "Carrying on your whole married life is hardly what I'd call loyal."

Jazz spoke softly. "Rusty explained he and Birdie had an agreement. So I didn't feel I took someone who belonged to somebody else. I was content to be the 'other woman' so to speak. Right now, Proposition 8, the anti gay marriage act, has stalled same-sex marriage in California. But when it becomes legal again, I want to get married."

Lucy's face tightened and her eyes narrowed. "Oh. So if gay marriage becomes legal it's okay for you to 'take someone who belonged to somebody else'?" She stabbed the air with finger quotes.

"No! I'd never do such a thing. Even with a divorce, Birdie would be taken care of, the same as always. She'd own this house and Rusty would provide for her every need. Money wasn't an issue. I just wanted him to retire so we could live openly. Proudly."

"And did he agree?" I asked.

"He said he'd discuss divorce with Birdie. He didn't want to do anything she couldn't agree to. He felt he owed her because she made his success possible."

Again, I'd been wrong about Russell Watson. He did respect Birdie and her feelings. He never would have forced her into a divorce.

Birdie walked back into the living room holding the crystal box and the envelope with *Jazz* written on the front.

"I found this in our safe deposit box. I think he intended to surprise you." She handed them to Jazz.

He opened the card first and read the message, eyes brimming. Then he opened the crystal box and gasped. He placed the diamond studded ring on his left hand. It fit perfectly. "Did he—you know—did he ever talk to you about divorce?"

Birdie shook her head. "No. But if he'd wanted to change our arrangement, it would have been fine with me."

Jazz Fletcher rose to his full six feet. Tears coursed down his cheeks. "You could have kept this ring, and I'd never have known Rusty intended to finally come out and marry me. But you chose to give me the one thing I wanted most. You are so generous. And so kind. Thank you."

Jazz bent over, folded his arms around Birdie, and began to weep.

CHAPTER 12

"Thank you for letting me know, Mr. Towsley."
Birdie hung up the phone. Monday morning arrived
and the coroner had just released her husband's
body.

She frowned and wrung her hands. "The mortician asked me to bring some clothes for Russell to
wear."

Lucy patted her arm. "We'll help you, hon."

Birdie led us to Russell's bedroom. She chose a
black cashmere suit. Caressing the jacket lapel, she
sighed. "This was his favorite. He wore it the evening
he met Alan Greenspan at the Watergate Hotel and
again the day he signed GyroTek, a multimillion-
dollar account."

She added a crisp white shirt and held up a pair
of gold and onyx cuff links. "These belonged to his
father. Russell was very proud of his heritage."

"Maybe you should give those to Denver when
you see him at the funeral."

Birdie hesitated. "I don't think Denver has ever

worn a pair of French cuffs. He was more of a jeans and cowboy hat type. But maybe you're right. Even if he doesn't wear them, he might want to pass them to his son." She put the links back on the dresser. "I'll use these silver ones instead."

Lucy pulled a black and silver striped necktie off a hanger in the closet. "Here's a nice tie. It matches everything perfectly."

Birdie reached for a strip of sky blue silk. "I think I'll use this, instead. He liked the fact the color brought out the blue of his eyes." She also collected socks, wing tip shoes, and underwear and handed them to Lucy to pack in an overnight bag on wheels.

Do underpants really matter when you're dead?

"Is this everything?" Lucy zipped the bag shut.

"Almost." Birdie gathered the Baltimore Album quilt folded at the bottom of Russell's bed and hugged it to her chest. "I want to make sure he stays warm."

Lucy's mouth fell open slightly. "Uh, I don't think that's going to be a problem, hon."

She can't mean to use her beautiful quilt as a shroud! Each of the twenty cream-colored blocks making up the quilt top were painstakingly appliquéd with either a wreath or a bouquet. The symmetrical designs featured plants, flowers, birds, and animals. Birdie had used primarily solid green and solid red fabrics, with just a sprinkling of multicolored prints. Great skill and hundreds of hours of beautiful hand stitching went into its creation. *Maybe I could persuade her to send her husband off in a more* utilitarian blanket. "I know you want to make sure Russell is comfortable, but are you sure you want to use this particular quilt?"

"Definitely. I finished this quilt in 1991 specifically for him. It's a reproduction of an old family treasure made in the early 1800s. His Watson ancestors brought it to Oregon in their covered wagon."

"Where is the original quilt now?"

"His brother, Denver, sold it in 1988. Russell's heart broke when he found out, so I used a photo of the original and made him a replacement. The project took three years from start to finish." She ran her fingertips over the bumpy texture of the quilt. "He used this on the nights he actually slept here."

How had the Watsons kept the secret of his double life for so many years? Lucy and Ray lived across the street, yet they never suspected a thing. Russell probably slipped out through the garage, which opened onto an alley behind the Watsons house. Nobody would have seen him drive away.

An hour later we found Jazz Fletcher waiting for us in the lobby of Pearly Gates Presbyterian Mortuary, wearing a pink linen jacket. The diamond wedding band sparkled on his left hand. He wasn't carrying the little Maltese today. Instead, he clutched a small brown leather duffel bag. He strode toward us, smiling, and kissed the air on either side of Birdie's cheeks. "*Merci beaucoup* for asking Towsley to notify me."

I pointed to his bag. "What's in there?"

He winked. "I'm sure you'll be relieved to know it's not a loaded gun."

Towsley appeared moments later. "Did you bring clothes for Mr. Watson?"

"I did." Birdie and Jazz spoke simultaneously. They looked at each other.

"I brought his favorite outfit," said Birdie.

Jazz hugged the duffel to his chest. "So did I."

Towsley's eyelid started to dance. He glanced from one to the other and tilted his head. "Why don't we all go to a consultation suite?" He guided us to a small room off the hallway, where we sat around a conference table. He remained standing. "I'll just give you some private time to discuss this among yourselves." Towsley quietly left, closing the door behind him.

Jazz spoke first. "Heavens, here we are in another awkward situation."

"We're just trying to write the final chapter in Russell's complicated life, dear. I'm sure we can work this out."

Jazz grabbed Birdie's hand. "You're so sweet. I want us to become best friends."

"Stand in line," Lucy said. She opened the overnight case and carefully laid Russell's somber outfit on the table. "Let's take a look at everything we have."

Jazz screwed his mouth sideways. "That is the fake Rusty." He opened his bag and pulled out light blue spandex cycling shorts, with matching canvas shoes. "Rusty always said he felt so free wearing these. He bought them during one fabulous weekend we spent at the Madrone Inn. We stayed in the Valentine Room. You know the one? With a heart-shaped bed and red satin sheets?"

The mind boggles.

The Madrone Inn was a popular tourist destination on the California central coast. A different theme inspired over-the-top décor in every room. To put it another way, if the Hearst Castle married a whorehouse, the Inn would be their offspring.

"And I made this for his seventieth birthday, the same year we adopted Zsa Zsa." He carefully laid out a lavender and green silk shirt featuring a print of Maltese dogs wearing various costumes.

He turned to us and smiled. "Ta da! This is the real Rusty."

Maltese shirt? Spandex with no underwear? Russell?

"Mercy!" Birdie grabbed her braid.

Lucy raised her eyebrows and looked at me. I tried to stop myself, but the laughter burst out of my nose. Lucy joined in. Soon we were howling helplessly.

"What's so funny?" Jazz lowered his eyelids halfway.

After a minute I wiped my eyes. "Sorry, Jazz. This outfit is just so—different from the Russell we knew."

"What are you going to do, hon?" Lucy asked.

"I want him to be comfortable." Birdie smiled at Jazz. "Let's go with *the real Rusty.*"

Jazz beamed.

"What about the Baltimore Album quilt?" I asked, hoping she'd change her mind.

"He might feel cold in those shorts. The quilt goes with him."

Darn! More fiber art lost to posterity. I thought about all the thousands of quilts that never survived the Civil War. During the four-year conflict, the families of many soldiers sent them off to the army with quilts for bedrolls. When the soldiers died in battle, those blankets often became their shrouds. A whole generation of hand stitching went with them into the ground.

Jazz touched a red fabric cardinal stitched to a green branch on the quilt. "This is beautiful. I'd love to be able to make something like this."

"Do you sew?" Lucy asked.

"*Mais oui.* I own Jazz, a men's boutique in West Hollywood. Maybe you've heard of my place?" He smoothed the sleeve of his pink jacket. "This is part of my summer line of resort wear. We dress some of the stars. Right now I'm working on a more youthful wardrobe for Johnny Depp."

Lucy fingered the Maltese shirt on the table. "This is beautifully tailored. French seams. I'm impressed."

He smiled. "I've noticed you have quite a flair for clothing yourself."

Lucy smiled back, obviously pleased with the acknowledgment. Today she wore a vineyard theme: grape colored amethysts in her ears, lavender blouse, purple trousers, and purple leather sandals in the same shade. For the hundredth time, I wondered how she always managed to find matching shoes.

Jazz gestured to her feet. "Could I offer a teensy

suggestion? Your color palette could use just a smidge of contrast. Maybe green shoes instead of purple? Maybe a yellow blouse? Too much matching is so nineties."

Lucy squinted one eye and pulled her head back. "I'll keep that in mind."

Jazz looked at my jeans and T-shirt and said nothing. I could be so insulted, but I knew he had a point.

Someone knocked softly on the conference room door. Towsley stepped inside. "Have we come to a decision?" He clasped his hands together and looked at Birdie.

She snatched the underwear from her pile of clothing and added them to the outfit Jazz brought. "I think Russell would feel most comfortable wearing these casual clothes."

Towsley collected them from the table. "Whatever you wish."

"And I want you to wrap him in this." Birdie passed the quilt to the mortician. "I trust this won't be a problem?"

The mortician's eyes widened in appreciation. "Not at all. Many families like to send their loved ones off with something meaningful. There will be plenty of room for this gorgeous piece of art in his casket."

Jazz stood. "Can we see him now?"

"I'm afraid it's too soon. He'll be ready for viewing at six this evening. Oh, and I've arranged for the decedent vehicle to leave in the morning. The driver's been briefed and will wait until you get here." He cleared his throat. "There's still time to hire a limousine for you ladies—in case you've changed your mind?"

"Thanks anyway." Lucy waved her hand. "We're fine."

Towsley nodded and left with Russell's things in his arms.

Jazz picked up his empty leather bag. "Well, I've got a lot of packing to do for Zsa Zsa and me. Meet you back here this evening. Au revoir." He threw air kisses at Birdie and left.

Lucy replaced Russell's unused outfit in the roll-on, and we headed back to Encino.

An hour later we sat in Birdie's kitchen eating tuna sandwiches on homemade bread when someone knocked on Birdie's door.

"I'll get it," she said.

"How are you, Mrs. Watson?"

Beavers? What was he doing here? Lucy and I jumped up and joined them in the living room. Arthur greeted his owner with a furiously wagging tail.

Beavers glanced at me and a corner of his mouth moved almost imperceptibly upward in a smile. Then he addressed Birdie. "I have news. Thanks to Martha, the Feds think they've ID'd the man who killed your husband."

A warm wave of pleasure washed over me. For the first time ever, Beavers acknowledged my role in solving a crime. "Who is it?"

"Name's Rene Levesque. A Belgian."

"What was he doing in Encino?"

"Long story. The FBI narrowed the field of possible suspects using the spiderweb tattoo and his approximate height from the surveillance video, but they didn't have any solid leads. Your information about him speaking French prompted them to contact Interpol. Turns out the bullets pulled from Mr. Watson's body were a match to other murders committed in France, Germany, Italy, and Florida—crimes definitely linked to Levesque."

"Great! Did they make an arrest?"

Beavers wagged his head. "He's a pro. Interpol's been after him for a decade." He reached in his pocket and handed me a photo of a middle-aged, dark-haired man with a cruel sneer and a spiderweb tattoo on the side of his neck. "Does this look like the man you saw outside the house taking pictures?"

I examined the face and tried to conjure up the figure standing behind the crowd of journalists and photographers. I shuddered at the flinty eyes staring from the picture. "This could be him, but like I told the FBI, I didn't pay much attention."

"Well, here's the bad news. Levesque doesn't rob banks. He's a professional assassin. Freelance."

"Dear Lord!" The color drained from Birdie's face.

"What makes you think robbing First Encino wasn't just a career change?" I asked.

"Witnesses heard Levesque threaten Mr. Watson with a *payback*. The Feds believe the robbery was just a cover for his real objective."

My stomach dropped to the basement. "Are

you saying someone hired Rene Levesque to kill Russell?"

"All the evidence points that way. Levesque may have pulled the trigger, but someone else paid him to do it."

"Oh my God! He almost got inside this house the other night. Who in the world would want to have Birdie killed? She'd never hurt a fly."

He turned to my white-haired friend. "Maybe you should consider accepting the offer of witness protection from the FBI, Mrs. Watson."

She pressed her lips together and shook her head. "That won't be necessary. We're leaving on a road trip first thing in the morning. I'm going to bury my husband in Oregon. If Rene Levesque comes here again, he won't find me."

"Leaving town is smart." He pointed to the picture in my hand. "Take the photo with you. Keep your eyes open while you're on the road. If you have the slightest suspicion anyone is following you, call 9-1-1 and head for the nearest law enforcement. Have them contact the FBI immediately. Call me too."

Had I crossed over into a parallel universe? An assassin was after Birdie? "What if he's been watching the house? What if he follows us to Oregon?" Somehow I had to convince Beavers to let me have Arthur for the trip. I took a deep breath. "Can we take Arthur with us? He acted so fierce when Levesque tried to break in. If he comes anywhere near Birdie again, the dog will recognize his scent and warn us."

Beavers locked eyes with me for five long seconds. Then he slowly reached down and stroked the top of the shepherd's head. "What do you say, Artie?"

The dog barked once and wagged his tail. Beavers ruffled his fur and leveled his gaze at me again. "Don't take any stupid chances, Martha."

"I learned my lesson the last time, Arlo. I'll take good care of him."

I hoped I could live up to my promise.

Lucy offered to help Birdie get ready for the trip, so Arthur and I returned to my house in the afternoon. Bumper met us at the door yowling and scolding me for abandoning him for the past week. But I could clearly see my neighbor Sonia had taken good care of him during my absence. I trusted her to continue his good care while I traveled. I'd have to remember to bring them both something special from Oregon. Maybe some Tillamook cheese for Sonia and a can of salmon for the cat. Or vice versa.

I spent the rest of the afternoon doing laundry and packing for the trip—including the loaded Browning semiautomatic pistol. God forbid we should encounter Rene Levesque, I wanted to be prepared.

CHAPTER 13

That evening, Lucy picked me up in her vintage black Caddy. For once, all three of us wore dresses. She seemed strangely quiet on the drive to Burbank. We pulled into Pearly Gates Presbyterian Mortuary by six, but Jazz Fletcher hadn't arrived yet. Birdie insisted on waiting in the lobby for him before viewing Russell's body.

"Sorry I'm late." Jazz rushed through the door, out of breath. "FBI Agent Lancet came by the house earlier this afternoon and grilled me for over an hour. It threw me way behind schedule. She acted nice, though. She said she was sorry for my loss. After she left, I had to make some rush decisions in packing. I completely lost track of time."

Usually an interview only takes a few minutes. "Why did she question you for such a long time?"

When he saw the mortician approaching, Jazz leaned over and whispered, "I'll tell you later."

Towsley steered us to a viewing room at the far end of a long hallway. "He's in a peaceful repose. I think you'll be pleased."

I must say, I had never been comfortable with the notion of staring at the dead. Jewish burials involved closed caskets, or bodies completely covered in a shroud. But my traditions were not Birdie's traditions. And since I wanted to be supportive, I steeled myself to face Russell Watson's corpse.

We arrived at the viewing room, and Towsley left us at the door. "Do take all the time you need. I've placed a few refreshments on the table against the wall. Cookies and coffee."

Really? Eating in the same room as a dead person?

Even though the hot July sun still shone outside, the drapes were drawn and the lights were dimmed to approximate twilight. Jazz reached down and grabbed Birdie's hand. He took a deep breath and led her forward toward the open casket in the front of the room. Soft strains of Bach wafted through overhead speakers.

I touched Lucy's arm, and we stopped walking, allowing the two principal mourners to approach the casket by themselves. As I suspected, Jazz dissolved into tears at the first sight of his beloved Rusty. His choking sobs tore at my heart. He and Birdie collapsed into each other's arms. Only the most hardened person wouldn't weep with them.

Like FBI agent Kay Lancet, who came out of the shadows in the back of the room. Her boots squeaked across the floor as she approached Lucy and me. "I understand the four of you are driving with the body to Oregon tomorrow?"

"Yes. We've arranged to follow the hearse all the way to McMinnville." I wiped my eyes and turned around to face her. She wore a loose-fitting gray pantsuit and no jewelry. Her hair, pulled back into a severe bun, emphasized her stunning cheekbones. A beautiful woman hid beneath that stern exterior. Hadn't Beavers said they knew each other? Now I wondered just how well.

Lancet rested her hand on her throat. "Detective Beavers thinks it's a good idea for you to take Mrs. Watson out of town. I don't."

Lucy pulled her chin back. "Why not?"

"I think she'd be safer in witness protection. Rene Levesque has avoided capture for over ten years. He's slippery and dangerous."

Lucy looked at me and tilted her head toward my purse. "Show her."

I opened my purse wide enough to expose the Browning semiautomatic.

Agent Lancet frowned. "Is this your gun, Mrs. Rose?"

"It's registered to me," said Lucy. "So is this." She opened her purse to reveal an even bigger Glock.

Lancet thrust her head forward and stuck out her hand. "What are you, the Over-the-Hill Gang? Why don't you hand me those guns right now before someone gets hurt?"

Lucy showed the agent a piece of paper from her wallet. "I don't have to. I have a permit to carry. See?"

"How did you qualify for this?"

"I do the books for my husband's business, which requires me to carry deposits to the bank. I'm from Wyoming, Agent. I grew up with guns. I can shoot a fly off a cow's back at forty paces."

Lancet grunted. "I'll bet your parents had a lot of unexplained bovine fatalities."

She turned to me. "What's your excuse?"

I looked at Lucy then back at the agent. "I'm carrying this gun for Lucy. I'm sort of like a caddy, only I schlep extra firepower instead of golf balls. In case she runs out of bullets."

"Get rid of it!"

Lucy reached over and transferred the Browning to her purse. "There. Are you satisfied?"

"Listen"—Lancet lowered her voice—"I know you're worried about your friend's safety, but so am I. We don't know why Levesque tried to break into her house. She'd be better off with professionals guarding her until he's caught."

I closed my purse. "I don't disagree, but this road trip is Birdie's decision. So if she wants to drive to Oregon, then we're going to take her there."

She pulled out two business cards and handed one to Lucy and one to me. "Call me every day. Let me know where you are. If you suspect you're being followed . . ."

"I know." I waved the card. "Call 9-1-1 and head for the nearest law enforcement. Detective Beavers already told us the same thing. Believe me, you'll get no argument from us."

The agent retreated to the shadows in the back of the room. Birdie and Jazz sat in folding chairs next to the casket.

I looked at Lucy and took a deep breath. "Shall we?"

She made the sign of the cross, and we approached the recumbent body of Russell Watson.

The first thing I noticed was how small he seemed in this roomy casket. The kill shots must have been in the torso, because his face and head were pristine. He might have looked like he was sleeping if it weren't for the slightly orange makeup. Birdie's green, red, and cream-colored appliquéd quilt was wrapped around him like a swaddling cloth, binding his arms inside. The collar of the lavender silk shirt printed with Maltese dogs peeked out sadly from the top of the blanket. I looked away and vowed to work hard to erase this picture from my memory bank.

Lucy and I sat, waiting for Birdie to signal she wanted to leave. A tall figure approached from the rear, and I tensed until I remembered Agent Lancet stood guard in the shadows.

I relaxed when I recognized Ivo Van Otten, president of First Encino Bank and Russell Watson's protégé. He stood quietly beside the casket, looking at his mentor and friend. Then he turned and spoke softly to Birdie, bending down so she could hear him. He shook hands with Jazz. Both men were tall, handsome, and very well dressed. They could have been featured in an ad for Dewar's or Mercedes-Benz.

There hadn't been time to announce the viewing in the paper, but thanks to social media, around fifty people showed up: several bank employees, four neighbors, and dozens of Jazz's and Russell's friends from West Hollywood. The friends seemed to gravitate toward Birdie like little children toward a favorite grandmother. And every single one of them hugged her before leaving.

Lucy hardly spoke. She was so busy texting.

"Is something wrong?" I pointed to the phone.

Her eyes filled with tears. "We just found out Junior's wife, Tanya, wants a divorce and is taking the kids with her to Hawaii. Junior now thinks she's been having a thing with her kung fu instructor."

Ray Junior was Lucy and Ray's oldest son. Junior had a degree in business administration and ran the Mondello family business—a string of busy auto repair shops in Los Angeles and Orange Counties. The Mondellos were a close-knit three-generation family. If Tanya took her three boys to Hawaii, it would kill the whole Mondello family. No wonder Lucy was crying.

Lucy closed her phone. "Junior never saw this coming. He's vowed to keep his boys here. We're scrambling to find him a good lawyer."

"I'm so sorry." I squeezed her hand.

When we finally left Pearly Gates, darkness had fallen. Night-blooming jasmine, so ubiquitous in Southern California, perfumed the air, and hundreds of crickets chirped. Some nights in Southern California were perfect, and this was one of them. A warm, silky breeze slid over my skin, and I suddenly missed the strong arms and the huge presence of Crusher. Even though he was six feet six inches of solid muscle, he'd always been gentle and tender with me. He left five months ago, and I hadn't heard one word from him since. I kept telling myself he was probably working an assignment and couldn't call, but new doubts began nibbling away at the edges of my confidence.

When I turned down his latest proposal of

marriage, he went back to working undercover for the ATF. Or maybe *Shin Bet,* the Israeli secret service. I never knew with him. At any rate, he'd grown tired of waiting for me to make a commitment.

But how could I? It wasn't the fact he was seven years younger than me. Nor was it the fact he was a rolling stone and had never been married and settled down. My romantic track record was dismal. Who was to say our relationship wouldn't end the way all the others had? Maybe it already had ended and I was just too stupid to realize it. An incredible sadness settled on me like a heavy blanket. What if he'd already found someone else?

"Martha? Martha!" I finally became aware of Lucy's voice. "We're home, hon." Birdie had insisted on being alone that night, so Lucy had driven straight to my house from the mortuary.

Thank goodness for the darkness. I didn't want my friends to see the tears soaking my cheeks. "I'm sorry, Luce. Must have dozed off."

She pulled the Browning out of her purse and handed it to me. "What Agent Lancet doesn't know won't hurt her."

I stuffed the gun in my purse and hurried out of her car toward my empty house. As soon as I walked in, my phone rang. For one wild moment I wanted it to be Crusher. "Hello?"

"How was the viewing?" Beavers. "I tried calling you at Mrs. Watson's house, but when nobody answered, I thought I'd try your home number."

"Hello, Arlo." My heart sank. Would I ever hear from Crusher again? "It was sad, of course."

His voice softened. "Do you want some company?"

Oh my God. I could be so tempted. "Nice of you to offer, but no, thanks. I need to turn in. We're getting an early start in the morning."

"You have everything you need for Arthur?"

"Yes, and thanks again for letting him come with us."

"I'll call you every night to check up on both of you while you're gone." I wasn't sure I wanted to hear from him every night, but I could understand his being concerned about his dog.

A half hour later I climbed into bed and turned off the light. Bumper curled up next to me, and Arthur stretched out on the floor. Just before I fell asleep, I realized I never did get to hear what Jazz told the FBI.

CHAPTER 14

Normally, Lucy, Birdie, and I would spend today quilting at Birdie's house. But this Tuesday morning we took our sewing projects on a 900-mile road trip to accompany Russell Watson to his final resting place.

At eight, I parked my Civic in front of Birdie's house. Arthur and I walked across the street, where Jazz helped Lucy's husband, Ray, pack the spacious trunk of her 1960 Cadillac with five pieces of luggage, bags of dog food, and Zsa Zsa's small leopard print dog bed.

"There will only be four of us in the car," I said. "Who's bringing the extra piece of luggage?"

Jazz raised his hand. He wore loose-fitting olive green trousers zippered tight at the ankles and a hand-tailored shirt pieced with floral prints and stripes. The pieces worked well together. "One for me and one for Zsa Zsa."

Lucy and I exchanged a look.

"I couldn't decide what to wear to the funeral, so I brought a few choices. And I wanted Zsa Zsa and me to have matching outfits, so I packed several things for her as well. Will that be a problem?" He pinched his eyebrows together and looked at Lucy.

"I think we'll be okay, hon. There's plenty of room in this big trunk." Lucy wore green twill pants and a green blouse. I blinked. Today her shoes were yellow.

Ray stood straight with his arms crossed and looked at each of us one by one: Lucy, Birdie, me, Jazz, and the two dogs. "You're not to take any chances. Do you hear me? Stick to the back of the other car like glue. Here." He bent down and picked up a box from the side of the driveway and handed it to Lucy.

"Inside are two-way radios and some extra batteries. One for your car and one for the driver of the hearse."

"Decedent vehicle, hon," Lucy corrected him.

"Okay. Whatever. Keep the channel open. You're to stay in contact at all times. I don't want you getting separated, especially if you have to make an emergency pit stop. Check all your gauges regularly. You don't want to run out of gas or overheat the engine. Although, I tuned this baby up pretty good last night." His voice softened. "She's purring like a kitten."

Arthur barked once.

"Lucy, honey, I want you to call me every day and tell me where you're staying for the night."

Where had we heard that before? If we called everyone every day, we'd have no time to drive.

"Keep those guns in your possession wherever

you go. Even to the john. You never know when you might need them."

Jazz, who'd been cuddling his dog, suddenly whipped his head toward Ray. "Lucy's armed?"

Ray crossed his arms again and leveled his gaze. "You don't have a problem with that, do you?"

Jazz clamped his lips together and shook his head. "Nope!"

"Good. Time to move out."

"Promise me you'll keep me updated about Junior." Lucy grabbed Ray's arm.

"I promise." He kissed his wife, who had to bend down slightly since her wedge heels elevated her four inches above her husband. He kissed Birdie and me on our cheeks. Finally, he shook hands with Russell Watson's lover, who also towered over him by a few inches. "I'm trusting you to take care of my girls, Fletcher."

Jazz pushed his shoulders back. "You can count on me, Ray."

"If you know how to use one, I could arm you with your own pistol."

Jazz's shoulders drooped a little. "I never learned. But don't worry; I took a class once in jujitsu."

Forty-five minutes later, we parked in the lot of Pearly Gates. The shiny black hearse sat in the driveway with the engine idling. A man in an ill-fitting black suit and fisherman's cap leaned against the driver's side door smoking a cigarette.

When he saw us get out of the car, he pinched off the end of the cigarette and put the butt in his pocket before limping in our direction. As he came closer, I saw his face was folded into a thousand creases. This man was way past retirement age. Would he be capable of piloting a hearse all the way to Oregon?

He removed his cap and smiled, revealing a row of crooked yellow teeth. He took one look at Birdie and smoothed his thin white hair back with the palm of his hand. "The name's Earl. I'll be taking you folks up to Oregon. May I ask which of you beautiful young ladies is Mrs. Watson?"

Oh, brother.

Birdie raised her forefinger. "I am." She briefly introduced the rest of us.

"At your service, ma'am. My deepest sympathies." He placed the cap over his heart and bowed deeply from the waist. I was afraid he wouldn't be able to stand up again.

I glanced at Jazz, who tapped his fingertips against his lips. Lucy looked at me sideways. We must all be thinking the same thing. Where did Towsley dig up this guy? I wanted to go inside and demand he find us a living driver.

Lucy clutched the walkie-talkie in her hands. I could tell she wasn't ready to hand it over just yet. "Earl, you look like you're in a little pain, hon. Are you sure you're up to this long drive?"

"Nothin' to worry about, Mrs. Mondello. My sciatica's acting up today, that's all. Comes from sittin' down my whole professional career."

"What did you do?"

"Bus driver. Forty years. And in all my years of hauling passengers, I never once had a accident." He slid his eyes over to Birdie and winked. "You can trust me to take care of your dearly departed."

She nodded slightly.

"So." He rubbed his hands together. "Let me brief you. We'll be driving a little slower than traffic, so the trip'll take us three days. If we leave now and don't stop too often, we should make Stockton by late afternoon. Tomorrow we'll drive as far as Ashland, Oregon. We'll easily make it to McMinnville on the third day. Mr. Towsley already booked hotel rooms at all three stops."

Lucy hesitated then gave him the walkie-talkie. "You know how to work one of these?"

"I reckon. We used something like this in Korea." He pulled up the antenna. "I drove a Army supply truck."

"Good. Keep it turned on. We'll be following right behind you. Since we have two dogs and an elderly woman with us, we'll be making frequent pit stops. So we need to stay in constant contact."

"Good thing you told me. Otherwise I woulda turned off my hearing aid. Saves on batteries, don'tcha know."

Lucy reached over and switched on his walkie-talkie. "Okay, let's get this show on the road."

Earl smiled again at Birdie. "Anything you need, just ask. Shame that a lovely woman like you should be all alone in the world."

Jazz put his arm around Birdie's shoulder. "Does she look like she's alone?"

Earl ignored him and put his cap back on. "Keep your headlights on. You'll be easier for me to spot in my rearview. Plus it might discourage other drivers from cutting in between us. Although, you'd be surprised how some meatheads have no respect for a funeral procession. They don't realize one day they'll be taking the same ride."

Five minutes later we headed down Alameda Avenue toward the northbound onramp of Interstate 5.

Lucy kept both hands on the wheel. "I'm getting one of my bad feelings about this Earl." She claimed to have ESP, but I maintained her intuitions sprang not from some sixth sense but from the challenges of raising five sons. "He's a little long in the tooth to be driving."

I had to admit, however, I shared her feelings.

CHAPTER 15

Birdie sat in the front passenger seat holding on to the grab bar above the door. I sat directly behind her, with my Double Wedding Ring quilt on my lap. Jazz also sat in the backseat, holding Zsa Zsa's yellow carry-all.

Jazz's phone rang. "No, Johnny absolutely cannot wear yellow. It makes his skin look too sallow. He needs pinks and blues. Just tell him I said so." He closed his phone and looked up. "Just between you and me, that man is beginning to show his age. It's a good thing I know how to dress him."

Arthur lay between us, panting and drooling. Every once in a while, he leaned over and snuffled the yellow bag. The little white Maltese popped her head out and he nuzzled her face with his enormous black nose. Zsa Zsa sneezed and shook her head. Today she wore a pink bow and a miniature green cargo jacket with tiny pockets.

"Her traveling outfit," Jazz explained.

Traffic crawled at fifteen miles per hour on Interstate 5 until we hit Sylmar in the north San

Fernando Valley. Once we approached the truck route, the semis and long-haul trucks veered to another road on the far right, relieving the congestion on the freeway. Earl kept the hearse in the right-hand lane and increased his speed to fifty-five miles per hour, about twenty miles per hour slower than the rest of the cars whizzing past us. At this pace we'd be lucky to get to Stockton by nightfall.

The megalopolis of Los Angeles gave way to the parched summer landscape of the Tehachapi Mountains. As we got closer to the Tejon Pass, known locally as The Grapevine, semis and tanker trucks merged onto the freeway again, surrounding our small procession. Fortunately, the truckers kept a respectful distance.

Birdie relaxed and let go of the grab bar. "I think I'll sew a little." She spread out her appliquéd rooster project and began to stitch a black and brown striped tail feather in place.

I quilted around a Wedding Ring pieced with two dozen wedges of different green fabrics.

Jazz watched my hands intently as I fell into the rhythm of running the needle in and out of the cream-colored background fabric. "Do you think I could try that sometime?"

His interest didn't surprise me. After all, he was a fashion designer and, judging from the workmanship on the silk Maltese shirt, a skilled tailor.

"Sure. You want to try now?"

"I'll wait until Zsa Zsa goes to sleep. She's feeling pretty frisky at the moment." He relaxed back in his seat and gazed out the window.

For the next several miles, we sat in silence.

I sensed the nose of Lucy's Caddy tilting forward and looked up to discover we were heading into a steep descent toward the San Joaquin Valley. Prominent signs on both sides of the highway pointed to runaway truck ramps.

Birdie's hand flew to the grab bar again, and she scanned the road nervously. Once we reached the valley floor, without being crushed by an errant semi, she relaxed and glanced over her shoulder. "How did you and Russell meet, Jazz?"

I'd been dying to ask the same question but was afraid to. I didn't know what details about Russell's other life Birdie was prepared to hear.

"We met at a musical in San Francisco twenty-five years ago." Jazz smiled wistfully.

Lucy glanced in the rearview mirror. "Ray and I went to a couple of those when we visited the Bay Area. We saw *South Pacific* and *Phantom*. Which show did you see?"

"A review at Finocchio's."

"The drag club on Broadway?"

Jazz smiled. "Have you been?"

"I'm surprised Russell would take the chance of being seen in a club for gays." Lucy held up her hand. "No offense, hon."

Jazz shrugged. "I know what you mean. But Finocchio's was world-famous. All kinds of people came. Straights and gays."

"Did you go there frequently?" Birdie asked.

"I should hope so. I worked there."

"You were a female impersonator?"

"I wish. Those people earned a lot more money than I did. No, I designed and made all their costumes."

Birdie shifted in her seat. "So how did you manage to meet Russell?"

"It was so romantic." Jazz's eyes glazed over. "During a break, I went to the bar for a drink. I spotted this gorgeous-looking middle-aged man and sat next to him."

Russell? Gorgeous?

"He smiled with those blue eyes of his, and my heart just melted."

"What was Russell doing in San Francisco?" I asked.

"Attending some conference at the Fairmont. We dated every night for the next four days."

"If you don't mind my saying so, there was quite an age difference between the two of you. What was the attraction?" Lucy had a knack for stating the obvious.

"He was fifty-one and so sure of himself. I was twenty-eight and still trying to make it in the fashion industry. When he offered to set me up with my own business in LA, I knew I had found my Prince Charming."

And you'd also found a gold mine. Would Jazz have fallen in love with the older man if Russell had been poor? I put down my needle. "Jazz, last night you never got around to telling us about your conversation with the FBI agent."

He sat straighter and shifted to face me. "Right. She asked me about our friends, my boutique, every aspect of our lives, really. She seemed especially interested in our finances. It's only when she asked if someone might've had a grudge, that I remembered Cisco."

"Who?"

"His real name is Francisco. Francisco Conejo. He owned the house next door. When the recession hit, he needed to refinance. Of course, none of the banks would give him money."

"Why?"

"He didn't have a steady income, and his mortgage was under water."

"Yes, that happened to so many people," said Birdie. "Russell felt proud of the fact he kept his bank out of the whole bad loan business."

Jazz nodded. "Exactly! So anyway, Cisco came to Rusty desperate for money. Rusty approved the loan, against his better judgment."

I had a hard time picturing Russell as a mortgage Santa Claus. "That seems really out of character, doesn't it? Especially if Russell was such a fiscal conservative."

"What can I say? Cisco was a friend and neighbor. I guess he caught Rusty in a generous moment."

"Something doesn't make sense. Why did Cisco hold a grudge? Seems to me he'd be grateful to the guy who bailed him out."

"He was. He used to bring us plates of divine Cuban food he cooked. Have you ever had fried plantains? *Délicieux!* Anyway, Cisco defaulted on his payments because he couldn't get a job. Between you and me, I don't think he looked very hard."

"Did Russell call in the loan?"

Jazz nodded. "Rusty had to foreclose. That's when the guy flipped out."

"Oh, dear!" Birdie tugged her braid.

"Cisco came over drunk one night, screaming and cursing. He said, 'Nobody takes my house from me. I'll get even with you. When you least expect it.' Then he called Rusty a bunch of names. When he saw me getting ready to do some jujitsu moves on him, he stormed out."

"When did this happen?"

"About a year ago. Agent Lancet promised to check his alibi."

Now we knew of two possible suspects who could have hired Levesque to kill Russell Watson: his brother, Denver, and Francisco Conejo. But what about the attempted break-in at Birdie's last week? Why would Conejo want her dead, too? Or was he after something else?

I gazed at the arid landscape. Some sections of the once-green farmland of the central valley now lay fallow and brown. As the historic drought became more severe, the state resorted to water rationing. Farms and orchards in the San Joaquin Valley, the largest consumers of water, were taking the biggest hit.

We'd been driving for two hours when we saw a blue sign announcing a rest area in five miles. Birdie put away her sewing. "I need to go, Lucy dear."

I sympathized. The older I got, the less able I was to go for long stretches without a pit stop. Lucy picked up the walkie-talkie and pressed a button. "Hello, Earl? Can you hear me?"

The radio crackled. "Roger that, young lady. Over."

"We're ready for a break, hon. Pull over at the rest stop ahead."

The right-hand turn signal flashed on the hearse in front of us, and Earl guided the vehicle off the highway to Buttonwillow. The truckers and other motorists walking around the area stopped and stared as he parked the slow-moving hearse discreetly at the far end of the parking lot. Lucy parked the large black Caddy next to him.

I couldn't wait to get out of the car and stretch my legs. My right hip ached from resting so long without moving. No wonder Earl walked with a limp. He'd spent his whole life perched in one position.

The Caltrans rest stop consisted of lavatories, a covered patio, benches, picnic tables, and a green space. A wooden display case covered in glass showed a road map of California. Next to a red dot on Interstate 5, a label in the shape of an arrow said *You are here.* According to the map, we'd covered a third of the distance to Stockton.

Lucy stood texting with a frown on her face.

I walked over to her. "Anything new?"

"Junior found a Beverly Hills lawyer." Beverly Hills was the code for expensive and ruthless. "He'll try to get a restraining order preventing Tanya from taking the boys out of LA County until the custody issue has been resolved."

"That should put your mind at ease, right?"

Her lips trembled. "Trouble is, we may be too late. Tanya left this morning with the boys and several suitcases. Junior has no idea where they went."

"I'm sorry, Lucy." If the boys were on a plane to Hawaii, no telling when the Mondellos would see them next. "Maybe they haven't left town. Maybe they're just staying at a friend's house."

"I hope you're right."

I gave her a little hug and walked over to the vending machines. I purchased a bottle of Arrowhead Mountain Spring Water and swallowed my fibromyalgia meds for the stiffness and pain in my hip. Then I gave Arthur a drink in his shiny aluminum bowl. Zsa Zsa drank out of a very small pink bowl with her name painted on the side. Her tags tinkled together on her rhinestone-studded collar as she lapped up the water.

"Is anyone else hungry?" Jazz asked.

When was I never hungry?

"I could eat." Earl removed his cap and smoothed back his hair with one quick swipe of the hand. "There's a pretty good place in Coalinga." He replaced the cap on his head and looked at Birdie. "It's about an hour farther up, if you can hold on that long."

As we walked toward the far end of the parking lot, Arthur strained at his leash and headed for the hearse.

"No! Leave it."

He must have smelled death coming from the back of the vehicle, even though Russell's casket was sealed tight. Police canines were trained to sniff out a lot of things, including dead bodies. Dogs could catch the scent of death from just a few molecules in the air. Seven months ago, Arthur dug up a human skeleton buried in someone's yard. I still hadn't told Beavers about that one.

An hour later we sat in the shade of an umbrella outside the Nothing Fancy Café. Arthur lay on the ground under the redwood picnic table, with Zsa Zsa at his side, waiting for clandestine handouts or a lucky crumb. I ordered a tuna sandwich and a Coke Zero. And to reward myself for not having eaten a burger with steak fries, onion rings, home fried chicken, or triple mac and cheese, I finished off my lunch with a slice of homemade apricot pie.

Earl barely spoke a word but kept sneaking glances at Birdie all during lunch. Finally, he took a sip of coffee and said, "So I guess you'll be living all by yourself now?"

Birdie sighed. "It takes some getting used to. My husband and I were together for over fifty years."

"It's a shame, pretty woman such as yourself. I'm a widower, too."

"You poor dear. I guess you know how it feels."

Birdie had no idea that he was flirting with her.

Earl reached up to adjust one of his hearing aids and winced. A shrill electronic whistle came from the vicinity of his head. "Ouch. I guess I need new batteries."

Lucy frowned. "You better fix that now before we get on the road, hon. In case we have to use the walkie-talkie again."

He patted his breast pocket. "Don't worry. I brought a whole card full of the little buggers. 'Course, batteries ain't gonna help if the hearing aids go bad. They're pretty old. It's tough to get the VA to spring for new ones."

Great. What if we have a real emergency on the road? What if his hearing aids suddenly die? I should've demanded Towsley find us a different driver when we had the chance. Now we were stuck with a deaf old man who kept hitting on Birdie.

CHAPTER 16

We reached Stockton by five that afternoon. The recession had hit the city hard. Windows of storefronts gaped like empty eyes with FOR RENT posters. Foreclosure signs stabbed the weedy front yards of several houses we passed. Economic distress screamed from every corner.

Earl's voice crackled over the two-way radio. "Can you hear me, Mrs. Mondello? Over."

Lucy pressed a button on the radio. "Yes. Can you hear me?"

"Roger. We're on Fremont Street. If you go straight, you'll run right into the Delta Waterfront Hotel. Your rooms are already reserved. Over."

"Aren't you going there too?"

"Negatory. The hotel refused to let me park overnight. Even in the freight zone. Bad for the image. Over."

"Well, how will we find you in the morning?"

"I'll be waiting for you outside the hotel at eight.

We gotta get an early start. Stockton to Ashland's a long haul. We're gonna drive through the Cascades. Over."

I leaned forward in my seat and spoke loudly so Earl could hear me. "What's the name of your motel?"

Static hissed again as he spoke. "Royal Palms. Have a nice evening, folks. Over and out."

The red light pulsed on the rear of the hearse, and Earl slipped into the left turn lane. Lucy tapped her horn twice in salute as we continued toward the hotel.

The Delta Waterfront Hotel towered seven stories overlooking the Port of Stockton. The western sun reflected from a hundred glass windows on the tall structure.

We pulled up under the porte cochere.

"Very ritzy," said Lucy.

The valet handed Lucy a green ticket. "Nice wheels. I seen one of these at a car museum once."

Lucy unlocked the trunk, while the rest of us got out and stretched. A uniformed bellman wearing white gloves wheeled a rolling platform on a brass frame toward the rear of the Caddy, where he unloaded our luggage—five suitcases, two bags of dog food, and Zsa Zsa's leopardprint bed. I hoped Towsley remembered to book pet-friendly rooms.

We ended up in three ground floor rooms with garden access to accommodate the dogs. Lucy and Birdie took the double next to my room, and we left the connecting door between us open so Arthur could get to Birdie if Rene Levesque followed us to Stockton. Jazz and Zsa Zsa took the room on the other side of mine.

We met up again in the hotel restaurant at six-thirty. Birdie and I still wore our traveling clothes, but Lucy and Jazz had freshened up. Jazz wore a white linen suit with a lavender T-shirt and yellow scarf hanging loose around his neck. He smiled when he saw Lucy. She had changed into a pink blouse and slacks with the same yellow shoes from the morning. "You look très chic, darling. Very fresh. Emeralds would really pop with that outfit."

"I'll be sure to ask Ray to run right out and get me some tomorrow."

Birdie laughed. "He would, too." She looked at Jazz. "What did you do with the dogs?"

He inclined his head in the general direction of our rooms. "They're keeping each other company at my place."

The hostess showed us to a table covered with a white cloth and sparkling wineglasses. I draped my purse, with the Browning inside, over the back of my chair. Lucy kept her purse, with the Glock, on her lap.

"Is anyone besides me going to have a drink?" Jazz ordered a cosmopolitan. The three of us women shared a bottle of chilled California chardonnay. Half an hour later, our dinner plates arrived, along with a bottle of rich California burgundy.

All during the meal, Birdie kept looking at her watch and Lucy kept checking her phone for new texts. Jazz had just pronounced his dessert of crème brûlée *magnifique* when Birdie said, "It's nearly time for *Rizzoli & Isles*. I don't want to miss one of the few summer series I really enjoy." She stood. "I already told them to put the dinner on my tab, so you can stay here as long as you like."

Lucy stood. "Okay. This is my cue to say good night too. Let's meet in the lobby at six-thirty tomorrow morning for breakfast."

"Lucy dear, you don't have to leave because of me. I'll be fine by myself."

Lucy patted her purse with the gun inside. "I don't think so."

Jazz and I watched them walk into the lobby.

He swallowed and turned to face me with deep creases between his brows. "There's something I have to tell you. But I need another drink first."

While we waited for the server to bring him a cosmo, he drummed his fingers on the table. Finally, his ruby red drink arrived in a martini glass with a slice of lime perched on the rim. As the server placed a napkin on the table, Jazz said, "Bring two more." He upended the glass and drained it.

His lips trembled and he fanned his face with his hand. "I need a little courage. I'm so ashamed of myself, I can barely say this out loud. You have to promise not to tell Birdie."

Good heavens. Do I really want to hear this?

I reached over the top of the table and gave his hand a reassuring squeeze. "Is it so bad?"

He pressed his lips together and nodded vigorously. "I had to tell Agent Lancet, of course. But, in all fairness, I think one of you should know as well."

The two cosmos arrived. He pushed one toward me. "You'd better have this."

What could be so horrible that I'd need a drink to fortify myself?

I raised the glass to my lips and took a sip. The cranberry juice and triple sec masked the slightly medicinal taste of the vodka. But I was already slightly buzzed from the two glasses of wine. I put the drink back on the table.

Jazz swallowed half his cocktail. He couldn't meet my gaze. Instead, he looked at the table and twirled the stem of the glass. I waited patiently for him to speak, bracing myself to hear his terrible secret.

He took a slow, deep breath. I could barely hear him over the clanking of dishes and the chatter in the room. "I think I killed Rusty." He glanced at me quickly to gauge my reaction.

"What?" Surely I didn't hear him correctly.

He drained the second half of his drink. If I had guzzled that much alcohol so fast, I'd be flat on my face. Jazz, however, merely seemed relaxed. I guessed that was one of the advantages of being a tall man. You could absorb more liquor.

"Why don't you tell me about it?"

"Promise you won't tell Birdie? I don't want her to hate me."

I nodded.

"Pinkie swear?"

"Come on, Jazz, out with it."

"About three months ago, a man walked into my boutique and said he liked what he saw. I thought he was just talking about the clothes. He ordered three custom suits and a half-dozen shirts. He was very friendly. Each time he came back for a fitting, he ordered more stuff."

"What's so bad about that? Didn't he pay for the clothes?"

"Oh, yes. He had gobs of money, and I thought he'd be a great advertisement for my clothing line since he's in the public eye. Anyway, he kind of flirted with me and"—Jazz cleared his throat and barely whispered—"I kind of flirted back."

He raised his hand defensively. "But it was innocent. I would never have cheated on Rusty. He was the real love of my life. Before I met him, I had the worst luck in the romance department. You know?"

"Unfortunately, I do. I helped put my ex-husband through medical school, then he cheated with someone else's wife and dumped me. None of my other relationships ended well, either. But, getting back to your story, how did your innocent flirtation lead to Russell's murder?"

"That client had a serious crush on me. He's young and famous, and I was flattered someone like him would find me attractive. I'm not getting any younger, you know."

"Welcome to the club. Who is he?"

"I'm sure you'd know him. He's a rapper."

"I seriously doubt that. The only rapping I'm familiar with is knuckles on the front door."

His eyes widened. "You've never heard of Li'l Ape Man?"

I think I'm getting that parallel universe feeling again. . . . "That's the guy's real name?"

"He's notorious! He's a great big blond Swedish guy. Sort of the Abba of gangsta hip-hop. Anyway,

Li'l Ape wanted to hook up. I said no, of course, but he wouldn't leave me alone. Even followed me home one night in his red Porsche. That's when the trouble started." Jazz rubbed his forehead.

I pushed my drink back across the table. "Go ahead. You need this more than I do."

"You sure?" He didn't wait for an answer. After-dinner drink number three went down as fast as the first two.

"Li'l Ape got out of his car and followed me to my door. He was determined to come inside. Rusty heard us arguing and opened the front door. He told Li'l Ape to leave or he'd call the police. That's when the brute pointed to Rusty and said, 'No one tells me what to do, old man. You better watch your back.'"

"How creepy."

"*Vraiment!* Anyway, he turned to go and whispered in my ear, 'No one ever says no to me.' Then he got in his car and drove away."

"How long ago did this happen?"

Jazz began to slur his words. "Three weeks. Since then, he's driven by my house every night and bombarded me with texts every day. I begged him to stop. I told him we were keeping a record of everything and were going to show it to the police."

"He sounds like a classic stalker."

"The next day Rusty was murdered." Jazz began to cry. "I think I'm the reason he's dead."

So now there were three suspects with three very different motives. Russell's brother, Denver, who wanted something that didn't belong to Russell; Francisco Conejo, a neighbor who blamed Russell for losing his house; and Li'l Ape Man, Jazz's stalker, who wanted Russell out of the way. Out of the three suspects, Li'l Ape Man was probably the only one who could easily afford to hire an international assassin.

The big question still remained unanswered, however. Why would any of them send the killer Levesque after Birdie too?

"Your secret is safe with me, Jazz. Birdie never needs to know. Although, I'm sure she wouldn't think less of you. Of course, if it turns out the rapper was the one who hired Russell's killer, everyone will know."

"Oh, *merci beaucoup*."

"Listen, Jazz. If Li'l Ape Man had Russell killed, it wasn't your fault. I'm sure Russell would want you to focus on the good things. He loved you. If you ever doubt that, all you have to do is look at the extravagant ring on your left hand. He obviously wanted to get married."

Jazz touched the ring and cried anew. "My life is in shambles. I'll never get over losing Rusty, and I'll never forgive myself for causing his death." He dabbed his tears with the end of his yellow scarf. The he grabbed my hand. "I'm so glad we're friends."

I took a deep breath. "Well, as long as we're sharing secrets, I've got one of my own."

His eyes widened, and he blew his nose into a cocktail napkin. "I'm all ears."

"You know Arthur's owner, LAPD Detective Arlo Beavers? He used to be my boyfriend, but we broke up a year ago. Then I started going out with someone else." How could I explain my history with Yossi Levy, aka Crusher? "My new boyfriend wanted to marry me, but I was too scared. So he left too—supposedly for a work assignment. But I haven't heard from him in five months."

Jazz reached over and brushed my arm in sympathy. "You poor thing."

"There's more," I said. "Now Arlo is acting like he wants to get together again. He's already texted me several times today. He claims he's checking up on his dog, but I think that's just an excuse."

"That's kind of romantic." He smiled.

I shrugged. "I've always been attracted to Arlo, but I don't want to cheat on Yossi if there's a chance we can still be together."

"You should just call Yossi and find out if he still likes you. Otherwise, you might be waiting around for years for a man who's never coming back."

"I've thought of trying to get hold of him again. But, in all fairness, even if Yossi comes back, I'm not sure I'm ready to get married."

"You need to make a decision before it's too late. You never know when life can throw you a curveball. Look at Rusty and me." He started crying again.

I was wrong about bigger men being able to hold their liquor. Jazz Fletcher was flat-out drunk. I helped him stumble back to his room and swiped his key card in the lock.

"You're the best, Martha."

We found Zsa Zsa curled up in her leopard print bed. Arthur lay on the floor next to her.

Jazz touched Arthur's head. "Nice doggie." Then

he fell across the bed and almost immediately
began to snore. I covered him with a spare blanket
from the closet. Then I picked up the phone and
ordered a wake-up call for his room. After taking
the two dogs into the garden for their last potty
break of the night, I returned with Arthur to my
room.

As promised, Beavers called to check up on me.
I managed to keep the conversation short. I was
tired and in no mood to chat.

Lucy walked in through the connecting door.
"Where've you been?"

"Getting an earful from Jazz. Have you heard
anything more about Junior?"

"No, nothing new. What were you and Jazz talking about?"

"Is Birdie awake?"

"No."

"Good. Jazz just dropped a bombshell, but he
made me vow not to tell Birdie."

Lucy sat on my bed. "Well, dish, girlfriend."

I told her about Li'l Ape Man.

"That's a real name?"

"I know, right? Anyway, we now have three possible suspects who could've hired Levesque to kill
Russell."

"But why would the big Ape hire someone to go
after Birdie? Does that make sense to you?"

"I'm thinking more and more that Rene Levesque
was sent to retrieve something from the house.
Something either valuable or incriminating. Do you

remember the red diary with the encrypted text and numbers we found in Russell's bedroom safe?"

"Yeah. Birdie brought it with her. She was actually studying it tonight, trying to decipher the code."

"Tell her to make sure nobody else besides us knows she has it. I have a strong suspicion that diary holds the key to Russell's murder."

CHAPTER 17

The hearse sat idling in front of the hotel at eight sharp Wednesday morning. This was our second day out, and I wondered how Russell's remains were faring in the summer heat. Would the air-conditioning in the car make a difference?

Today we all dressed in blue denim. Lucy wore an orange blouse tucked into her jeans and pink shoes. Birdie wore a short-sleeved white T-shirt with her overalls and Birkenstock sandals, with white athletic socks. I wore a pink T-shirt with my size sixteen stretch denim jeans.

Jazz sported sunglasses, tight-fitting blue jeans, and a blue striped shirt with the cuffs perfectly rolled back. Even Zsa Zsa wore a tiny blue denim sundress with tiny white buttons. He examined each of us and threw up his hands. "Thank God we're not carrying banjos."

Lucy pressed her lips together and checked her cell phone. "Let's just get the heck out of here."

Whoa. Someone was in a foul mood this morning. Had something happened back home?

"Have you heard anything more about Tanya and the boys?"

"Nothing." She tucked her phone into her purse. Lucy turned down my offer to take a turn at the wheel. "I need to feel in control of something today. Might as well be the driving."

We settled back in our usual positions in the Caddy and followed Earl onto Interstate 5 heading north.

Birdie shifted sideways in the front seat and smiled at Jazz over her shoulder. "You're unusually quiet this morning, dear. You just picked at your eggs. Didn't you sleep well?"

"It's never the same as your own bed, is it?" He sipped a cup of coffee to-go from the hotel breakfast bar.

Especially when you were nursing a hangover.

His phone started playing "We Are Family." He opened it and appeared to be staring at a picture of something. "Oh, God!" He gasped and then punched in a number. "No, no, and no! Those prints are all wrong. How many times do I have to tell you? He's Deep Winter, not Clear Summer. Put him on the phone."

Jazz's voice turned to honey. "Johnny, I forbid you to choose those prints. They scream airstream trailer on the road to Mississippi. Right now I'm thinking Urban Pirate is the way to go. When I get back, I'll fix you up with a wardrobe that's truly chic. *D'accord?*"

He closed the phone and rolled his eyes. "Movie stars."

Zsa Zsa seemed to be happy snuggling on the

seat next to Arthur. The huge shepherd sniffed at her dress and whined.

I reached for my Double Wedding Ring quilt and adjusted it in the hoop. "Would you like to try your hand at quilting, Jazz?"

"Absolutely. Do you have a thimble?"

I passed the quilt over to him along with the sewing kit. He tried to wear my metal thimble, but his fingers were too big.

"Does anyone in the front seat have anything larger?" he asked.

Birdie reached into her supplies and found a leather finger cot. "Try this, dear."

The arthritis in Birdie's hands had swollen her fingers, so her thimbles were considerably larger than mine. Jazz was able to jam the more pliable covering onto the middle finger of his right hand.

I leaned toward Jazz to give him a tutorial. "I find the easiest way to keep the stitches flowing is to position my left hand under the quilt and use those fingers to guide the needle back up through the batting to the quilt top." I could have saved my breath. Jazz had already filled the needle with perfectly spaced stitches.

"Ta da!" He smiled and showed me his handiwork. "Am I doing this right?"

I kept forgetting Jazz was an experienced tailor. "Excellent. You're a natural."

"I'm going to make a quilt when we get back to LA. Maybe you can give me some pointers."

Lucy glanced at him in the rearview mirror. "We all will, hon. If you're serious about learning how to quilt, you can join the three of us on Tuesday mornings."

Jazz put the palm of his hand over his heart. "Me? Really? I'd love to!"

Birdie twisted the end of her braid. "You know, dear, a quilt doesn't have to be made out of cotton, and it doesn't have to be used as a blanket. You can use whatever fabric you want. You can hang it on a wall, decorate a tabletop, or turn it into clothing. And if you don't like traditional piecing or appliquéd designs, you can make up your own. Look up Art Quilts on the Internet, and you'll see thousands of exquisite pieces of fiber art. You'll be limited only by your imagination."

Jazz pulled out his phone again and launched a search. He began scrolling through dozens of photos of fiber art, turning the phone slightly so I could also see the screen. "This gives me an idea. I'm going to make Johnny a quilted coat with wide lapels and a swallow tail." He smiled. "What do you think?"

I could easily imagine Johnny Depp in such a getup. "I think it's very Urban Pirate."

Jazz beamed. "I'm also going to use the fabrics from all the shirts I sewed for Rusty over the years and make a quilt. I'll sleep under it every night so I can always feel close to him."

I handed him a spool of white quilting thread. "Many people do that. They're called memory quilts. I made one for my daughter, Quincy, out of her childhood dresses when she went away to college. She still uses it. And I've seen some gorgeous quilts made with old necktie collections."

"Maybe I could do that, too," he said.

I showed Jazz how to copy my stitching pattern. "Outlining a quilt pattern with stitching is called echo quilting. Block pieces are sewn together using a quarter inch seam allowance. So if you're echo quilting near a seam, try to stay at least a quarter of an inch away from it to avoid having to push your needle through multiple layers of fabric. Of course, some people like to stitch in the ditch. That's when you quilt right inside the seams. Those stitches sink down and become invisible."

Jazz continued to echo quilt around a ring pieced in red wedges. He was off to a good start, so I turned my attention to the farmland rolling by. Soon my mind wandered back to Birdie's recent conversation with Denver. He'd be waiting for her when we reached our destination to talk about what he wanted back from Russell. Would she be safe?

The morning traffic slowed as we headed toward Sacramento, moving at an uneven pace. Birdie removed something from her tote bag and I caught a flash of red—the diary. "I've been trying to make sense out of the cryptograms. I'm sure Russell used a simple substitution cipher."

Jazz perked up. "What are you talking about? What are cryptograms?"

"That's where the letters of the alphabet are replaced by other letters. But so far, I'm stumped. There aren't enough encrypted words for a pattern to emerge. If I can spot a pattern, I can begin to crack the code."

"I still don't get it," Jazz said. "What was Rusty doing making up codes?"

Birdie glanced at me and pursed her lips. I could tell she realized she shouldn't have mentioned the diary in front of Jazz. We were supposed to keep it secret.

However, since the cat was out of the bag, I decided we might as well let Jazz know what was going on. He might even be able to help us make sense of what Russell had written. "Birdie found this diary in their home safe. Russell appeared to be keeping a secret record of some sort. She's trying to figure out what it is."

Jazz blinked several times. "How does a cryptogram work?"

"Well, suppose you were faced with a paragraph of encrypted words. They'd look like gibberish. So the first thing you'd do is find the letter that appears most frequently. In the English language, that letter is *e.* You'd plug the *e* in the encrypted paragraph. Then you might see that it occurs at the end of several three-letter words. The most common three-letter word is *the,* so now you know which letters stand for *t* and *h* and you can plug those in. At this point you know three letters in the paragraph. From there you might see other patterns emerge that allow you to guess at other words."

Lucy waved a hand. "Sounds too hard for me, hon. I'm not that good with words."

Birdie turned her face toward Lucy and smiled. "The process is intuitive, but with practice, I'm sure you'd catch on, dear. Unfortunately, Russell's diary doesn't have whole paragraphs. The encrypted words are in a list. There's not enough context to guess at patterns."

Jazz reached his hand toward Birdie. "Can I take a look?"

She passed the red diary to the backseat.

"Yes, this is definitely Rusty's handwriting." He flipped through the pages. "You're right. This list doesn't give you much to go by. But here on the first page are two words in English. *Crazy Plot.* What do you make of that?"

Birdie twisted the end of her long white braid. "I think he left a hint of what the diary is all about— a list of evidence of some sort."

Was this what Denver Watson wanted back? Did the diary refer to something Denver had done or was planning to do? Or did the list document all the times Li'l Ape Man had texted, stalked, and harassed Jazz? What about Francisco Conejo? How could he be connected to this mysterious record?

Jazz handed the diary back to Birdie and sniffed. "Do you think this is what got him killed?"

Birdie nodded. "Yes. That's why it's so crucial to crack his code. At any rate, I need to make a stop soon."

Lucy contacted Earl on the two-way radio, and he led us to a sprawling truck stop on the outskirts of Sacramento, with a restaurant, mini mart, showers, and a parking lot the size of two football fields.

As soon as Lucy parked the car, she checked her cell phone.

"Any news?" I asked.

"Junior stayed up all night calling all their friends, but nobody's seen her." I looked at Lucy's face reflected in the rearview mirror. She raised her hand and briefly swiped away a tear. "I'm so afraid she's absconded with those boys. What if she never intended to go to Hawaii? What if she just said that to throw us off the trail? They could be anywhere." Tears now spilled down her cheeks. "Ray Junior is so close to his boys. His heart is breaking, not to mention mine and Ray's."

"Listen, Lucy, how old is the oldest boy? Nine? Ten? He knows how to use the phone. He'll call his dad."

Birdie patted Lucy's arm. "Martha's right, dear. When he realizes what's going on, he'll get in touch."

"I hope so." She helped Birdie walk to the restroom.

Jazz and I also headed for the restrooms, but he stopped suddenly and grabbed my arm. "Oh my God. Red car at two o'clock." A tall man wearing a T-shirt and baseball cap got out of a bright red sports car at the far end of the parking lot and headed for the mini mart.

"Jazz." I put my hand on his arm. "Is that the red Porsche you were telling me about? Is that Li'l Ape Man?"

He turned to me, face ashen. "I can't be sure. He's too far away. What'll I do?"

Great. Now we not only had to worry about an assassin following Birdie, we had to worry about a crazed stalker following Jazz. "Well, we could sneak over there and find out."

"And then what? You've got to think this through, Martha. He's dangerous."

"Don't forget, I've got a Browning." I patted my purse.

"How could I forget? You almost shot me."

By the time we came back out of the restrooms, the red car at the far end of the parking lot had vanished. Jazz walked the dogs and Earl stood by the hearse smoking a cigarette.

When he saw Birdie, Earl limped toward her. "How was your room last night, pretty lady?" He leaned toward her. "Did you sleep okay?"

"It was quite pleasant, thank you." Birdie still seemed clueless that Earl was hitting on her. "And you? Did you get some rest?"

He dropped his cigarette and ground it under his shoe. "It was okay. But a man gets lonely. Sure would be nice to share a bed with someone again."

Lucy edged over to where I stood and whispered, "Should we rescue her?"

"He's probably harmless. I think she can handle herself. And anyway, there are more serious things to worry about right now. Jazz thinks he might have seen Li'l Ape Man following us in a red sports car."

Lucy covered her mouth at the news. "Good Lord! That's all we need."

"Let's hope it turns out to be nothing. But just the same, keep your eyes peeled while you're driving. I'll also be on the lookout."

I stopped Jazz before he got back in the car. "I just told Lucy about Li'l Ape Man so she can watch to see if he's tailing us. I think it's time you tell Birdie about him too."

"I'm so upset." His voice quivered and he fanned

his hand in front of his face. "Do you think we should call the FBI agent?"

"Not yet. Not until we know for sure that was him."

Jazz stood for a few seconds gazing at the large semis and their drivers. Then his expression lightened. "You know, I'm feeling inspired right now. Instead of Urban Pirate, maybe I could do Johnny in Trucker Chic with lots of leather, plaids, and denim. I could embellish with grommets and chains. What do you think?"

"Don't make any hasty decision."

CHAPTER 18

We caravanned back to Interstate 5, and our solemn procession moved at a stately fifty-five miles per hour in the far right-hand lane. Once we hit the open road, the other cars passed us at considerable speed. Several red cars flew by, none of them a Porsche.

Jazz cleared his throat. "Birdie, I have something to tell you. I hope you don't think any less of me because of it."

She looked over her shoulder and raised her eyebrows. "What is it, dear?"

Jazz told her about Li'l Ape Man. "It's only fair you know, since he might be following us. I'm so sorry if I've put everyone in jeopardy."

"Jazz dear, it's not your fault you have a stalker. Let's just hope you're wrong about spotting him earlier."

Jazz brought his fingertips to his lips and threw Birdie a little kiss. "Thank you." He picked up my Double Wedding Ring quilt again and began stitching. I turned awkwardly in my seat so I could watch out the back window for a red Porsche. I barely noticed the farms, orchards, and ranches of the north Sacramento Valley. We reached Red Bluff around one and cruised by an old brick building built in the neo classic style with fluted white columns and a carved stone pediment. Beyond that lay a row of stores with false fronts straight out of the early twentieth century.

The walkie-talkie hissed to life with Earl's voice. "Just to your right is Peggy's Picnic Palace. It's famous around these parts. If it's okay with you folks, I'll park around the corner and meet you there. Over."

Lucy pressed a button on the two-way radio. "Will do."

We stopped in front of a wooden storefront painted white. A sign in blue letters announced PEGGY'S PICNIC PALACE, GOOD OL' HOME COOKING. Light blue and white checked curtains hung in the window.

"It's charming," said Birdie. "I hope they'll let us go inside with the dogs." We pushed the glass door open and trooped inside.

"Nope. No dogs allowed," said Peggy, a heavy middle-aged woman in a hairnet. Her gold polyester uniform strained over her large breasts.

"I can see why you'd be concerned." Jazz looked around and flashed a dazzling smile. "Your restaurant is perfect." He closed his eyes and took a deep breath. "And it smells divine in here."

The woman's frown disappeared under the handsome man's compliments.

He leaned in a little and bent his head closer to

hers. "It's just that this is no ordinary German shepherd. He's a decorated police canine and extremely well behaved. What if we sat right by the door and put him under the table? If at any time you change your mind, I promise I'll take him outside. No arguments." Jazz failed to mention the tiny Maltese hiding in the yellow tote bag over his arm.

Peggy gave him a coy grin. "Well, I s'pose just this one time. But if he barks or disturbs my customers, out he goes."

He gave her shoulder a little squeeze. "You're the best."

About twenty diners chatted around tables covered with checked cloths matching the curtains. None of them seemed a bit concerned over Arthur's presence. Earl joined us and removed his cap before sitting down. "Friend of mine recommended this place. Said the food's real good." He smiled at Birdie. "I hope it meets with your approval, little lady."

She smiled. "I'm sure it will."

"Good, because I can't tell anymore." He patted the package of cigarettes in his breast pocket. "The smokes destroyed my sense of taste and smell."

I ordered Peggy's Wednesday lunch special: three crispy pieces of fried chicken, potato salad, corn on the cob, hot biscuits, and apple pie for dessert. Peggy cooked everything from scratch with fresh ingredients. It was beyond good. All during lunch I slipped tidbits under the table for Arthur.

Earl looked at Birdie. "I'll bet you're a good cook. You know what they say. The way to a man's heart is through his stomach."

Lucy put down her fork and nudged me under the table. "I thought you couldn't taste or smell."

I avoided her gaze to keep from laughing.

The old man shrugged. "That's right. But if anyone took the trouble to cook for me, I'd show her a lot of appreciation." He winked at Birdie and finished the last of his coffee. Then he pushed back from the table. "We better git to gitten, folks. We've got at least another three hours of driving ahead."

Birdie insisted on paying the bill and gave Peggy a generous tip.

Peggy wrapped a couple of biscuits in a paper napkin and handed it to Jazz. "For the dog." On the inside of the napkin was her name and a hastily written phone number.

Back in the Caddy, I turned sideways to fasten my seat belt and caught a flash of red out of the corner of my eye. A sudden jolt of electricity traveled down my spine. A Porsche? I whipped my head toward the back window for a better view, but whatever I had glimpsed was gone. *For heaven's sake, Martha, stop being so paranoid.* I decided not to alarm the others just yet.

Back in the car, Jazz made a phone call. "Did that shipment of silk from Thailand come in yet? Only seven bolts? Call Pradeep and find out where the other three are." He ended the call and rolled his eyes. "I leave for five minutes and everything falls apart. I swear, you can't depend on anybody these days." He sighed. "That's one of the many reasons I loved Rusty. He was so steady and reliable."

"I know what you mean, dear. That's why I loved him too."

Wasn't that why Birdie married Russell in the first place? She needed an anchor to ground her after that traumatic near-death experience in India.

By four in the afternoon we reached the town of Yreka and entered the Cascade Mountain range.

"There's Mount Lassen." Birdie pointed to a majestic snow-capped peak in the distance. "We'll be in Ashland in another hour."

I had been too busy glancing out the rear window to enjoy the forest scenery. My muscles had tensed rock solid with anxiety. The fibromyalgia had blossomed into a full-blown assault.

Really, Martha. How likely is it that some big Swedish rapper in a red Porsche is stalking Russell Watson's gay lover, or that an international assassin is after a seventy-six-year-old widow with arthritis? Get a grip. No one's going to attack us today.

I swallowed my pain meds, sank back in the seat, and closed my eyes. Every muscle in my body ached and my head throbbed. *Please don't let there be any more drama. Just let me crawl into bed soon.*

"Wake up, Martha. We've reached Ashland." Jazz gently shook my arm.

My jaw had fallen open and my chin was wet with drool. I hastily sat up and wiped my face with the back of my hand. "I must have fallen asleep."

"Really, girlfriend?" Lucy stared at me in the rearview mirror. "I never would have guessed from your snoring."

"I don't snore!"

Jazz bobbed his head rapidly. "Yes, you do, but not a lot."

Ashland, Oregon, was the home of the renowned

annual Shakespeare Festival. Theater lovers came from all over the country to enjoy the professional performances. Towsley had booked us into the Hotel Falstaff near the site of the festival grounds. Earl gave us directions to the hotel over the two-way radio. "I'll pick you folks up again at eight in the morning. Over."

"Where will you be staying?" Lucy asked.

"I'm bunking overnight at the Alas Poor Yorick Mortuary."

It's a good thing I'd eaten a large lunch. The hotel served only one menu item each night. Wednesday's choice was bangers and mash—pork sausage, mashed potatoes, and mushy peas. Since I didn't eat pork or mushy peas, I just ordered coffee and dessert, a pasty English pudding made with raisins and currants called Spotted Dick.

Don't ask.

We didn't have adjoining rooms this time, so Arthur and I stayed in the double, guarding Birdie while Lucy slept down the hall.

Birdie barely spoke through dinner and just pushed the food around her plate. When we got back to our room, I heated some water in the coffeepot and handed her a cup of tea. "How're you doing?"

She sighed. "I've often dreamed of coming back here. But nothing's the same. This town is unrecognizable from the little place it was in the sixties. There's no place for me to park my memories."

"Do you want to visit Aquarius?"

She looked down and massaged her hands together. "It's much too late for that, dear." Tears coursed down the wrinkles in her cheeks. "I made my choice a long time ago. I traded the only man I truly loved for a life of safety and stability."

My heart squeezed in sympathy. "This must be very hard on you. Are you having second thoughts?"

She wiped her eyes with a tissue. "Not just today. I've often wondered over the years if I made the right choice."

"But didn't you tell Lucy and me before that you and Denver continued to see each other as part of your arrangement with Russell?"

"Yes. It wasn't the best situation, but it was the only one we had." Birdie stared into the distance, wrapped in old memories. "We were so passionate. But everything stopped when Feather got pregnant. Denver wasn't happy about leaving me, but he wanted to do the right thing for the sake of the boy. 'Set a good example. Give him a stable home,' he said. In his own way, Denver turned out to be as conscientious as Russell."

Conscientious? Sleeping with two women? "So that was the end of your romance with Denver?"

Birdie dabbed at her eyes with the tissue and nodded. "He did the responsible thing."

"Are you prepared to see him tomorrow?"

She wrung her hands again. "I'm worried sick."

"Birdie, do you have any idea what Denver meant when he said he wanted something Russell had that didn't belong to him?"

She pushed her brows together. "The only thing I could think of were the bearer bonds. I think they belonged to Russell's parents. Maybe Denver believes he's entitled to those bonds, or at least half of them."

"What'll you do if he asks for them?"

Birdie sighed. "Whatever's right."

Could Denver Watson have had Russell killed for hoarding the bearer bonds? Could he have sent the killer to Birdie's house to retrieve them? If Birdie decided to keep the bonds, would Denver try to harm her?

The three of us would have to stick to Birdie like glue once we got to McMinnville. We couldn't allow Denver to get her alone. We couldn't let the wolf lure the sheep away from the safety of the herd. Thank God for the Browning and the Glock.

While I waited for Birdie to finish taking her shower, my cell phone rang.

"Everyone okay? Where are you?" Beavers.

"Arthur's fine. We're staying in the Hotel Falstaff in Ashland."

"I've been thinking. Maybe I'll meet you in McMinnville. It's not that far from the Rez over on the coast. I haven't visited my cousins in a while. You might like to see it, too."

Oh my God! Beavers was referring to the Siletz Indian Reservation where he grew up with his grandparents. He often talked about taking me there when we were dating.

"I don't think that's a good idea, Arlo. You and me."

"Think about it, Martha. We could start out slow. Just friends. See how things develop. We were so good once."

He was partly right. When we were dating, we were great together, at least in the beginning. I felt safe. Cared for. He treated me with respect, but not like a person with her own opinions and desires. Eventually I came to feel constrained by his rigidity. Beavers had to be the one in control at all times. In the end, I couldn't live with that. And he couldn't live with my independence.

"I'd be lying if I said I wasn't tempted, but my first obligation is to Birdie. Thanks for the offer, though."

"Just think about it."

CHAPTER 19

I woke up Thursday morning with a roaring appetite. The breakfast buffet at Hotel Falstaff included a full English board of eggs, sausage, bacon, kippers, baked beans, broiled tomatoes, mushrooms, toast, butter, marmalade, and tea. I avoided the pork and the beans but loaded my plate with everything else. My mood soared after such a satisfying meal, and I looked forward to a pleasant drive to McMinnville.

Lucy kept texting all through breakfast. Finally she turned off her phone and pressed her lips together.

I poured some milk into a fresh cup of tea. "What's the news?"

"Junior hired a private detective. So far they know Tanya and the three boys boarded a flight to Oahu two days ago." She looked at me and set her jaw. "She paid for *five* tickets with her credit card."

So Tanya *did* run away with her kung fu instructor. I had never seen my tall friend look so pissed.

After breakfast, Lucy rolled my luggage out to

the front of the hotel while I took Arthur for one last walk. Five minutes later the German shepherd and I joined the others waiting outside. Overnight temperatures had dipped to fifty degrees, and the morning air was still chilly. Lucy wore a faux mink vest over a long-sleeved T-shirt. Birdie wore a blue cardigan she knitted about ten years ago. Jazz was dressed in a gray suede jacket with a lavender wool scarf hanging around his neck. Zsa Zsa wore a matching lavender sweater with a rhinestone barrette holding her topknot.

I was glad I'd brought my thick Aran cardigan. "I'm surprised at the cold."

Birdie pulled her sweater tighter around her body. "Don't worry, dear. It's July. Even though the nights are cool, daytime weather in these parts reaches the upper eighties."

Lucy looked around. "Where's Earl?"

Jazz rubbed his hands together. "It's eight-fifteen. Shall we call that mortuary where he's staying?"

"I don't think that's necessary." I pointed to the long black vehicle driving slowly up to the curb. Earl parked and walked toward our group, limping a little more than usual. The circles under his eyes and sallow skin suggested he'd suffered a bad night. "Sorry I'm late, folks. My sciatica. Didn't get to sleep until the wee hours. Overslept."

Birdie tilted her head. "You look a bit peaky this morning. Did you manage to have some breakfast?"

He removed his cap and smoothed back his sparse white hair. "No time. But I stopped at Tony's Tacos and got a breakfast burrito and large coffee to go."

I guess if you'd lost your sense of taste and smell,

a breakfast burrito was as good as kippers, eggs, and mushrooms.

Earl shifted his weight to one side and winced in pain. "You folks ready? The drive from here to McMinnville will take all day. If we don't stop too many times, we'll make it by late afternoon or early evening."

When we got back to LA, I'd give Towsley a piece of my mind for sticking us with a sick old man. "Earl, are you sure you're up to the trip?"

Instead of answering my question, he turned to Birdie and winked. "Don't you worry, pretty lady. This old dog has a lot of life left, if ya know what I mean."

Lucy rolled her eyes.

Jazz sidled up to Birdie and put a protective arm around her shoulder. "Lively old dog? Kudos to your veterinarian."

Back in the Caddy, Lucy continued to drive, Birdie brooded over the code in the diary, and I quilted my Double Wedding Ring.

Jazz made a phone call. "What did Pradeep say about the missing shipment from Thailand? Omaha? As in Nebraska? They're not even in the same zip code. Whatever. Just make sure we get them back before they get blown away in some tornado."

Jazz closed the phone and gazed out the window. "Everything's so green. Rusty often talked about how beautiful it is up here. I think he missed it more than he'd admit."

Birdie turned sideways in her seat. "Wait until we get farther north. That's where the really dense forests are. You can pick wild berries starting in late spring."

Jazz held Zsa Zsa to his chest and stroked her under her chin. "Rusty said his family came here in a covered wagon over the Oregon Trail. Where is that, exactly?"

"Let me see." Birdie ticked off her fingers. "The trail started in Independence, Missouri, and cut through Iowa, Kansas, Nebraska, Colorado, Wyoming, Utah, and Idaho before ending in Oregon City."

"Where's that?" he asked.

"Near Portland. Russell's ancestors traveled due west from there and claimed farmland in the area around McMinnville. His roots go way back."

I put down my needle and snapped, "But not as far back as the Native Americans!" Arlo Beavers was half Native American. He had talked about how poorly his people were treated by the American government, even as late as the 1970s. He maintained that his people were the true owners of the land. "Russell's family—along with every other settler, miner, and industrialist—stole from the Indians. That's hardly something to be proud of."

Birdie sighed. "I know what you mean, Martha dear. How the pioneers treated the Native Americans was always a sore point between Russell and me. Basically, his ancestors stole their land."

Jazz nodded. "I agree. Plus, you could say that about every square inch of this country, couldn't you? None of it rightfully belongs to us."

Oh my God. Jazz and Birdie were just alike. Russell Watson had a type!

Lucy squirmed in her seat. "Good grief!" she exploded. "I'm stuck in a car with a bunch of bleeding hearts. Get over it! What do you want? To give this country back to the Indians? It's far too late for that. You can't take back the past. You just have to move on."

Whoa! Normally, my Republican friend avoided political conversations with Birdie and me. Her distress and worry over her son's family had shortened her temper and fouled her mood. We sat in awkward silence following her angry outburst.

We passed Medford and approached Grants Pass when the two-way radio crackled to life with Earl's voice. "Do any of you folks need to stop? Roseburg is more than an hour ahead."

Birdie spoke gently. "Please tell him yes, Lucy. Better safe than sorry."

Just as we pulled off the road into a gas station, a red sports car sped past and disappeared around the corner. We stepped out of the car and I tugged on Jazz's suede jacket sleeve. "Was that you-know-who?"

He attached a lavender leash to Zsa Zsa's collar and put her on the ground. "I couldn't tell. Shouldn't we contact the FBI agent?"

I shook my head. "And tell her what? If it is Li'l Ape Man, he's playing a stalker's game. He's showing just enough of himself to make you afraid but not enough to be identified. Keeping you in the dark is all part of the psychological torture. On the other hand, it could be a coincidence that a red sports car passed us just now. If we're going to

contact Agent Lancet, we need more than flashes
of red."

During our break, Lucy walked away from us for
a private conversation on the phone. Then she
walked past us and sat in the car by herself.

I whispered to Birdie, "I don't know what's upset
her more. Our conversation, or Ray Junior's missing wife and children."

Birdie adjusted the strap on her overalls. "Best to
just let her work it out on her own right now. She'll
talk when she's ready."

Ten minutes later, we headed north again on
Interstate 5. The air in the Caddy was thick with
resentment. My hopes for a pleasant ride to
McMinnville vanished. Birdie appeared to be writing something, and I resumed my quilting. Jazz
produced a sketch pad from his tote bag and drew
jackets with wide lapels and baggy slacks with pleats.

Lucy finally broke the silence. "My bad feeling is
coming back. Did anyone get a close look at Earl
back at the gas station? He seemed sick to me."

I knew what she meant. The old man's appear-
ance hadn't improved, despite the breakfast burrito
and coffee. His hands seemed a little shaky, and
beads of sweat had peppered his upper lip.

Birdie raised her hand. "Yes, I saw the same
thing. I asked him if he was all right, and he assured
me he felt fine."

Forty-five minutes later, the hearse started to
drift toward the left-hand lane in front of us.

I gasped. "Holy crap! What's he doing?"

Lucy honked her horn, and the hearse jerked to

the right in a sudden corrective move. "Something's not right."

I sat at the edge of my seat on high alert, straining forward against the seat belt. Jazz and Birdie did the same thing. After another minute, Lucy slammed on her brakes as the hearse in front of us veered to the right and shuddered to a stop on the side of the highway.

Lucy steered the Caddy off the road and parked in front of the black hearse. "I *told* you I had a bad feeling."

We all jumped out of the car and rushed to the driver's side of the hearse. Earl opened the door and stood. The skin on his face had turned an ugly color of green. He removed his cap and loosened the skinny black tie around his neck. "I think I'm going to be sick."

The four of us immediately jumped backward. Earl staggered on shaky legs toward the brush on the side of the road, leaning on the car for support. He clutched his stomach, bent forward, and puked into the bushes. He stood, spat a few times, and pointed to the driver's seat. "Water."

Lucy, Birdie, and Jazz stood still, unwilling to breach the inside of a decedent vehicle. Who could blame them? I took a deep breath and walked to the open driver's door. The inside of the hearse smelled like a mixture of beans, coffee, stale cigarette smoke, and something else. I retrieved a bottle of water from the console and handed it to Earl.

He rinsed his mouth, spat again, then drank a few sips. With shaking hands, he pulled a handkerchief from his coat pocket and mopped the sweat from his face.

Birdie responded with her customary concern. "Do you think it was the burrito?"

Earl clutched his left shoulder and slumped against the fender. "Pain. Can't breathe."

Jazz covered his mouth. "Oh my God. He's having a heart attack. I'll call 9-1-1."

Lucy ran over to the old man and put her arm around his shoulders. "You have to tell them where we are." She looked around frantically. "Where is that, anyway?"

Birdie scowled in concentration. "I think we're about fifteen miles outside of Roseburg. By the time the paramedics figure out where we are and respond, we could already be at the hospital. It'll be faster if we take him ourselves."

Lucy opened the passenger door of the hearse and settled Earl into the seat. She slammed the door shut and stood back and scowled at me. "Martha, you have to transport him." All eyes turned in my direction.

I shuddered. "Seriously? Why me?"

Lucy put her hands on her hips. "I have my own car to drive. Besides, hanging out with dead bodies is your specialty."

Jazz and Birdie both looked at the ground, avoiding my gaze. Lucy was still angry, but I had to admit she was right. Even if Birdie hadn't lost her license, it would be cruel to ask either her or Jazz to chauffeur Russell's body. Like it or not, I was going to have to transport Earl to the hospital.

Jazz said he'd use the GPS on his phone to guide

us to the hospital in Roseburg. I slid into the driver's seat and attempted not to think about the big mahogany casket behind me. The leather was still warm from when Earl sat there just a couple of minutes earlier. I adjusted the rearview mirror, brought the driver's seat slightly forward, and pushed the button on the walkie-talkie. "Okay, let's get this show on the road."

I pulled onto the highway behind the Caddy and rolled down my window. The air inside the hearse was stale and unpleasant. At first I sat stiffly behind the wheel but relaxed when I realized that piloting the big vehicle wasn't any more difficult than steering an extralong station wagon. The old man sat gasping and moaning next to me. I reached over and tried to give him a reassuring pat on the hand. "Hang on, Earl. We'll be at the hospital in just a few minutes."

His words came out in a raspy voice. "Going too fast." I glanced at the speedometer. Lucy was eating up the road at seventy miles per hour, and I was right on her tail.

"That's the whole idea, Earl. We're rushing you to the emergency room. Hardly any cars are on the highway right now. Just try to relax and focus on steady breathing."

"Someone needs to call my wife."

"You're *married*?"

Earl moaned in response.

The chutzpah of this old guy: lying to a vulnerable widow while he was away from his wife! Was there no one left in this world who was faithful? Almost every man I'd ever been with had cheated on me. Except for Yossi Levy, my latest romantic interest. And since I hadn't heard from him in over five months, I could only assume he'd found someone else too. I briefly thought about calling Beavers and accepting his invitation to go to the Rez, just to spite Yossi. But I just as quickly rejected the idea and focused instead on staying a safe distance behind Lucy's Caddy.

Twelve minutes later Lucy turned on her right blinker. On the side of the highway, a blue sign with a big *H* pointed us in the direction of a nearby hospital.

We followed the arrows on the big red EMERGENCY signs in front of Mercy Medical Center. A team of doctors and nurses waited for us right outside. I discovered later that Jazz had the presence of mind to phone ahead.

Lucy got out of the Caddy and pointed them to the passenger side of the hearse. After a moment's confusion, they opened the door of the death vehicle and placed the living Earl on a gurney.

He raised his head and looked at me. "Don't let me die alone. Call Wanda. Call my wife."

As they wheeled him away, Lucy crossed her arms. "That old Lothario is married?"

I nodded.

She curled her lip. "It figures!"

I wasn't proud of my feelings, but, at that moment, I was glad to be driving in a different car from my angry friend—even if it meant hauling the mortal remains of Russell Watson the rest of the way to McMinnville.

CHAPTER 20

Jazz and Birdie joined Lucy and me by the door of the emergency room.

Birdie wrung her hands. "What'll we do now?"

I glanced at my watch. "It's noon already, and we're not even halfway to McMinnville. We can't stick around the hospital. Let's grab some food to go and forge ahead."

Lucy crossed her arms. "I agree. The sooner the better."

I held a clipboard, holding a map and papers that I had picked up from the hearse's console, next to the driver's seat. "The way is clearly plotted on this map. When we get to the Salem area we'll leave Interstate 5 and head northwest on the 22."

Birdie frowned. "But what about poor Earl? He said he's all alone in this world."

Lucy's eyes narrowed. "He lied, Birdie. Earl's married to someone named Wanda. He's her problem now. Let's get the heck out of here."

I handed the map to Lucy. "You take the lead. We'll reverse the order of our little procession. Jazz can navigate. I'll be right behind you, with Arthur to keep me company."

As soon as I brought the German shepherd close to the hearse, he began to bark. "Easy, boy. I know you can tell there's a body in the back, but it's supposed to be there. Calm down. You can sit up front with me, okay?" He jumped up on the side of the hearse and barked again.

"For heaven's sake. If you're going to act that way, you'll have to go back to the others." I marched Arthur back to Lucy's Caddy. "Sorry, everyone, but I can't cope with a hyper dog right now. I need to focus on driving."

Zsa Zsa wagged her tail and jumped up and down when Arthur climbed onto the backseat of the Caddy again.

We grabbed burgers at the nearest McDonald's and stopped at a gas station to fill our tanks. I emptied the ashtray and threw away the food wrappings and empty cups Earl had accumulated along the way. As soon as we hit the road, I rolled down the windows for ten minutes to freshen the stale air inside.

When I rolled the windows back up, I thought I detected a faint sickly sweet odor. Was it coming from the coffin? Surely not. Russell had been embalmed before we left. His remains should keep for the three-day trip. And anyway, the coffin had been sealed.

My mind raced. What if Towsley cheated? What if he skipped the embalming part? Now I understood why he hired Earl. A man with no sense of smell wouldn't be bothered by the decay occurring in the box directly behind the driver's seat.

Either I was imagining that smell, or something was rotten in Denmark. Either way, I'd have to hang on until we got to McMinnville.

We had just passed the small town of Cottage Grove when I noticed a car in my rearview mirror, less than a quarter of a mile back. We were traveling sixty-five miles an hour, but the car rapidly closed the distance behind me.

The highway was clear around us, but the car headed straight toward the back of the hearse. I leaned on the horn to warn Lucy and steered toward the right-hand side of the lane.

Red. The car was close enough for me to see it was red. The driver pulled alongside of me and pounded his horn in a maniacal staccato. All of a sudden, he darted into the space between the hearse and the Caddy, forcing me to hit the brakes. The hearse skidded onto the shoulder of the road. The tires lost traction, and the long car began to rotate. My heart pounded in my throat.

The world spun around in shades of black. Green. Red.

Am I going to die?

The seat belt dug into my left shoulder and chest as my body continued to travel forward at sixty-five miles an hour. My shoulder slammed sideways against the door. A big, white pillow punched me in the face. Then all was quiet.

I kept my eyes closed and conducted a mental survey of my body. Nothing seemed to hurt. Maybe it was the adrenaline. Maybe I'd hurt later. I opened my eyes. I couldn't see past the pillow in my face.

Familiar voices. "Martha! Oh my God! Are you okay, hon?" Lucy didn't sound angry anymore. Just scared.

A strong arm pushed the air bag out of my face. Jazz. He reached across and unhooked my seat belt. "Come on, Martha. Let's get you out of here. Can you stand?"

"I think so."

He grabbed me under the arms and lifted me to a standing position. "Anything broken?"

I shook my head and looked around. Lucy's Caddy was parked in front of the hearse on the soft shoulder of the highway. The Porsche was gone. "Where is that creep?"

Jazz clenched his fists. "He spun out clear across to the other side of the highway. Almost got hit himself. Too bad they missed. When his car stopped, he straightened out and laid rubber."

I remembered what Detective Beavers and Agent Lancet had told us at the beginning of our trip. *If you see anything suspicious, call 9-1-1 and head for the nearest law enforcement.* A part of me drifted away from my body, and I heard myself speak in an eerily calm voice. "It's time to call Agent Lancet. Her card's in my purse. We also need to notify local law enforcement."

The cars on the highway began to slow as they drew near the scene of our accident, but none of them stopped. Just the opposite. They suddenly accelerated past us.

Jazz walked toward the driver's side of the hearse.

"I'll get your purse." He groped around until he found my shoulder bag.

I unearthed Agent Kay B. Lancet's card and handed it to him. "Better call her now."

Lucy wrinkled her nose and sniffed. "What is that smell?" She used her hand to fan the air in front of her face.

Jazz frowned and turned down the corners of his mouth. Birdie sniffed and looked horrified. The sickening odor I thought I'd detected before now permeated the air; the overwhelming stench of death left unattended.

I put up my hand. "You and Jazz better stay here, Birdie. Come on, Lucy."

I took my tall friend's arm and walked with her toward the back of the hearse. The rear door had popped open, allowing the coffin to fly out the back. The big casket now lay gaping open on the ground. No wonder none of the other drivers on the highway stopped to help us.

The good news was that despite my worst fears, Towsley had not cheated Birdie. Russell's body had been perfectly preserved by the embalming fluids.

The bad news was I now understood what Arthur tried to tell me when he jumped on the side of the hearse and barked. Russell wasn't alone. On top of his body lay the source of the awful smell—the decomposing corpse of a strange man with dark hair.

And plainly visible, despite the bloating and discoloration of his skin, was a spiderweb tattoo on the side of his neck.

Lucy and I took one look at each other and walked back to the Caddy. Jazz had one arm around

Birdie, while he talked on his phone. "Northbound. We just passed signs pointing to Cottage Grove. Don't worry, we're not going anywhere."

He closed his phone and pinched his brows together. "That was 9-1-1. I also left a message for Agent Lancet. Dare I ask what's back there?"

There was no gentle way to tell them Russell's remains lay exposed on the ground. "I'm afraid the coffin lid popped open when it slid out of the back and onto the ground."

Birdie gasped. Jazz covered his mouth with his hand.

"I'm sorry, but it gets worse. Someone stuffed another body inside the coffin on top of Russell."

Birdie sagged backward into Jazz's chest.

"The upside is we don't have to worry about Rene Levesque anymore."

CHAPTER 21

Sirens screamed in the distance, heading toward us from both directions. Once I knew help was on its way, the adrenaline subsided, and my knees began to shake. The quaking became more violent as it traveled up my body. When it reached my neck, the muscles seized up into a mother of a spasm. My head throbbed so badly, I thought my eyes would explode out of their sockets. "I've got to sit down."

Lucy helped me walk back to the Caddy, where Zsa Zsa and Arthur huddled together on the backseat. We sat in our usual places, with the doors open, and waited for the police.

I rummaged through my purse for my migraine meds. "Is there anything to drink?"

Birdie handed me an unopened plastic bottle of Arrowhead Mountain Spring Water. "That was Jazz's crazy stalker, wasn't it?"

I swallowed my pills and rubbed my pounding temples. "Who else? That creep tried to kill us."

Lucy turned in her seat to look at me. "He's got to be the one who hired Russell's killer."

"I don't know." I closed my eyes. "He seems perfectly capable of committing violence all on his own. The sooner Birdie can decode the diary, the sooner we'll know for sure."

The Cottage Grove Police parked behind us in a black and white SUV and proceeded to put flares on the road, diverting the traffic from the accident. The Lane County Sheriffs parked in front of us in a green and white car with a gold stripe on the side and hurried to examine the bodies and the coffin. Three dark blue Oregon State Police cruisers parked next to us on the highway, shielding our morbid tableau from curious drivers. A tall trooper assumed control of the scene. He seemed older than the rest, and I guessed he was a senior officer. A small bulge in his lower lip suggested he had squirreled away a pinch of Copenhagen.

"How are we going to explain all this?" Lucy asked.

I kneaded the back of my neck. "Very carefully."

Two state troopers cautiously approached the Caddy. A young trooper stood on the passenger side of the car, while the tall one in charge bent down and spoke to Lucy in the driver's seat. "License and registration, please." He examined her papers and handed them back. "Was anyone injured in the accident?"

I raised my hand. "Me."

He looked in the backseat, where I sipped from the bottle of water. His name tag read FRANKLIN. "Don't worry, ma'am. Paramedics are on the way." He raised his head and scanned the area. Then he looked back in the car. "Did you folks see where the driver of the hearse went to?"

I raised my hand again. "That would be me."

His eyes widened. "Come again?"

"It's a long story, Officer."

He pushed his brows together, and his face conveyed a warning. "This better be good. There's enough evidence lying on the ground back there to arrest all of you."

I took a deep breath, and the words tumbled out like a landslide on the Pacific Coast Highway. "We were attacked just now by a famous Swedish rapper in a red Porsche who's been stalking Jazz for a month." I pointed to Russell's lover, who nodded vigorously and hugged Zsa Zsa to his chest.

"Right. He have a name?"

"Li'l Ape Man."

Trooper Franklin didn't even try to hide his laughter. "Okay, lady, you need to step out of the vehicle and take a breathalyzer."

I took a drink of water, trying to ignore the pounding in the right side of my head. "Please, just hear me out first."

"This should be good." He turned his head to the side and spat.

"We suspected Li'l Ape Man had been following us for the last couple of days but didn't call the authorities. In hindsight, we should have. He appeared out of nowhere just now and deliberately ran us off the road."

Jazz stroked Zsa Zsa's head. "That's my fault. He's crazy about me."

The trooper wrote something on his notepad. "Explain the bodies back there."

"The real body is Russell Watson, her husband." I pointed to Birdie. "The other body is an international assassin who is wanted by Interpol. We were afraid he was coming after us, too."

"An international assassin."

Lucy, who'd been silent throughout the questioning, finally spoke up. "His name's Rene Levesque. He's murdered people all over Europe and Florida."

I cleared my throat. "Whoever hired Rene Levesque to kill Russell also hired him to steal something from Birdie, but we foiled his plan with a police dog and a frying pan."

"Really. So how did he end up dead in another man's coffin?"

"I guess the mastermind had no further use for him. He must have known Russell's body was going to be buried out of state. What better way to get rid of the only witness?"

The trooper narrowed his eyes at me. "Why were you driving the hearse in the first place? How do I know you weren't the ones trying to get rid of the body?"

Birdie twisted the end of her braid. "My friends here were helping me escort my husband's body from LA to McMinnville. He wanted to be buried with his ancestors up there in the old family plot."

Jazz twisted the diamond band on his left hand. "The Watsons traveled the Oregon Trail in a covered wagon."

"And stole land from the Native Americans," I muttered under my breath.

"And?" The trooper rolled his hand impatiently as if he were directing a traffic snarl at an intersection.

I took another sip of water. "Unfortunately, the hearse driver had a heart attack near Roseburg this morning. We left him in the emergency room of Mercy Medical Center. You can check that out too. His name is Earl. I don't know his last name, but he's married to Wanda—and he cheats on her."

The officer parted his lips as if to speak then closed his mouth again.

I took a deep breath. "We couldn't just leave Russell's body in Roseburg. Getting him buried is the whole purpose of our trip. So I volunteered to drive him the rest of the way. Believe me, I wasn't happy about it. Once I sat inside the vehicle, I detected a bad odor that Earl had missed because he lost his sense of smell from smoking. Personally, I think that's why the mortician hired him in the first place."

The trooper closed his eyes and ran his hand over his face.

"Tell him about the FBI." Jazz poked my arm.

"You need to know the FBI has jurisdiction over this case because Russell Watson was killed during a bank robbery. However, the LAPD is also searching for Levesque because he tried to break into Birdie's house. By the way, the LAPD detective working on the break-in was raised on the Siletz reservation right here in Oregon. He's my ex-boyfriend." I watched Trooper Franklin closely, hoping I'd scored some credibility.

He just slowly shook his head and glanced at his partner, so I kept talking.

"The night of the attempted break-in, I heard the man swear in French. That detail, along with the spiderweb tattoo on his neck, enabled the FBI to identify Levesque. Here. I can show you his picture."

The trooper put out a restraining hand. "Stop. Keep your hands where I can see them." He looked at each of us. "All of you have to come to the station while I check out this cockamamie story. Get out of the car."

I stood and clipped a strong black nylon leash to Arthur's matching collar. "I'm bringing my dog. Remember I told you about my ex-boyfriend, the LAPD detective from Oregon? This police canine belongs to him. I think he deserves some professional courtesy."

Arthur stood obediently beside me, ears pointed forward on alert.

Jazz placed Zsa Zsa inside her yellow tote bag and draped it over his arm. "My little princess can't be left alone, either."

Trooper Franklin made me blow into a breathalyzer three times before he reluctantly acknowledged my sobriety. The other state troopers searched the car. One of them removed the keys from the ignition of the vintage Caddy and opened the trunk. When the younger trooper reached for my purse, my stomach dropped to my knees. I had forgotten about the Browning inside.

He held up the gun. "Take a look at this."

Another trooper had opened Lucy's purse and

pulled out the Glock. "We've got another one over here."

Lucy held up her hand. "Those guns are registered to me. I have a permit to carry both of them. Look in my wallet."

With a little digging, Franklin read the paper in her wallet. "This permit isn't valid in Oregon. And anyway, what is your firearm doing in her purse?"

Lucy briefly glanced at me and raised her chin. "Isn't it obvious? We didn't know the assassin was already dead. We wanted to protect Birdie."

"Here's something else that's obvious. I'm confiscating these weapons." He turned to the other troopers. "Search 'em."

A chunky blond female trooper with a large derriere patted down Lucy, Birdie, and me, while the young trooper frisked Jazz. When they were satisfied we were unarmed, they stepped back and gave us back our purses, minus the pistols.

Trooper Franklin gestured toward the backseats of the dark blue patrol cars. "We're taking you to our field office in Springfield."

Birdie wrung her hands, and her eyes brimmed. "But what's going to happen to my poor husband? You can't leave his body exposed like this."

"His body will be taken to the medical examiner's office in Clackamas. On the off chance your wild story checks out, his body will be released. You can make arrangements with a local mortuary for transport to McMinnville."

"What about my car?" Lucy pointed to the Caddy.

"It'll be towed to our office."

I asked Jazz for Agent Lancet's card and handed

it to Trooper Franklin. "We've already called her. She's probably on her way to Oregon as we speak. But you should call her anyway. She'll vouch for us."

The police radio clipped to Franklin's shoulder crackled to life. He walked away from us to speak to dispatch. When he returned, he spat and looked straight at me. "I don't believe it. An FBI chopper is on the way with agents from the Portland office. They've verified at least part of your story."

"Of course they have, because it's the truth."

"Lady, I've got to say, I've heard some lunatic explanations in my time, but yours tops them all."

He gestured toward an ambulance waiting on the road above us. "You said you were injured. Maybe you should get checked out by the paramedics."

I shook my head. "No, thanks. I prefer to stay with my friends."

As I walked toward the backseat of a patrol car, I heard the young trooper speak to his chunky blond colleague. "Wow. Li'l Ape Man. I know the dude these old ladies are talking about. He had this cool rap that was all over the radio for months."

"Yeah? Which one was that?"

"'Bite My Swedish Meatballs, Yo.'"

CHAPTER 22

The state police field office in Springfield, Oregon, was located right off Interstate 5. A narrow strip of verdant lawn lined the sidewalk in front, and a row of alders delicately camouflaged the small one-story facility. Once inside the station, curious stares greeted our little group—three senior women with a German shepherd and a tall man carrying a tiny Maltese with a rhinestone barrette.

A blowsy secretary snickered as we passed, but a hard stare from Franklin shut her up. Somewhere between Cottage Grove and Springfield, he'd gotten rid of the Copenhagen, and his lip was flat again. He opened the door to a conference room and gestured for us to enter. Then he and the young trooper joined us.

Lucy, Birdie, Jazz, and I arranged ourselves in a protective huddle at the far end of a long table laminated in brown wood-grained plastic.

Jazz leaned over and whispered, "I'm surprised, with all the trees in Oregon, they don't use real wood for their furniture. And what's with these beige walls? Don't they realize that color paint, along with those fluorescent lights, sucks the life right out of a person's cheeks?"

Franklin cleared his throat. "The ETA for the feds is about a half hour." He crooked his thumb toward his young partner. "Posner here will stay with you while you're waiting. I'll be back." He left abruptly and closed the door.

Young trooper Posner stood awkwardly. "Is anyone thirsty?"

Jazz flashed a smile. "It's three in the afternoon. We normally take tea at this time. Maybe some scones and crème cakes to go with?" He turned his face to us and winked.

Posner didn't get the joke. He nodded, stuck his head out the door, and shouted, "Madonna!"

The blowsy secretary shouted back, "Yeah?"

"I need you!"

A minute later, she appeared in the doorway. "What?"

Posner whispered something under his breath. She thrust her neck forward and stared at us. "Seriously?"

"Just do it, please."

Ten minutes later, we each had a disposable cup of tepid water, with a Lipton tea bag floating inside, and a small package of chocolate chip cookies from a vending machine.

"You know, I've been thinking." Jazz opened a packet of sugar and stirred his tea with a white plastic spoon. "Trucker Chic is too casual. I mean, how would I dress Johnny for the Oscars? I'm getting a whole new take on his wardrobe. Detective

Debonair. I'm going to redo the Smokey Bear trooper hat in forest green felt and stick a partridge feather in the brim. Luckily, I've been saving a bolt of dark green cashmere for just the right project. I think that fabric would rock in a suit with wide lapels."

Lucy sipped her tea. "Sounds an awful lot like Robin Hood to me, hon. And way too matchy-matchy."

Birdie and I looked at each other in disbelief. Could this be our Lucy speaking? The one who always dressed with a theme? The one who had an extensive collection of color-coordinated shoes that matched every outfit in her closet?

Jazz pursed his lips. "Hmm. I see what you mean. Maybe I could do the whole look in midnight blue instead. With a peacock feather and an iridescent shirt."

Lucy nodded with approval. "I think you're on to something."

Trooper Franklin came back in the room around four, followed by two male FBI agents wearing gray suits and blue ties. They introduced themselves as Tucker and O'Neal.

"Make yourselves comfortable, folks. We're going to be here awhile. We're waiting for Agent Lancet's flight to land in Eugene."

Birdie raised her hand. "Have you apprehended Li'l Ape Man yet?"

Tucker shook his head. "No, ma'am. But author-ities in all the surrounding states have been alerted. Unless he drives his car into the Pacific Ocean, we'll catch him."

Over the next two hours, the agents interviewed us one by one. During that time I received a worried call from Beavers.

"Kay told me about the accident. Are you hurt? Is Arthur okay?"

"We're fine, Arlo."

"I can fly up there tonight."

Dealing with Arlo Beavers was the last thing I wanted to do right now. "Please don't. Honestly, we're fine. I'll give you an update tomorrow."

We ordered pizza from a local restaurant. I requested one with anchovies, instead of pepperoni made from pork, and shared it with the dog. Despite his owner's instruction not to feed him people food, in my book, Arthur deserved a treat for being so well-behaved.

Agent Lancet finally showed up as we finished the last of our dinner. "I've just come from the forensics lab down the hall. The second body has been positively identified as Rene Levesque from a thumbprint they managed to lift from the corpse. Clearly, you can stop worrying about him as a threat. However, the person who hired him is still at large." She looked at Birdie. "We have to assume he might come after you, even now."

Jazz picked up the last slice of pizza with a paper napkin. "Don't you think he just did?"

Lancet blew out a breath. "Yeah. I'm leaning toward the Swedish rapper for obvious reasons. Running you off the road was a desperate act."

"He really became obsessed with me," Jazz said. "Like Glenn Close in *Fatal Attraction*."

I wasn't convinced that such a violent man would

bother to hire someone else to do his dirty work. Besides, how did he, or anyone else, for that matter, get access to Russell's coffin? "So, are you ruling out Russell's brother, Denver, and Jazz's neighbor Cisco Conejo as the possible mastermind? Seems to me they both held equally strong grudges that could've led to murder for hire."

Lancet shook her head. A strand of brown hair slipped out of the bun at the nape of her neck and fell down the side of her face. "The problem is, we haven't found any evidence linking them to the murder. But we do have clear proof the rapper attempted multiple murders today. Yours. Sometimes the simplest explanation is the best. Li'l Ape Man is our most likely suspect."

She was right, of course. The creep did attempt to kill us today. Still, I wasn't ready to eliminate the other two suspects from my list. Not until we knew for sure what was in that diary.

Soon Birdie would come face-to-face with one of the suspects. Russell's brother, Denver, said he'd meet her in McMinnville. What if Agent Lancet was wrong about the Swedish rapper? What if Denver Watson hired Levesque to kill his brother and steal back the bearer bonds? Now, more than ever, Birdie needed to break the code of secrets in Russell's red diary.

Birdie reached over and grasped Jazz's hand. "What about Russell, Agent Lancet?"

"The body's in Clackamas right now." Lancet's voice softened. "You can arrange for him to be picked up tomorrow." She looked at her watch and addressed Trooper Franklin and her colleagues at

the FBI. "It's eight. Why don't we let these folks go
to a hotel now? They've been through a rough day."

Franklin reached in his shirt pocket and returned the keys to Lucy's Caddy. He also handed
over her two guns. Then he gave us directions to
the nearby Hilton Garden Inn. "We've booked
separate rooms for each of you. They're not a pet-
friendly hotel, but they won't give you trouble
about the dogs."

I ruffled the fur on the back of Arthur's neck.
"How'd you manage that?"

He grinned. "I asked for professional courtesy."
The bump was back under his lower lip. As we left,
I thought I saw him slip a small piece of paper to
Jazz. *Really?*

Arthur and I stayed in a single on the ground
floor, near an outside door. I walked him for the last
time that night and left a bowl of water on the floor
in case he got thirsty. Then I took a long, hot
shower in hopes of easing the soreness in my muscles, climbed into a clean pair of flannel pajamas,
and took another Soma. My room phone rang.

"Are you feeling any better, dear?" Birdie's voice
sagged with concern and fatigue.

"A little. I'll feel a whole lot better after a good
night's rest."

Birdie yawned as she spoke. "I know what you
mean. But as tired as I am, I can't seem to settle
down. I'm going to work on the diary for a while.
I'll meet you at eight in the morning for breakfast."

I turned off the lamp next to my bed, and Arthur
crawled up next to me, burping anchovy breath in
my face. The phone rang again. I opened my eyes,

surprised to find the room flooded with morning sunlight.

"Hey, girlfriend, you all right?" It was Lucy. "We've been waiting in the restaurant for the last fifteen minutes and got worried when you didn't show up."

The digital clock on the nightstand read eight-fifteen. Even if I hadn't seen the clock, my bursting bladder would've confirmed I'd slept more than ten hours straight. My body hurt all over. I was in for a few bad days from the trauma of the accident. Every nerve ending burned and ached. "Oh, crap! I forgot to ask for a wake-up call. Can someone come and walk the dog while I get dressed?"

At twenty minutes to nine, we ordered big breakfasts from a laminated plastic menu. I looked around the booth and realized nobody wore denim today. Even Birdie. If all went well, we'd be burying Russell this afternoon.

Lucy and Jazz each wore peach linen. Birdie wore a long cotton dress left over from the seventies, printed with yellow flowers on a soft blue background.

When she saw me staring at it, she fingered the fabric on her sleeve. "This was one of Russell's favorites."

I also wore a cotton dress, only mine was calf-length and rather plain. I purchased it because the solid green brought out the color of my eyes.

I ordered two eggs sunny side up and a stack of pancakes soaked in melted butter and syrup made from Oregon marionberries. A half hour later, I added milk to my third cup of coffee and sank back in the red leatherette cushion of the booth. "What do you want to do now, Birdie?"

With the back of a teaspoon, she spread the last drop of marmalade from the little plastic bucket onto the crust of her English muffin. "I called the mortuary in McMinnville last night to explain why we didn't show up yesterday. They'll pick up Russell from the medical examiner's office this morning and be back in McMinnville by the time we get there. I told them to be sure to wrap him back up in his quilt."

"And I called Agent Lancet this morning," said Lucy. "So far, nobody's spotted the red Porsche."

Jazz smoothed the sleeve of his peach and white striped shirt. "I'm worried that he's still lurking around somewhere watching us. I had nightmares all night. Poor Zsa Zsa didn't know what to think." He looked around the restaurant to make sure nobody else was watching. Then he reached into his yellow tote bag and caressed the little Maltese.

Today Zsa Zsa wore a dress sewn from the same peach and white striped fabric as Jazz's shirt.

Lucy took out her cell phone and sent a brief text. In the frenzy of events yesterday, I had completely forgotten about Ray Junior's missing wife and children.

"What's the latest, Lucy? Any news from Tanya and the kids?"

She closed the phone, looked up, and sighed. "Trey called his dad last night." Trey was what they called Ray Junior's son, Ray Mondello, III. "They're okay, but they're understandably confused. Junior's flying to Hawaii today to try and talk Tanya into coming home with the boys."

The sadness in Lucy's eyes tore at my heart. I began to get an idea about how I could help her. "Does this kung fu guy have a name? What do you really know about him?"

"His name is Nick Evans. He's originally from Hawaii. Tanya met him two months ago. That's all we know."

Two months didn't seem like a long enough time to be familiar with someone. "What kind of man runs off with a married woman and her children after such a short time? He's up to something bad."

Lucy frowned. "I don't think you'll ever convince Tanya of that."

"Then we need to find some dirt on Nick. Something Ray Junior can use to persuade Tanya to come home."

"How are we going to uncover something a private investigator couldn't find?"

"Don't worry," I said. "I've got a plan."

I scooted out the end of the booth. "We should probably get going. Since I overslept, I still have packing to do." I had left Arthur in my room eating his morning kibble out of the stainless steel bowl. He'd need another walk before we got started. "Arthur and I will meet you guys out in front in twenty minutes."

As I folded yesterday's clothes and put them in my suitcase, I kept thinking about something Birdie just said. She'd asked the mortician in McMinnville to be sure Russell was wrapped up in her Baltimore Album quilt again. I revisited the scene of yesterday's disaster in my head and realized, with a sinking feeling, that wasn't going to happen.

When Levesque's body was added to the casket, the prize-winning reproduction of a Watson family heirloom had been removed. Birdie's Baltimore Album quilt was missing.

CHAPTER 23

It was Friday and, once again, I'd be missing Shabbat dinner that night with Uncle Isaac. I called him on my cell phone as we headed north on Interstate 5 toward McMinnville.

"Shabbat Shalom, Uncle Isaac."

"Good *Shabbos, faigela.* So how did it go yesterday, the funeral?"

There was no way I was going to tell him about the accident and the extra body we found. "Uh, we ran into a little glitch on the highway and ended up spending the night in Eugene. But we're on our way now."

The anxiety in his voice was instantaneous. "*Nu?* What kind of glitch? Are you okay?"

"It was nothing. A flat tire and a busted thingamajig. We had to wait overnight for a part." *God forgive me for lying to an old man.*

"*Baruch haShem.* For a minute, I was worried. I heard on the news yesterday some *meshuggena* celebrity tried to run a bunch of elderly people off the road in Oregon. They say he's still on the loose."

What nerve! Elderly? To the media, anyone over forty was elderly. "What else did they say?"

"They said he's Swedish. I'm surprised. They're usually such a quiet people."

"Don't worry, Uncle Isaac. Oregon's a big place. Chances are we'll never run into him. I'll see you when we get back to LA next week."

I closed my phone and caught Lucy looking at me in the rearview mirror. "Flat tire? Waiting for parts? Don't look now, girlfriend, but your nose is growing longer."

"I know, I know." I rolled my eyes. "But what was I supposed to tell him? Apparently the whole thing was on the news last night. Thank God they didn't divulge our names."

I called my daughter, Quincy, in Boston but only got her voice mail. I wished her a Shabbat Shalom and asked her to call me later.

"Oh, for pity's sake! Why didn't I see this before?" Birdie waved a sheet of paper in the air with alphabets written in pencil. "I think I've broken the code."

Thank goodness. Birdie was a seasoned puzzle solver. Her years of working cryptic crosswords were about to finally pay off.

"Just as I thought." She beamed. "It's a simple substitution code. A shift cipher with a key phrase. It works like this. First, you write out the alphabet in the usual way. Then right under each letter you write out the cryptic alphabet, beginning with a key word or phrase, which can have no repeated letters. After you write the key, you insert the rest of the letters of the alphabet in their normal sequence. You still end up with twenty-six letters, but they've been shifted over."

"Huh?" Lucy glanced at Birdie.

"Remember Russell wrote the words 'C*razy* P*lot*' in the front of the diary? That phrase was the key that unlocked the cipher."

I reached forward. "Can I see that?"

Birdie handed me the sheet of paper on which she had written:

A B C D E F G H I J K L M N O P Q R S T U V W X Y Z
c r a z y p l o t b d e f g h i j k m n q s u v w x
bqgy = JUNE
zyayfryk = DECEMBER

"Congratulations, Birdie, this is brilliant." I handed the sheet back to her. "So, what does the diary reveal, besides dates?"

She sighed. "Give me some time to work it out. I've only just cracked the code."

"I think we're in trouble." Lucy kept looking in the rearview mirror. "We're being followed. Black SUV. Two cars behind."

Jazz and I turned in our seats and strained to look out the back window. Sure enough, the SUV trailed directly behind a white Prius. "I see him. How can you be sure he's following us?"

"After yesterday? I'm constantly checking the road. He's been pacing our speed, only allowing one car between us the whole time."

Jazz hugged Zsa Zsa and stroked her nervously. "Do you think Li'l Ape Man changed cars? Do you think he's still after us?"

I pulled out my cell phone. "We're not going to take any chances. I'm calling Agent Lancet right now." She picked up on the second ring, and I put her on speaker. "I think we're being followed again. We're approaching Albany."

"Describe the car."

I twisted around in my seat to look again. "Black SUV. Lucy says it's been on our tail since we left Springfield."

She laughed. "Don't worry. You're quite safe."

The car pulled out from behind the Prius and sped up. "Oh my God, it's coming after us. I'm getting the Browning out of my purse."

"Are you crazy?" Lucy shouted. "If I get any bullet holes in this car, Ray is going to kill me."

Jazz looked horrified. "You and a gun? Not again!"

"Did I hear someone say they still had the Browning?" Lancet was still on the phone and had heard everything we just said.

"No!" we all said together.

The SUV pulled up next to us and the window on the passenger side slowly rolled open. A woman's right hand waved from the passenger seat. Then I saw her face. Agent Kay Lancet.

She spoke into the cell phone she held in her left hand. "You didn't think we'd let you go back on the road without providing security, did you?"

"Good grief!" Lucy's hands loosened their death grip on the steering wheel and she slumped in her seat. "She could have warned us. I almost had a heart attack."

A wave of relief washed over me, and I started

breathing again. "You're on speaker. We can all hear you."

"Keep your guard up. You're doing great. Mrs. Watson, I called the ME's office in Clackamas. They released Mr. Watson's body to Yoder Brothers Mortuary early this morning. Everything should be ready for you by the time we get to McMinnville."

"How long will that be?" Lucy asked.

"Not more than an hour and a half. Relax, folks, and enjoy the beautiful scenery." Lancet ended the call and the SUV dropped behind us once again.

Lucy turned off the highway into the Walmart in Albany for a pit stop. The SUV pulled up next to us in the parking lot, and Agents Lancet, Tucker, and O'Neal got out. "We'll be going in with you."

Jazz shrugged. "Fine with me." He turned to Agent Tucker and offered a friendly smile. "Does everyone in the FBI wear gray suits?"

"Don't know. Never thought about it."

"What about off duty? Do you ever do colors?"

"No."

Jazz raised an eyebrow. "Well, if you ever decide to branch out, consider sticking to slightly grayed pinks and blues. You're definitely a soft summer."

Tucker grunted in response and gestured for O'Neal to accompany Jazz into the store.

I touched Agent Lancet's arm and indicated I wanted to talk to her alone. We waited until everyone disappeared inside Walmart.

"Agent Lancet, Kay, there's a problem I'm hoping you can help me with."

"I will if I can."

I told her about Lucy's daughter-in-law, Tanya,

running off to Hawaii. "She took the boys out of state without their father's permission. The thing is, she's only known her kung fu instructor for two months. What kind of man would run off with a married woman and her three children? I'm certain he's up to no good."

"This sounds like a civil matter to me, Mrs. Rose."

"Please call me Martha. Isn't it kidnapping? Isn't that a federal crime?"

"No. It's a federal crime only if they were taken against their will. But if she went willingly, it's a matter for the family courts."

"Lucy's son is flying to Hawaii to persuade Tanya to come back home with the boys. I thought that if he had some dirt on the kung fu character, Ray Junior could convince her that she'd made a big mistake."

"Well, they could always hire a private detective to do some digging."

I groaned. "They did, but he turned up nothing. You, on the other hand, have access to all kinds of databases."

She pulled her head back. "We don't investigate people when no crime has been committed, Martha. You're asking me to use the resources of the federal government to spy on one of its citizens."

"Please, Kay. Just take a look. If you turn up nothing, nobody needs to know you looked in the first place. But what if he's done this before? What if he's a serial killer? What if this is a huge scam designed to extort money from the Mondello family? Wouldn't you want to catch the guy?"

She briefly closed her eyes then frowned at me.

"Tell me everything you know about him. Name, where he worked. A photo would help. I'll see what I can do, but I can't promise anything."

I gave her an impulsive hug. "Thank you! The Mondello family has been torn apart by this. They'll be so grateful."

She held up her finger. "This is totally off the record. Do you understand what I'm telling you?"

I nodded. "I won't even tell Lucy about it. This is just between you and me." I felt a sudden sense of lightness as we turned and joined the stream of shoppers headed toward the entrance of Walmart. If Nick Evans was a bad guy—and I was sure he was—the FBI would have a record of him somewhere.

Once again I had noticed Lancet's stunning cheekbones and large eyes. I suspected when her long brown hair wasn't bullied into that severe bun, she'd turn out to be quite an exotic beauty. I cleared my throat. "So how long have you known Arlo Beavers?"

"Why?"

"I don't know. He said the two of you go way back."

She continued walking, looking straight forward. "We do."

I hesitated asking my next question. She'd have every right to shut me down, but I took a deep breath and asked anyway. "You seem to be on very friendly terms. Did you ever date?"

She slowed her pace and stared at me. "Why do you ask?"

"Well, I used to go out with him. Now he seems

interested in rekindling a romance. I just wondered what your experience might have been."

She stopped walking altogether and regarded me for a long moment before she spoke. "If you must know, we used to be married."

My mouth fell open. This was Beavers's ex-wife? While I dated him, he never spoke about her except to say he had once been in a bad marriage. I had just assumed he had been a victim of some floozy. But how bad could it have been? Kay Lancet seemed like such a decent, capable woman.

With a flash of insight, I understood. Lancet wasn't the kind of woman who'd allow herself to be manipulated, and neither was I. The problem was, Beavers had a hard time tolerating not being in control. After all, didn't the same kind of power struggle end my relationship with him? If Crusher were truly gone forever and I were foolish enough to start dating Beavers again, chances were history would repeat itself. But I still needed confirmation that I was seeing things clearly.

"Did you ever think he might be a little overbearing?" I asked as we entered the store and headed toward the restrooms.

She gave a short laugh. "Oh, yeah. But Arlo's a decent guy. And a hell of a good cop. I really don't care who he dates. I've got no skin in that game anymore."

I nodded and pushed open the restroom door. Neither did I.

CHAPTER 24

We left Interstate 5 near Salem and headed west on Highway 22. Lucy drove in silence. Her mood had improved since yesterday's outburst, but she still seemed more stressed than I'd ever seen her. She was a no-nonsense pragmatist, the kind of person who could step in and fix a problem while others were still debating what to do. I could only guess that waiting helplessly while her son dealt with the disappearance of his family must have been killing her.

Birdie had abandoned whatever she'd been working on earlier. The closer we got to McMinnville, the quieter she became, just staring out the window. She jumped a little when her cell phone rang. "Oh, Rainbow. Have you settled in? Good, good. We're going straight to Yoder Brothers Mortuary. Then we'll caravan to Pioneer Cemetery." She listened and then said, "Last night Denver said he'd meet us all there. Yes, I'm very nervous. Okay. See you soon." The call ended and she said,

"That was Rainbow. I called her yesterday after the accident to let her know we'd be a day late."

I became hyperalert. "Birdie, you never mentioned Denver called last night."

She turned slightly in her seat. "He didn't call me. I called him. I wanted to also let him know why we were arriving a day late."

Jazz looked up from the sketch pad, where he was drafting a design for yacht wear. "Are you talking about Denver Watson, Rusty's brother? You're in actual contact with him?"

"Yes."

Jazz sniffed his disapproval. "It's just that they didn't get along. I don't think they've spoken since their mother died. I'm surprised he's coming, that's all."

Birdie rubbed her fingers together. "They had a complicated relationship, dear. They may have been angry with each other, but they were brothers. We should allow Denver to pay his respects without judging him."

That was vintage Birdie speaking; always ready to accept and forgive. But had she forgotten the potential danger awaiting her? Denver said he wanted something back from Russell. She figured out it must be the bearer bonds belonging to his parents. How far had Denver been willing to go to get them? Did he hire Levesque to kill his brother and steal the bonds from Birdie's house? Birdie had confided Denver was the only man she'd ever truly loved. Was the memory of their shared past blinding her to the dangerous realities of the present?

We continued to drive past vineyards and farms.

At the transition, north on Highway 99, Birdie said, "It won't be long now."

Sure enough, we passed a road sign that read MCMINNVILLE, 20 MILES. The afternoon sun was high overhead, and a few wispy clouds swept across an impossibly blue sky. The black Caddy ate up the last bit of highway with the same effortless power as when it crested the Grapevine just north of LA.

Jazz closed his sketchbook and slipped it in an outside pocket of the yellow tote bag. "Do you know how to get there, Birdie?"

"The cemetery is actually a little farther up the road, right outside the tiny town of Lafayette. But first we have to stop at the mortuary in McMinnville."

About five miles outside our destination, the unmarked black SUV sped up and took the lead. We followed the FBI car past gently rolling fields, some lined with neat rows of heavy grapevines, others carpeted with green. The fields eventually gave way to the manicured campus of Linfield College. White stone columns dressed the stately old red brick buildings and, for a moment, I felt we could be in Indiana or Ohio. "I had no idea it was so beautiful up here."

Jazz sighed. "Rusty always talked about this place with mixed feelings. It has been his family's home for generations. He called it 'bucolic.' But he wasn't comfortable here as a gay man."

We drove slowly through the small town. I'd googled McMinnville before we left LA, and learned the streets had been laid out by the town's settlers during the great migration west before the Civil

War. City parks provided generous green spaces with old-fashioned streetlights along the pathways. Turn of the twentieth century architecture preserved the quaint feeling, including a Carnegie library built in the late 1800s and old storefronts turned into restaurants with outdoor cafés.

"Look!" Lucy pointed to a wooden sign hanging above the entrance of a large store: MILLER'S, SINCE 1943. FABRICS, NOTIONS, SEWING SUPPLIES was painted on the windows where antique quilts and brand-new sewing machines were displayed. "Maybe I'll find more of those tiny polka dots that work so well as a background fabric."

She didn't need to say anything else. Lucy, Birdie, and I had one cardinal rule: if we found a new quilt shop, we had to check it out. There was nothing that excited a quilter more than stumbling upon a new store, because every shop had its own personality.

Cotton cloth manufacturers typically produced several fabric collections every year, each in many different colorways. With offerings from dozens of manufacturers, quilters could choose from hundreds of different designs. However, no single fabric store could carry every possible pattern and colorway. Therefore, each store offered its own unique selection of dry goods.

Fabrics, like fashions, reflected seasonal trends. Some years, certain colors were plentiful while others were hard to find. During the 1980s, most colors were grayed and dull. In the 1990s, Amish quilts became popular. The simple geometric designs used by the Amish featured solid fabric in clear colors set against dark backgrounds. Manufacturers introduced solid and print fabrics in colors that were truer and brighter. Around the turn of the twenty-first century, reproduction fabrics from the 1930s reflected both pastel and bright colors from that era. Then around 2005, reproduction fabrics from the 1800s trended into popularity. Colors became grayed again—completing the circle.

Exploring a new quilt shop held for us the promise of discovering unique treasures and an opportunity to add fresh fabrics to our collections. I knew we'd be back here in the next day or so.

We followed the SUV into the parking lot of Yoder Brothers, a one-story red brick building. Gravel crunched under the tires as we stopped at the far edge near a tangle of wild blackberry vines. Lancet sent Tucker and O'Neal to check out the building while she stood next to Lucy's Caddy.

My body was stiff from sitting so long without a break. Pain shot down my hip when I stood. I grabbed Arthur's leash and limped with him to a nearby cypress tree where he relieved himself. Then I poured some water into his stainless steel dish and gave him a well deserved drink.

Jazz unfolded himself from the backseat and carried Zsa Zsa to a soft patch of dirt where she squatted. He praised her copiously.

Lancet sauntered over to me and spoke quietly. "While we were driving, I got a hit on VICAP." She was talking about the Violent Criminal Apprehension Program database the FBI maintains.

I whipped my head around in surprise. "That was fast. How bad is it?"

Jazz was approaching us with Zsa Zsa in his arms. "I'll tell you later."

When everyone was ready, we moved toward the entrance. Birdie hung on Lucy's arm. Agent O'Neal offered to stand outside with Arthur, so I handed over the leash and grabbed Birdie's other arm. If Denver Watson waited inside, I wanted her to have plenty of support and protection.

My eyes took awhile to adjust to the dim interior. Another figure standing nearby appeared as a shadow at first. Gradually, I made out a buck-toothed man in a black suit with a solemn expression.

He glanced at Agent Tucker for a nod of approval then approached us with nervous steps. Clasping his hands behind his back, he looked at the three of us. "Mrs. Watson?"

Birdie tilted her head. "I'm Mrs. Watson."

Bucktooth nodded once. "I'm Milton Yoder, proprietor of Yoder Brothers, at your service. If you follow me to my office, I have some papers for you to sign. Then we can arrange for you to take one last look at Mr. Watson if you wish."

Lucy and I kept hold of Birdie, and Jazz walked with us into the Spartan office of Milton Yoder. Every surface was clean, dusted, and completely devoid of any decorative item, with one exception. Behind the desk hung a picture of praying hands holding a cross on a chain.

Jazz sat next to Birdie, facing Yoder, while Lucy and I stood behind their chairs.

While Milton Yoder explained the paperwork to

Birdie, I leaned over and whispered to Lucy, "I have to tell you something before Birdie goes in and looks at Russell again." I pulled her by the sleeve and led her back near the door.

"What?" she whispered back.

"The quilt was missing." I could tell by the look on her face she didn't understand what I was saying. "The Baltimore Album quilt. In Russell's coffin. When we discovered Levesque's corpse, didn't you notice? In order for the killer to fit him in there with Russell, he had to remove the quilt."

Lucy's eyes widened and she mouthed, "No!"

I dipped my head slowly. "Birdie's quilt is missing, and I forgot to tell her."

"Maybe she'll want to skip the part about looking at him again," Lucy whispered.

Birdie finished signing the documents and handed the pen back to Yoder.

He tapped the papers on the desk to make a neat pile and stapled them together. "Do you wish to view Mr. Watson again?"

Lucy and I exchanged a worried glance.

"After everything that's happened, I want to make sure it's my husband we're actually burying today, and not someone else."

Yoder looked at Jazz. "Perhaps your son could make the identification?"

Jazz sat up straight. "Russell Watson was not my father. He was my fiancé."

Yoder's eyes clouded over.

"Birdie," I hastily interrupted. "I hate to see you go through that again. Why don't you let me look for you? It'll only take a minute. Then we can leave for the cemetery and do what we came to do."

She gave me a grateful smile. "That's so thought-ful, dear. We'll wait right here until you're through."

Lucy winked at me and gave me thumbs-up. Crisis averted.

As Yoder led me down the hallway, I asked, "Are any other mourners here besides us?"

He clasped his hands again. "Yes. I believe a brother is here as well as a few friends. They were told to wait in the chapel by the authorities. I must say, I've never handled a funeral where the FBI was involved. We're a quiet little town here." He looked at me accusingly. "Christian. God-fearing."

Without another word, he opened the door of a small room where Russell's mahogany coffin sat on a low platform. The top had two deep scratches it must have received when it fell out of the back of the hearse. Someone tried to disguise them with a darker stain.

Yoder raised the lid. "Please confirm this is the deceased, Russell Watson."

I took a deep breath and peeked inside. Sure enough, I'd been right about the quilt being miss-ing. Russell's orange makeup was smeared, and his clothes reeked of the decomposing corpse that had lain on top of him for three days. I gagged and quickly backed away. "Were you really going to allow Mrs. Watson to see her husband in this condi-tion?"

He shrugged. "We could clean him up for a fee."

Oh my God. Will this nightmare ever end?

"Just close him up good and tight and get him in the ground as fast as you can. If you don't want to be part of the biggest lawsuit in the history of your God-fearing town, you will never—I repeat, never— breathe a word of his condition to Mrs. Watson. Do I make myself clear?"

Yoder blinked and nodded. We returned to his office, where my friends chatted quietly.

I forced myself to smile at Birdie and Jazz. "You can both relax. Russell's tucked away nice and safe. He's ready to make his final journey." *And the sooner the better.* "Shall we go?"

Birdie's shoulders slumped with relief. "Thank heavens. Yes, let's go. I'm ready."

"Follow me to the chapel, please." Yoder gestured toward the other end of the hallway and threw me a dirty look as I followed Russell's widow out the door.

Lucy and I each flanked Birdie and escorted her down the hall. Jazz fell in next to me. The four of us linked arms and marched toward the door of the chapel, knowing Denver Watson waited inside.

CHAPTER 25

A dozen men and women turned in the polished wooden pews to look at us as we entered the chapel. One man sat alone in a middle pew, staring intently at Birdie. He bore a strong resemblance to Russell Watson.

An elegant blonde in a short upsweep rushed over to Birdie. She wore an expensive cream-colored pantsuit and blouse. Diamonds dripped from her ears, fingers, and wrist. I recognized the scent of Bvlgari Rose Parfum hovering around her in an intoxicating cloud. I guessed she was around Lucy's age, somewhere in her very well-preserved sixties.

She and Birdie hugged each other for several seconds.

Finally, Birdie pulled back a little so she could look at her friend. "Rainbow! I'm so glad to see you. How was your flight?"

"Comfortable. It helps to have your own jet."

This former hippie owns a jet?

"You holding up okay?" she asked.

Birdie shrugged. "Fine, all things considered."

The elegant blonde bent down, whispered something in the older woman's ear, and pointed to the man in the middle row. When Birdie looked his way, he stood and slowly ambled toward her. The fringes on the sleeve of his brown suede jacket danced as he raised his arm to remove his hat. Underneath his Stetson, his hair was white, like his brother's, but longer; combed behind his ears and curling over the collar of his denim shirt.

His blue eyes sparkled as they gazed at Birdie. "Hey, Twink."

All the wrinkles in Birdie's face seemed to relax and disappear, and a soft smile curled her lips. "Denny."

I looked at Lucy, who seemed as perplexed as I was. This guy didn't seem like a threat at all. Denver Watson looked about as far away from vengeful as a man could get. Was this just a ploy to charm the vulnerable Birdie out of a quarter of a million dollars in bearer bonds?

He took her hand and brought it to his lips. "We've got a lot of catching up to do."

Reluctantly, Lucy, Jazz, and I stepped away to give them a little privacy. We moved to one of the back pews.

The blonde joined us and offered a slender hand with a French manicure. "I'm Sandra Prescott." She smiled. "But my friends call me Rainbow."

"I'm Martha Rose." I introduced the others. "I'm happy to meet you. Birdie's told us a little about you. All good, of course."

She smiled. "Well, she's told me a *lot* about you.

I can't imagine how we avoided running into each other all those times I visited LA."

Lucy waved her hand. "She probably wanted you all to herself, hon."

"This is a terrible business about Russell, isn't it?" Rainbow scowled and lowered her voice. "I can't help feel I'm somehow responsible."

What was it with Russell Watson that so many people wanted to take responsibility for his death? First Jazz and his secrets and now Sandra Prescott, aka Rainbow.

"Care to elaborate?"

She shook her head, and every short blond hair stayed perfectly in place. "Not now. But we'll talk later, Martha. Birdie's told me you're very good at solving crimes."

"Why don't you go to the FBI with your suspicions? I hear they're also pretty good at that sort of thing."

"I have my reasons." Rainbow stopped speaking when Birdie waved us over. "We'll talk."

The four of us joined the older couple, although Jazz hung back a little. Birdie introduced Lucy and me as her quilting friends. She reached for Jazz's hand and pulled him in closer. "This is Jazz Fletcher, your brother's longtime partner and fiancé."

The scowling Jazz hesitated for a moment then stiffly shook Denver's hand and said, "You look like him, in a taller, cowboy sort of way."

Denver regarded his brother's lover. "I'm sorry for your loss, Fletcher."

Jazz nodded once but said nothing. Clearly his knickers were in a twist about something. Jazz must know more about what happened between Russell and Denver than he was saying. What was it?

The things I had to find out were piling up. What were Denver's true intentions toward Birdie, and why was Jazz so upset? Why did Rainbow feel responsible for Russell's death, and how did the red diary figure in?

One by one, the other mourners in the room walked up to Birdie. Some old friends showed up, including a woman in a pantsuit with her white hair gelled into a spiky Mohawk hairdo. Rainbow introduced her as Nancy King and explained she'd been trained by Russell to take over the financial management of Aquarius when he left. Others introduced themselves as Watson cousins, including Carol Anne, a registered dietician, and Johnny, an air traffic controller.

Yoder approached Birdie and said, "Mrs. Watson, I'm told your minister is waiting at Pioneer Cemetery. It's time to leave. Your car will follow right behind the hearse."

Birdie hadn't wanted a chapel service but had asked an old friend of hers from the commune to officiate at the graveside. "I'm ready."

"Ladies and gentlemen—" Yoder cleared his throat and raised his voice over the quiet chatter.

The room fell silent.

"We will now proceed to Pioneer Cemetery, five miles up the road. Please turn on your headlights and form a line with your cars behind Mrs. Watson's car."

Our funeral procession crept at thirty-five miles per hour up Highway 99. Denver and Rainbow followed directly behind Lucy's car in a late-model Dodge pickup truck.

"Did you know this cemetery is haunted?" Birdie asked.

"Get out," Jazz said.

"The story is legend around here. Back in the 1800s, Lafayette was the county seat. A local man, Gus Marple, was tried and convicted of murdering his mother's boyfriend. They say the mother, Anna, who was a witch, put him up to it."

"Mothers and sons," Jazz said. "I could write a book."

"Watch it!" Lucy warned. "I've got five boys of my own."

"Anyway," Birdie said, "they hanged Gus right there in the cemetery. Anna watched her only son die. When it was over, she cursed the town of Lafayette. She condemned it to burn down three times. Since then, the town has been destroyed by fire twice."

Lucy, who swore she had a sixth sense, listened to the story closely. "What about the third time?"

"They're still waiting."

The hearse made a left-hand turn on a dirt road outside the hamlet of Lafayette. A small wooden sign nailed to the scaly trunk of a western white pine tree read PIONEER CEMETERY, ESTABLISHED 1850. Our cars snaked carefully through the neglected graveyard, where wild grasses and weeds grew knee-high. Over the decades, a relentless army of trees from the surrounding forest had invaded that resting place, swallowing the graves as it progressed. Their roots strangled many of the headstones, reducing them to jagged rubble. The surviving grave markers were so worn by the frequent rains of the Northwest, they appeared to be nearly un-readable. A few of the oldest headstones were still discernible several yards deep into the forest.

Yoder stopped near the tree line at the edge of the cemetery, just behind a battered blue Ford Taurus on the narrow road. A woman wearing a flowing white caftan emerged from the Taurus, car-rying a large cardboard carton with holes punched in the sides. Her gray hair, crowned by a wreath of flowers, fell loosely to her waist. She placed the carton by an open grave and made her way quickly toward us.

She and Birdie fell into an embrace.

"Phoebe dear. How long has it been?"

"When did you and Russell leave Aquarius? Forty years ago? More?"

Birdie introduced us. "This is my old friend, Phoebe Marple."

Marple? As in the ghost's family?

Denver and Rainbow joined them, and Phoebe embraced each in turn. "I'm so glad the universe has brought us back together again."

Three women wearing identical purple robes emerged from Phoebe's Taurus, carrying shallow drums and rawhide mallets. They drifted toward the grave and stood together at the foot.

Lucy scanned the area and whispered, "I thought Yoder said the minister was already here."

Jazz tilted his head in Phoebe's direction. "I think he was referring to the head forest fairy over there."

Phoebe grabbed Birdie's hand. "Are you ready?"

"First, I want you to meet someone." Birdie walked over to Jazz, took his hand, and led him to the circle of friends. "This is Jazz Fletcher. He was the love of Russell's life. They were going to be married."

Phoebe searched Jazz's eyes and in the gentlest of voices said, "I am so very sorry for your loss. I can see the love. I can feel the suffering."

Jazz's whole posture slumped, and he covered his face with both hands. Through his tears, he managed to choke out, "Thank you."

Phoebe didn't hesitate to hug him as warmly as she had hugged her old friends. "Pain, like pleasure, is transitory, Jazz. You will eventually achieve a new balance. But for now, let your tears flow."

While Birdie talked to her friends, I inspected the Watson family plot. Unlike the rest of the cemetery, someone had paid to keep the weeds cut and the trees from invading. Although weathered, the ancient headstones were still readable. I studied the ones closest to where I stood.

ISAIAH WATSON, 1807-1870, GONE TO THE LORD

SARAH, 1818-1850, WIFE AND MOTHER

JOSIAH WATSON, 1836-1837.
AN ANGEL TAKEN TOO SOON

Poor Sarah hadn't been entitled to a last name or an epitaph on her tombstone. Back in those days, a married woman rarely had an identity of her own, apart from her husband's. Even Sarah's friends might have addressed her as "Mrs. Watson," according to the convention of the times.

Yoder and three assistants rolled Russell's casket out of the back of the hearse. They placed it on heavy industrial straps suspended over the freshly dug hole.

Yoder nodded at Phoebe. "We're ready whenever you are."

She stationed Birdie and Jazz on one side of the grave and Denver and Rainbow on the other. Then Phoebe took her place at the head of the grave. She closed her eyes and spread her arms wide in a welcoming gesture. "We call the spirits of the departed, who sleep in this sacred ground, and upon the elemental deities. Come forth!"

The three purple-robed women beat the drums. "Arise ye souls from glad repose," they chanted.

Lucy nudged me with her elbow.

Phoebe opened her eyes and looked toward the sky. "We entreat you. Gather round your kin Russell Watson and welcome his spirit into the generations."

"Welcome, welcome," pulsed the chorus and drums.

Eyes closed once again, Phoebe began to sing in a reedy voice, "I Shall Be Released."

Bob Dylan?

Yoder's face wore a disapproving scowl.

Phoebe lowered her arms when she finished, and all her commune friends snapped their fingers in applause, while the chorus tapped a rapid rhythm on the drums.

Jazz looked bewildered.

"Would anyone like to say a few words about our friend Russell?" Phoebe asked.

Slowly at first, people began to recall the ways in which Russell Watson had touched their lives, or the role he played in arranging loans to family and friends over the years. Cousin Johnny recalled fishing trips on the Columbia River all the boy cousins had taken with their grandfather.

Birdie began to speak softly. "Russell and I dated each other in college. At the time, I didn't know he was gay. When we went to live in Aquarius, we both found happiness with other people, but we always remained best friends. Around the time Russell left Aquarius, I traveled to India, where I had a traumatic experience that changed my life. When I returned to the States, I suffered a kind of breakdown. Nowadays you'd call it PTSD. Anyway, Russell offered me a sheltered life and promised to always care for me and keep me safe. So we married."

All the time Birdie spoke, Denver never took his gaze off her. I read both anguish and rage on his face.

Birdie cleared her throat. "For more than forty years, Russell kept his promise. I never wanted for anything material. He worked hard to keep me financially secure. And I kept my half of our arrangement by protecting his secrets. We depended on each other. About twenty-five years ago, Russell fell in love with a talented young man, Jazz Fletcher." Birdie grabbed Jazz's hand. "They were going to be married. After all those years, Russell was finally ready to come out of the closet."

She stepped forward and put her other hand on the coffin lid. Her voice quavered. "But then he was murdered. I'm so sorry, Russell dear. You deserved better."

All eyes were focused on Jazz, who had removed Zsa Zsa from the yellow tote bag on his arm and was now holding her to his chest.

He looked around nervously. "He was my knight in shining armor. He was my everything." Tears streamed down his face. "I don't know how I'll live without you, Rusty." Jazz buried his face in Zsa Zsa's long white fur and sobbed.

Birdie patted his back.

Right on cue, the ladies in the robes pounded out a slow dirge and moaned in high, arching voices, "Ahhh. Ohhhh."

Denver cleared his throat. "I'd like to say something. Russ was my brother, and I had a brother's love for him growing up. Now I realize he may've helped some of you financially, but he was also a selfish, self-centered SOB who took something that should have been mine."

Everyone gasped. Jazz stopped crying and became a thundercloud, opening and closing his fists. Birdie put a calming hand on his arm.

"Didn't see that coming," Lucy whispered in my ear.

Denver's face had hardened. "Wherever he is right now, he's got a lot to answer for."

Agent Tucker had emerged from somewhere in the background and deliberately placed himself in Denver's line of sight. Denver clamped his mouth shut and took a small step back from the grave. He bumped into Agent O'Neal, who'd materialized right behind him.

Phoebe continued unruffled. "Let us now help our friend on his journey to an eternal oneness with the universe." Phoebe signaled the four men, who loosened the straps under the coffin and slowly lowered Russell Watson into the ground.

Jazz renewed his sobs.

Removing a little leather-bound book from a pocket, Phoebe read, "Spirits of the forest, spirits of the earth, sky, water, and fire—we commend this soul into your care. Guide him on his journey to the universe. Show him the way."

She paused and turned the page. "And now I speak to the soul of Russell Watson. Hark! Depart not in regret, but sally forth with joy, safe in the knowledge all is as it should be."

Drums boomed again as Phoebe bent down and opened the cardboard box. Several pigeons cooed inside. With an elaborate arm gesture, Phoebe commanded them to "Fly!" But the birds just sat.

"Fly!" she ordered them again. They still didn't move, so she lifted the box and turned it upside down. Six fat pigeons slid to the ground. Five of them waddled toward the tall grass, looking for food. The sixth rolled into the grave and landed on top of Russell's coffin. He lifted his tail feathers, deposited a runny white glob, and flew out of the hole.

Lucy's body, next to me, was shaking with silent laughter.

Phoebe scowled and swiveled her head as if she were looking for something. "That's not funny, Gus!"

She's talking to the ghost!

Phoebe closed the slender book, put it in the pocket of her garment, and reached for a long-handled shovel. Thrusting it in the mound of dirt next to the grave, she scooped a small amount into the hole. It landed with a soft thud on top of the mahogany casket. She passed the shovel to Birdie who, with shaking hands, did the same. Jazz couldn't bring himself to bury his lover. He handed the shovel to Rainbow, who performed the task quickly and efficiently. Denver thrust the shovel deep into the dirt and poured a heaping amount of soil on top of his brother. Twice.

When everyone had had a turn with the shovel, Yoder made a short announcement. "Please join the family immediately following for a reception and tea at the Yamhill Country Inn on Evans Street."

My stomach had been growling throughout the service. It was two in the afternoon and we hadn't eaten since breakfast. "Are you as hungry as I am, Lucy?"

"Is the Pope Catholic?"

"Did you see how angry Denver Watson is? We have to keep an eye on Birdie."

"Don't worry, girlfriend." Lucy tucked her arm through mine and walked me back to the Caddy. "We can multitask. Eat and worry at the same time."

CHAPTER 26

We parked in front of a charming, Victorian-era hotel, the Yamhill Country Inn. A wide porch, populated with white iron tables and wicker chairs, wrapped around the front and sides of the well-kept building. Stained-glass flowers and fruit adorned the windows along the façade.

"We had a lot of buildings just like this in Wyoming," said Lucy as she pushed open the heavy oak door.

Antique Edwardian sofas and chairs upholstered in dark green velvet sat in the lobby. William Morris wallpaper featured a background of light green papyrus plants. Pairs of white cranes faced each other with outstretched wings and necks curved symmetrically, forming the shape of a heart.

Lucy's gaze slid around the room and she sighed. "This looks just like my granny's house in Gillette."

The proprietor, a pleasant woman in a lace blouse, came out from behind an old mahogany bar-turned-reception desk and addressed Russell's brother. "Hello, Denver. We have your reception set up in the Rose Room."

Denver removed his hat. "Much obliged, Ruthie."

The woman escorted our group to a private parlor off to the side. "The servers will arrive shortly. Please make yourselves comfortable."

Four round tables, each surrounded by six chairs, were covered in crisp white linen and set with bone china. Crystal vases of summer roses and forest ferns sat in the middle, completing the genteel ambiance. The other mourners began arriving in small groups, including the head forest fairy and her purple chorus. Agent Lancet stood quietly just inside the door. Tucker stationed himself in the lobby. O'Neal stayed on the porch with Arthur.

Denver led Birdie to the table closest to the window and pulled out her chair. "You'll like the view, Twink."

Jazz quickly claimed the seat on her other side. He seemed as determined as Lucy and I were to not leave Birdie alone with Denver Watson.

Rainbow, Lucy, and I arranged ourselves in the other three seats.

Lucy placed her napkin in her lap. "This place is gorgeous, hon. How'd you know about it?"

Birdie smiled at Russell's brother. "Actually, I didn't. Denny made these arrangements. Since he lives here, he knows just about everyone in town."

Denver Watson reached over and gently clasped

Birdie's hand in both of his. "Right now, there's only one person I want to know."

Jazz shifted in his seat and twisted his mouth to the side.

Two servers came in the room bearing silver trays and passed around crystal flutes of bubbling champagne.

Rainbow stood. Something about the woman exuded control, and the room became silent. "I'd like to propose a toast to Russell Watson, our husband, brother, fiancé, cousin, and friend."

Denver frowned and pushed his glass away.

Everyone else stood and responded, "To Russell."

When we sat down again, Denver got up and walked to a corner of the room where a scuffed instrument case stood against the wall. He removed a well-used acoustic guitar, sat back down at our table, and announced, "I'd like to dedicate this song to Birdie." He looked at her and the room fell silent. In a heartbreaking voice, he crooned words of love and longing from "Unchained Melody."

Birdie covered her mouth with her hands, and tears streamed down her face. When he finished, her voice was nearly drowned out by the applause in the room, "You remembered."

"How could I forget?"

I nudged Lucy's foot under the table, and whispered, "I don't like where this is going."

She nodded and whispered back, "I think we're too late. Birdie and Denver are on a runaway train."

The servers offered a parade of several savory

and sweet finger foods. They also provided endless pots of tea.

Denver gestured for the server to fill our glasses. "You have to try our local Pinot Noir. We grow some of the best grapes in the world."

I had to admit, the man was charming, regaling us with funny stories about the strange food concoctions Birdie and Rainbow sometimes prepared in the commune. "The weirdest one was the feta cheese tacos with dried figs wrapped in kale leaves. But they turned out to be everyone's favorite."

Rainbow laughed. "They still are. Kale tacos are one of our biggest sellers."

I thought about the hundreds of little taquerías in the barrios of LA. "You own a taco stand?"

"Yes." She smiled. "A few of them."

By the end of our meal, the volume had been turned up on the conversations and laughter filled the room. Several people came to our table for private conversations with Birdie and Denver. An older man with a long gray ponytail, wearing jeans and a tie-dyed Nehru jacket, walked over to Rainbow and kissed her on the cheek.

"Cody!" She brightened. "You haven't changed a bit."

He ran the palm of his hand over his very receding hairline and laughed. "Neither have you. You're still the prettiest woman in the room." He squatted down next to her chair and lightly stroked her arm. "I hear you found your pot of gold, sweet cheeks."

As they reminisced, I turned my attention to

Jazz, who clutched Zsa Zsa in his arms and looked miserable.

I pointed to the little Maltese. "She looks adorable, Jazz. I'm sure Russell would love what she's wearing."

Jazz had changed her into party clothes on the way over from the cemetery. She wore a pink velvet dress with eyelet lace ruffles, a rhinestone collar, and a pink ribbon in her hair.

His lower lip trembled. "Thank you for noticing." He pulled off a tiny piece of salmon from the top of a cracker and fed it to the dog on the tip of his finger.

When the servers began to clear the empty plates, Birdie announced to our table, "I've changed your hotel reservations. We were originally booked into the Comfort Inn, but I thought the four of you might have more fun staying here. This is a literary hotel. Each room is decorated in the style of a famous author, including a selection of their books for you to read. Martha, you're staying in the Faye Kellerman room. Lucy, you're in the Tony Hillerman." She turned to Jazz and winked. "And you get the Truman Capote room."

Jazz rolled his eyes. "I get it. The gay guy gets the gay author. Well, for your information, I happen to be a huge fan of Nicholas Sparks. So, which room did you choose for yourself, Birdie?"

She looked down and blushed. "Actually, I won't be staying here. Denver has invited me to be a guest at his ranch."

The hairs stood on the back of my neck. How could I persuade her to stay with us where she'd be safe? "I thought it would be fun to take a run at that great fabric store tomorrow. And what about Rainbow? She's flown all this way to see you. Don't you want to spend some time with her?"

Birdie held up her hand. "I know what I'm doing, Martha dear. I'll see you in a couple of days. If you need me, you can call my cell phone."

My mind raced for a way to keep her with the three of us. I also wanted to ask her about the diary but didn't want to alert Denver of its existence. I stood and walked over to her chair. "Can I talk to you for a sec?"

I guided her out into the lobby. "What about the diary, Birdie? The key to Russell's murder is in that book, and you're the only one who can decipher it."

She smiled and pulled the diary out of a pocket in her vintage blue dress with the yellow flowers. Inside the book was a folded piece of paper. "I was going to give this to you before I left. I haven't had time to decode the entries. But you won't have any problem. The substitution code is on that paper. All you need to do is plug in the right letters."

Lucy was right. Birdie and Denver were on an express train, and there was nothing I could do to stop it.

"What about Feather, Denver's wife? Won't she be unhappy when he brings you home?"

Birdie waved her hand dismissively. "Feather got bored and left him and the boy decades ago. Denver raised Ethan on his own from the time he was six."

"What about Ethan? What will he think?"

Birdie's face softened. "Ethan was killed in Afghanistan. Denver is all alone."

Loneliness and grief. That was the hook that Denver was using to catch the tenderhearted Birdie and reel her in. That and the passionate love they once shared. Denver Watson had pushed all of her buttons. It was hopeless to try to make her stay with us.

"You'll call if you change your mind or things don't work out at the ranch?"

My old friend lightly squeezed my hand. "Be happy for me, dear. This is my last chance."

I hugged her tightly. "You deserve so much happiness, Birdie. I promise I'll try to stop worrying."

We walked back into the Rose Room.

Birdie put her hand through Denver Watson's arm and looked at Jazz, Lucy, Rainbow, and me. "I'll be in touch."

Then the two old lovers turned and walked out of the hotel.

After Birdie left, Rainbow lowered her voice and said, "You seem worried. Don't be. Denver didn't kill Russell, if that's what's bothering you."

I bit my lip. "How can you be so sure?"

"That's what we need to discuss." She looked at her watch. "It's four-thirty now. I want to freshen up and take a short nap. Let's meet in the lobby for drinks at seven."

"What about Lucy and Jazz?" I asked.

Rainbow shook her head once. "Best if you come alone for now."

"Where are you staying?"

"Here. For some reason Birdie booked me into the J.K. Rowling room. I hope it's not filled with stuffed owls." She flashed a smile. "See you at seven." Then she turned and grabbed the hand of the man in the ponytail and tie-dyed Nehru jacket and headed toward Hogwarts.

CHAPTER 27

I waited for everyone to leave the Rose Room before I approached Kay Lancet, still standing at the door. "You just let Birdie go off with Russell's brother? Why didn't you stop her?"

"On what grounds? I don't have the authority to do that. Don't worry. We still have eyes on her. I sent Tucker to surveil them."

"You must be hungry," I said. "You stood by the door all throughout the meal."

"We ate in the car on the way over, plus I snuck quite a few of those tiny egg rolls and a couple petit fours." She looked down and brushed chocolate crumbs from her chest.

I tried again. "Let me buy you a drink. I want to know what you discovered about Tanya's kung fu instructor."

We found a small bar next to the dining room on the other side of the lobby, ordered our drinks, and sat at a table for two. Lancet held a frosty mug of a local brew she ordered for the name alone—Vlad the Imp Aler. I sipped another cup of tea.

The agent swallowed a long draft of Vlad and wiped the foam from her upper lip with a cocktail napkin. "Hmm. Tastes almost like lemons. It's different. I'll say that much."

She took another swig and watched me fidget impatiently with my cup. "Okay, I won't keep you guessing any longer. He's got a sheet. Nick Evans is his real name, but he's used aliases before: Nick Henderson, Andy Freeman, and Rocky Freeman. He started in his teens boosting cars and graduated to fraud and grand larceny. Now he's found a pathway to legal extortion. Tanya isn't his first."

"His first what?"

"Evans seduces vulnerable women and persuades them to leave their husbands. He takes them to Hawaii to 'start a new life' then contacts the husbands and offers to return them for a fee."

"What if the husband doesn't want her back?"

"Evans is smart. He only targets women with young children. Even if the husband doesn't want the wife, he usually wants his kids. And he'll send money to get them back. Strictly speaking, it's not kidnapping and it's not extortion."

"So what can we do?"

"Already done," said Lancet. "I asked one of the guys in the Honolulu office to go talk to Evans and Tanya together. He made sure she knew about the other six women he'd seduced with the same con." Lancet chuckled. "I understand there was a lot of screaming and packing of suitcases."

"So I can tell Lucy?"

She nodded. "Yeah."

"What a relief. I don't know how to thank you, Kay. You've helped the Mondello family avert disaster. You maybe even saved a marriage."

She looked at me sideways and brought the mug to her lips again. "Don't know about the marriage thing. These situations rarely end well. After all, the woman wasn't kidnapped. There must be a reason she did a bunk."

I smiled at her use of British slang. "You're right. Once you stop being able to trust someone, a relationship can never be the same."

She peered at me over the rim of the beer mug. "Are we talking about Arlo here?"

"He's just one among many. Was he unfaithful to you, too?"

She laughed. "Only after I cheated on him first."

I studied the woman sitting before me. Why had she strayed outside her marriage? Did her behavior give Beavers permission to become a cheater? I decided I didn't want to know. After all, I wasn't ever going to become involved with Arlo Beavers again.

"What about Li'l Ape Man?" I changed the subject. "Have you caught him yet?"

Lancet finished her beer. "The good news is you can stop worrying about him. The bad news is he's not in custody. Immediately after he ran you off the road, he drove to Eugene, hired a private jet, and flew to Canada. From there he changed planes and flew to Stockholm. The Justice Department wants to extradite him for stalking and attempted murder, but we're looking at a long process before he ever sees the inside of a U.S. courtroom."

Since the FBI agent was so forthcoming with information, I continued to probe. "What do you know about Sandra Prescott, aka Rainbow?"

"What makes you think . . ."

"Come on, Kay. I know you're too good a cop not to vet everyone."

Lancet shrugged. "She's on her way to becoming a billionaire."

My mouth fell open. "Are we talking about the same woman? The former hippie who owns a couple of taco joints?"

"Yup. You want to know more? You'll have to ask her yourself." Lancet stood and stretched. "Thanks for the beer. You need to retrieve your dog from O'Neal so we can go back to the office."

Arthur was lying on the front porch next to Agent O'Neal's chair. When the shepherd saw me, he trotted over, wagging his tail. I thanked O'Neal for watching him, and walked back inside. The clock behind the reception desk read five o'clock, dinnertime for pooches. I asked for the key to my room and assured the lady in lace that Arthur was well trained and completely housebroken.

Blue and white striped wallpaper greeted us in the Faye Kellerman room. Two posters hung on the wall. One showed a Jerusalem skyline. The second pictured a dark-haired girl harvesting oranges on a kibbutz. A sky blue matelassé spread covered a dark, four-poster bed and a silver Hanukkah menorah sat on a shelf next to a dozen books in Kellerman's mystery series. I guessed this was someone's idea of how a room with a Jewish theme should look—blue and white like the Israeli flag. Shabbat would begin at sundown, and the hotel would never allow me to light candles. Too big a fire hazard. I'd just have to be satisfied with hanging out in a blue and white room with "Jewish" posters.

I fed Arthur a cup of kibble and a cube of cheese I'd saved from high tea. Then I sat in an overstuffed reading chair and dialed Lucy's cell phone. I couldn't wait to tell her the good news about the kung fu instructor.

"You asked Agent Lancet to investigate Nick Evans? So that's what happened. I just got a text from Ray Junior saying he's bringing Tanya and the kids back home. Thanks for doing that."

"Thank Kay Lancet. She did all the work."

Lucy's voice sounded lighter already. "In spite of high tea this afternoon, I know I'll be hungry again in a couple of hours. Jazz and I are going to check out the dining room later. Do you want to join us for a late supper?"

"Sorry, but you'll have to do without me. Rainbow said she wanted to talk alone. Something about Russell."

"Why can't I come?" Lucy sounded hurt.

"I have no idea. After all, we only met a few hours ago. Don't worry. I'll fill you in afterward."

"Well, call me as soon as you get back to your room."

We ended our conversation, and I checked my watch. I had an hour and a half before my meeting with Rainbow downstairs. I'd use the time to check out the diary entries. I unfolded the paper with

Birdie's notes, grabbed a pencil, and began to decode the letters in the diary. I started with the first column, which consisted of all letters. Then I moved to the second column of mixed letters and numbers. The third column consisted of all numbers. When I had finished I studied what Russell had recorded.

Five Star Packaging	December 17, 2011 –	500
Sunset Enterprises	June 4, 2010 – June 10, 2011	500
Wong Technologies	December 11, 2009 – December 3, 2010	500
Northwest Development Corp	June 26, 2009 – June 11, 2010	500
Tracy Freight Lines	December 12, 2008 – December 4, 2009	500
Landsdown Nurseries	June 20, 2008 – June 19, 2009	500
Mississippi Solar	June 15, 2007 – June 13, 2008	500
Freitas Salvage	December 8, 2006 – December 14, 2007	500
Davis Plumbing	June 16, 2006 – June 22, 2007	500

The first column listed names of various companies, and none of them seemed to be related to any of the others.

The dates in the second column showed a curious pattern. The entries were made in either June

or December going back to 2006. All but the most
recent item had two dates exactly a year apart. For
example, the oldest entry, Davis Plumbing, recorded
the period of June 16, 2006 to June 22, 2007. But
Five Star Packaging, displayed only one date, December 17, 2011. I guessed it was because a year
hadn't yet passed.

The third column displayed the same three-digit
number of 500 starting in 2006. Did that number
represent a dollar amount from some kind of financial transaction? If so, it probably was a multiple of
thousands, and 500 would be banker shorthand for
$500,000.

Arthur walked over, rested his chin on my knee,
and stared at me until he had my attention.

I reluctantly looked up from the diary. "What?"

The dog's ears swiveled forward, and he tilted
his head.

I knew that beseeching look. "Okay, I'll get your
leash." Two minutes later I stood in the parking lot
holding one end of his tether while the shepherd
anointed a rhododendron bush.

When we returned to the room, my phone rang.

"I'm calling for my update." Beavers.

"The funeral was . . . different. We all came back
to the hotel for high tea. Birdie's fine. Arthur's fine.
I'm still sore from the accident yesterday, but I'll
live." I paused for effect. "And I had a nice conversation with your ex-wife."

Silence.

"Arlo? Are you still there?"

"So Kay told you? What else did she say?"

"Nothing I didn't already know—that you're a hell of a good cop."

He cleared his throat. "So have you thought about joining me on a trip to the Rez?"

"I haven't changed my mind, Arlo. You and I together in that way would be a very bad idea. I'm happy just being your friend. Can't we keep it that way? Casual?"

"I don't know if I can do *casual*."

I also had my doubts. Arlo Beavers was a serious and intense guy. Gray areas made him nervous. Simple friendship might be too hard for him to handle. "Well, I'd sure hate to lose you as a friend," I said. "Not to mention Arthur."

We said an awkward good-bye, and I looked at my watch. It read five minutes before seven. Time to discover why Rainbow felt responsible for Russell's murder.

CHAPTER 28

Sandra Prescott, aka Rainbow, relaxed on one of the green velvet sofas in the hotel lobby. She'd changed into a gauzy white blouse and bright cotton maxi skirt. Next to her sat the man in the gray ponytail and the tie-dyed jacket, who'd accompanied her to the J.K. Rowling room after tea.

As soon as he saw me approaching, he kissed Rainbow on the mouth. "Catch you later, sweet cheeks." He stood, gave me a brief smile, and left.

Rainbow also got up. "You're right on time, Martha. I know we said drinks, but I've had a very busy afternoon and I'm ready to eat. How about talking over a nice, big steak? There's a place just down the street. We can walk from here." Without waiting for an answer, she turned and headed for the heavy oak doors. This was a woman who liked to be in charge.

The décor of McGinty's Steak House felt as familiar as an old flannel shirt. The walls were paneled in dark wood and the booths upholstered in red leather. The food must be good because the place

was packed on this Friday night. People waited
shoulder to shoulder in the bar for a table to become
available. Rainbow approached the maître d', who
took one look at her and seated us right away in a
small booth near the window.

He presented a wine list. "It's an honor to serve
you, Miss Prescott."

When he walked away, I asked, "You've been
here before?"

She studied the wine list and smiled. "Everywhere I go, people try to get me to invest in their
businesses. That maître d' is actually the owner
and a friend of Denver's. When he heard I was
going to be in town, he offered to comp my dinner
tonight. I think he's hoping I'll buy this place."

"Will you?"

"Take a look around. McGinty's is too old-
fashioned. I predict we'll be served food with a lot
of rich sauces, even on our steaks. This cuisine may
be okay for a small town, but it's not what I do. I'm
merely here as a courtesy to Denver."

"How did you get into the restaurant business in
the first place?"

She put down the wine menu. "After I left Aquarius in 1980, I went back to California and opened
a vegetarian restaurant in The City."

Bay area natives referred to San Francisco as The
City, never as 'Frisco. "Is that where you're from?"

"Close enough. Palo Alto. Anyway, I took advan-
tage of the growing demand for organic and fresh
food. I called my place *Lechuga*. It's Spanish for let-
tuce. It became so popular, I opened two more.

Then I franchised my brand and eventually went global."

Who hadn't heard of the very popular *Lechuga* restaurants? "Oh my God. I love your food. I often have lunch at the one in Encino. You're the CEO of all the *Lechuga*s in the world?" Lancet was right. Sandra Prescott must be knocking on the door of the billionaire's club.

She smiled. "Guilty. I'm the sole owner of Rainbow Enterprises. We not only have the restaurants, we own organic farms around the world and sell a product line of frozen meals and packaged foods. I try to keep all my investments green, like solar and wind farms. I feel an obligation to give back. My Rainbow Foundation makes microloans to women in developing countries."

"And you've kept in touch with some of the people from Aquarius all these years?"

"Of course. We're family. I've also employed a few. Nancy King, for instance. You met her briefly this afternoon. She took over the books when Russell left the commune. In 1980 she went to Harvard Business School. Now she's my CFO. She's the one who found the problem."

The maître d'/owner reappeared at our table, waiting for Rainbow to order the wine.

She scanned the menu and pointed with her finger. "Let's begin with a bottle of this chardonnay and move on to the merlot with our dinner course."

Two minutes later our wineglasses were filled. A basket of warm baguette slices and an array of assorted spreads lay on the table before us, including pesto sauce, mushroom pâté, an olive tapenade, and a pot of garlic butter.

"Did we order this?" I asked.

Rainbow laughed. "The chef is in charge of our menu. When I called earlier, the only thing I told him I wanted was steak. The rest of the meal will be as much of a surprise to me as it is to you."

I spread a generous spoonful of tapenade on a slice of crusty baguette. "What makes you think you're responsible for Russell's murder?"

Rainbow chose the pâté. "Rainbow Enterprises is one of First Encino's biggest customers. I like doing business with people I know and trust. At least I thought I could trust Russell. We were looking for a new packager to handle our frozen meals. I suggested Nancy ask Russell for a recommendation. A loan officer at the bank gave Nancy a referral. It seems a packager in the Bay Area had just received a huge expansion loan."

Rainbow took a bite of bread and washed it down with a sip of chardonnay. "I'll let Nancy give you the details, but it turned out the company doesn't exist."

"That's really bizarre."

"I thought Russell should know about it, so I called him immediately."

"When was that?"

Rainbow closed her eyes in concentration. "About two weeks before he was killed. He apologized and said he'd look into it. A week went by, and I didn't hear from him, so I called him again. He said he couldn't talk about it."

I helped myself to a fried cake made of flaky salmon, onions, and breadcrumbs, which reminded me of gefilte fish, only ten times better. One crisp bite told me I had to make this for my uncle Isaac. "I imagine Russell felt under a lot of pressure to fix the problem and keep you satisfied."

"I'm sure he did. But I have to admit, I was more than a little annoyed. I felt, at the very least, I deserved an explanation."

The servers came back to our table with tiny shrimp in a salad, which I politely declined. Rainbow didn't seem to notice. She chewed a bite and then said, "He just apologized and said, 'This is a confidential bank matter.' I immediately called Nancy into my office and told her to find out everything she could about Five Star Packaging. I was determined to discover why Russell was being so secretive."

Two thick steaks arrived on very hot plates, along with a selection of creamed spinach, cauliflower topped with melted Tillamook cheddar, steamed baby asparagus spears, garlic mashed potatoes, and baked yams dripping with a clear glaze. I helped myself to the asparagus and yams. Everything else contained dairy, and I avoided mixing meat and dairy together in the same meal.

The knife cut through my filet mignon like butter, and I raised a bite to my lips. "What did you find out about Five Star?"

Rainbow was already chewing a piece of meat. She washed it down with merlot and said, "The company didn't exist before December of last year. Therefore, the whole story about doing well and needing to expand had to be pure fiction. At first I thought the bank was being scammed by an expert con artist. But I quickly dismissed the idea."

"Why?"

"Because I know Russell. He would never have approved a loan without vetting a company thoroughly. No way could a brand-new company without any assets get past Russell's scrutiny. I realized that someone inside the bank must have made that loan, knowing Five Star was bogus. Someone inside the bank was working the con and pocketing the loan money. And this was why Russell couldn't talk about it."

"I'm sure you've been quizzed by the FBI like the rest of us. Did you tell them about this?"

She shook her head and took a large drink of wine.

"Why not?"

"It was Russell's job to report embezzlement to the FBI, not mine."

I forked the last bite of meat into my mouth. "I don't think the FBI knows, Rainbow. They've never questioned any of us about it."

She closed her eyes. "I feel responsible for Russell's murder. I may have gotten him killed by bringing the scam out into the open. Either the embezzler killed him to keep from being exposed, or worse." She paused for effect. "Russell himself could have been the embezzler."

I wasn't convinced. "Really? If he was the thief, how could that get him killed?"

She put her fork down. "We know he didn't report the bad loan. What if he used those two weeks to cover his tracks and make it look like someone else was responsible? What if he had an accomplice? What if the accomplice knew he was about to be thrown under the bus and killed Russell?"

More than ever I thought Agent Lancet should be told. She had the resources to get to the truth. "You have to tell the feds what you know."

"Not until I know whether Russell was involved." She crossed her arms. "If it turns out he was the thief, the bank would have every right to then turn around and sue his estate for the missing money."

I finished her thought. "And Birdie would end up having to make restitution."

She nodded. "They'd take every penny from her."

I could see her point. Birdie would not only lose everything, she'd be publicly embarrassed. "So what do you want me to do?"

"Talk to Nancy King. See if you can't figure this thing out. If it turns out Russell had nothing to do with the theft, then I'll go to the FBI with what I know."

Our dinner plates were replaced by dessert plates and the side dishes cleared to make way for a selection of rich desserts. I managed to find room for the steaming chocolate soufflé after I decided to overlook the meat-and-dairy-in-the-same-meal thing.

"Tell me your secret," I said. "How do you keep your figure and still eat like this?"

She sipped espresso from a white demitasse. "I normally eat only the foods I advocate: fresh, organic, and vegan. But every once in a while, I get an overwhelming urge to just pig out."

I could relate. After such a huge meal, I felt rather porcine myself.

The maître d' came back to our table with a bottle of Courvoisier and two round snifters. He poured our drinks and stood nervously. "I hope you enjoyed the meal, Miss Prescott."

Rainbow swirled the brandy in the snifter, took a sip, and bestowed a reassuring smile. "I can't remember when I've enjoyed a meal as much. Many, many thanks to you and my compliments to your talented chef."

A wave of relief passed over his face. "About my proposal?"

Rainbow stood and extended her hand toward me. "I think my friend here has slightly over-indulged herself tonight and needs to return to the hotel. May I call you in the morning? We can have our discussion then."

He made a little bow. "Of course! I look forward to hearing from you."

Rainbow shook his hand and thanked him again, and the two of us left McGinty's.

On the walk back to the Yamhill Country Inn, I said, "You know, Russell's murder may not be connected to the embezzled funds. You saw how his brother, Denver, was so angry today at the funeral. He maintained Russell took something that didn't belong to him, and Denver wanted it back."

Rainbow stopped walking and put her hands on her hips. "And what do *you* think he wants?"

"Birdie found over a quarter of a million in bearer bonds in their home safe. Some were issued as far back as the 1940s. I'm guessing they belonged to Russell's parents. Denver could have hired Rene Levesque to kill Russell and take back the bonds from Birdie's house."

Rainbow laughed. "Denver has enough money of his own. I can't picture him killing his brother over a few bonds. Martha, I think Denver has already taken back the thing that Russell stole from him."

I sighed. Rainbow had just confirmed what I had already begun to suspect. "The 'thing' Denver wanted back was *Birdie.*"

She smiled, slipped her arm through mine like an old friend, and continued walking. "You should have seen them in the old days. They were devoted to each other, and so much in love. But she was a wreck when they returned from India. Denver, on the other hand, didn't seem fazed. He wanted to hitch around the country and hop freight trains with nothing but his guitar, a backpack, and Birdie on his arm. He didn't realize how traumatized she was from that horrific railway disaster they survived."

That confirmed what Birdie had already told Lucy and me. She had a breakdown and opted for the stability and security that Russell offered.

Rainbow sighed. "I was sad to see her choose the path she did. But I also understood."

We walked the rest of the way in silence. Denver wasn't entirely off the hook for Russell's murder. The killer had mentioned a "payback" right before he shot Russell. Could Denver have sent the message

he was taking Birdie back? On the other hand, if
Rainbow was correct, the payback could have come
from an embezzler who was about to be exposed.

When we reached the hotel, Sandra Prescott
pushed open the doors. "I'll introduce you to
Nancy King tomorrow at ten."

I returned to my room and took Arthur outside
one last time before bed. Then I called Lucy, but
she didn't answer, so I left a message that I'd tell
her all about McGinty's in the morning. I opened
the diary and studied the entries again. Were all
the companies on the list fake? What about the
peculiar dates of June and December? Did Russell
uncover 4.5 million dollars in bogus loans, or was
this a record of his own thefts?

CHAPTER 29

Saturday morning I got up at seven, threw on my stretch denim jeans and a T-shirt, and took Arthur for a walk. I needed the exercise after last night's pig-out at McGinty's. My body was still stiff and sore from the accident on Thursday, but the more I moved, the better I felt. After twenty minutes, we were on Third Street. "Hey, Arthur, let's try to find the fabric store. It won't be open yet, but we can look in the window."

The dog wagged his tail and trotted happily beside me down the sidewalk.

He stopped to pee on a lamppost in front of a shop displaying beautiful handmade jewelry. The sign on the window said:

YAMHILL COUNTY ART ASSOCIATION
FEATURING LOCAL ARTISTS

I stepped closer to the window and admired the clever way the maker had fashioned hammered gold around bright blue turquoise stones to make a pair of earrings. As I peered through the glass into the interior of the shop, a bronze sculpture caught my eye. The bust of a long-haired woman looked remarkably like the young Birdie we saw in the photograph from Aquarius. I gasped when I read the tag next to it: "DENVER WATSON, 1980."

More and more I could see how Birdie and Denver were kindred souls. Both were creative in different ways: Birdie with her quilting, gardening, and cooking, and Denver with his music and sculpting.

A voice spoke behind me. "It's gorgeous, isn't it?"

I whipped my head around. The wind lifted the long white hair around the face of a woman I didn't recognize. She wore an ankle-length Madras skirt and a white peasant blouse. Around her neck hung a strand of tiny puka shells: love beads. Her face wore a blissful smile, and her eyes sparkled.

"Birdie!" My mouth fell open.

Her delighted laughter told me she had meant to astonish me. "Hello, Martha dear."

"You look wonderful. Ten years younger. No, fifteen years." I gave her a hug. "I don't even have to ask you if you're happy."

Her laughter tinkled again in the morning air.

I looked up and down the street. "Where's Denver?"

She pointed to a Dodge pickup that had pulled to the curb across the street. "His kitchen lacks baking supplies, so we're on our way to the market. When I saw you and Arthur, I asked him to stop so I could say hello."

I looked at the truck and waved. The man in the

cowboy hat smiled and waved back. We hugged one last time, then she limped across the street with her arthritic knees. Denver hopped out of the truck and helped her into the cab. I waved again as Birdie and her lover drove off. I wanted to be happy for them. I didn't want to believe he had killed his brother. Because if he had, Birdie's heart would surely break.

I returned to the hotel, where I spotted Jazz walking Zsa Zsa outside. He wore a long-sleeved green print shirt tucked into yellow cargo shorts. The Maltese wore a matching green dress and bow in her hair. Even her leash was green. When she saw Arthur, she yipped loudly and ran toward him, broadcasting a rapid hello with her tail.

"You're up bright and early." I smiled.

Jazz yawned. "Yesterday was *très émotionnel*. After Lucy and I had supper last night, I went straight to bed. Where'd you go?"

"Down the street to McGinty's Steak House with Rainbow." I paused for a beat and then asked, "You know, Jazz, I couldn't help but notice yesterday you seemed particularly unhappy about Denver Watson. Is there something you haven't told us?"

The tall man looked at the ground and re-arranged the dirt with the toe of his white canvas espadrille. "It's just that Rusty didn't trust him. He told me years ago Denver had threatened to out him."

"I can certainly see how that would cause a lot of hard feelings between brothers," I said.

Jazz rolled his eyes. "Denver was pissed at Rusty for taking Birdie away and threatened to retaliate.

Rusty was terrified his colleagues would discover he was gay. His career would've been over, and Denver knew it."

Russell was right. In the early days, he would've been a pariah if his sexual preferences were known. Especially in the corporate world. Living under the constant threat of exposure must have been excruciating.

"But Denver never said anything, did he?"

Jazz shook his head. "But he inflicted mental torture with his threat. I hate him for making Rusty suffer."

"What about the big argument when their mother died? Do you know what that was all about?"

"Family! It was all about money. Denver cheated Rusty out of his inheritance."

I thought about Denver's guitar and the beautiful bronze bust in the window of the Yamhill County Art Association. "He doesn't seem the type to be preoccupied with money."

"Does anyone? As the oldest brother, Rusty was supposed to get the ranch. But Denver wanted it."

"Couldn't they have split it? Each own half?"

Jazz drew a line across his throat with his finger. "Denver said since Rusty didn't have kids, the ranch should go to his son, Ethan."

I thought about the bearer bonds dating from 1943. "But Russell did get something from the estate, right?"

Jazz nodded. "He settled for some bonds, but they weren't worth half as much as the property."

"So Russell just let him have the property?"

Anger twisted his mouth. "Rusty was afraid that if

he didn't agree, Denver would make good on his threat to expose him."

I pressed him further. "It was pretty clear yesterday that you disapprove of Birdie's relationship with Denver."

A storm flashed in his eyes. "Don't you? I mean, it's been decades since they were together. What does she really know about him now? And what does he want with her, anyway?" He crossed his arms. "Birdie's way too nice. I'd hate to see her hurt."

I agreed. After more than forty years of leading a quiet, sheltered life, Birdie was on her own again, and vulnerable. On the other hand, if she and Denver truly loved each other, who were we to stand in their way? Didn't she say this was her last chance?

"I ran into Birdie on my walk this morning. She looks happier than I've ever seen her. Almost transformed."

Jazz just grunted. We settled the dogs back in my room to keep each other company and joined Lucy in the dining room for an eight o'clock breakfast. How was it, that so soon after that huge meal last night I was actually looking forward to eating again?

After the server left with our orders, my orange-haired friend favored us with a warm grin. Her mood had vastly improved since she learned Tanya and the kids were coming home. "I talked to Ray Junior last night. He blames himself for what happened. He said he paid too much attention to the business and not enough to his family. He wants to try to mend his marriage and get closer to his kids.

They're staying in Hawaii for the next two weeks. Junior rented a house in Kailua."

"That's great news, Lucy. I'm so happy things are working out. I ran into Birdie this morning on my walk. You wouldn't believe how happy she is. Maybe life is finally working out for her, too."

"Not everything is working out," Jazz said. "We still don't know who's behind Rusty's murder."

A busboy stopped briefly at our table and filled our coffee cups.

Golden hoops swung in Lucy's ears as she leaned forward. "I've been puzzled about something. An unknown person hired an assassin to get rid of Russell. Then that same person got rid of the assassin and stuffed him in Russell's coffin. How could he pull that off?"

Good question. "I've been wondering the same thing. Let's think this through. We know Levesque's body was added after the viewing on Monday night and before we left LA on Tuesday morning. The killer either broke into the mortuary in the middle of the night or was let in by someone who works there. Then he, or they, opened the coffin and removed the Baltimore Album quilt to make room for the new body."

Jazz raised his eyebrows. "That pretty quilt is gone? Does Birdie know?"

I shook my head. "Lucy and I didn't want to upset her. Anyway, I believe the unknown mastermind killed Levesque because he didn't want to leave any witnesses behind. I think he stashed the corpse without any help because he didn't want witnesses to Levesque's murder, either."

The server brought our orders. A bowl of fruit for me, an omelet for Lucy, and waffles for Jazz.

Jazz reached for a bottle of dark purple syrup. "Well, he'd have to be really strong to carry a dead body into the mortuary all by himself and place it in the coffin."

"Who has the muscle to do that?" Lucy asked.

I fished out a fresh marionberry from my bowl. "Who's on our list of suspects with a motive to kill? Jazz, what about Francisco Conejo, your angry neighbor?"

"Cisco?" Jazz briefly waved his hand. "He's a short little Cuban drama queen. No way could he lift a body. He pitched a royal fit when he lost his house, but I never believed he would actually try to hurt anyone."

"What about Li'l Ape Man?" Lucy asked.

Jazz put his fork down and adjusted the cuffs of his shirt. "He's a huge Swede. He could easily throw a corpse over his shoulder, with those muscles of his. I should know." He blushed. "I measured his body several times during his custom fittings. He could've killed Rusty as payback for not being allowed to have his way with me."

I still wasn't ready to rule out Denver. Although he'd slipped from the top of my list. "Remember, Russell's brother said he wanted something back that Russell had taken from him? It's obvious what that was. He wanted Birdie. It's possible Denver had Russell killed as payback for stealing Birdie away and to clear the way for him to move in and take her back."

"And it looks like he's succeeded." Jazz clenched his jaw.

"Why now?" asked Lucy. "Why not ten years ago? Or twenty?"

What was it Birdie told me yesterday about Denver's son? "Ethan Watson was killed in Afghanistan. Denver's in his seventies and has no family left. Maybe he wanted to spend whatever time he had left with the woman he loved."

"Makes sense," said Lucy. "Denver lives on a ranch, right? I come from a long line of ranchers in Wyoming. They're as tough as nails from hard work, like tossing around hundred-pound bales of hay all day long. Even into their seventies. Judging from the looks of Russell's brother, he could easily lug a corpse."

Now was the time to show them what I'd discovered in Russell's diary. I removed the little red book from my purse and handed it across the table. "This diary suggests yet another possible suspect for Russell's murder. As you can see, with the help of Birdie's substitution alphabet, I deciphered his notes."

Lucy peered at the list. "Good job, hon. But this information is as clear as mud. What does it mean?"

Jazz studied the book and also looked perplexed. "This has nothing to do with Li'l Ape Man or Cisco, as far as I can tell. None of it makes sense to me, either."

"First of all," I said, "no one but the three of us has ever seen this. Not even Birdie. And I'd like to keep it that way for now."

Jazz handed the book back to me. "How'd you get this?"

"Birdie gave the diary and code to me yesterday after tea. She hadn't had the chance to decrypt the entries. I did that last night. I think what we're looking at is a record of embezzled money going back several years and totaling 4.5 million." I repeated Rainbow's story about Five Star Packaging and Russell's secrecy.

"Rainbow thinks two things could have happened during the last two weeks of Russell's life," I continued. "The first possibility is he was doing what he claimed, attempting to find the embezzler. If that proves to be the case, he was killed before he could talk."

Lucy picked up her coffee cup. "Did she tell this to the FBI?"

"Not yet."

Her cup clattered back to the table. "Good grief. Why not?"

I knew Jazz wouldn't like what I was about to say. "Because of the second possibility. If the real embezzler turns out to be Russell, he could've been using that time to cover his tracks and implicate someone else. Possibly an accomplice. If his partner in crime discovered what he was doing, he could've killed Russell to prevent being exposed. That would also explain the 'payback' remark."

Jazz looked up sharply. "Rusty wasn't a thief!"

I closed the diary and put it back in my purse when the server came with the check. "Think hard, Jazz. Did Russell talk about missing money, or embezzlement, or anything like that during those last two weeks?"

Jazz gazed off in the distance and frowned. "He seemed more preoccupied than usual. Little things upset him." His face relaxed. "I do remember he talked about how much he looked forward to our anniversary. . . ." He fondled his diamond wedding band.

"Did he ever mention Rainbow by name? Or her CFO, Nancy King?"

"Rusty never talked about his clients. He had too much integrity to gossip. Anyway, why don't you just give the damn diary to the FBI and let them sort it out?"

"Believe me, I'd like to," I said. "But if they determine Russell was involved in the theft of all that money, the bank could turn around and sue his estate to recover the stolen funds. Four and a half million dollars is at stake. Maybe more. Any assets you shared with Russell, such as your business, bank accounts, investments, home, or car could be seized right along with Birdie's assets. Do you want to take that risk?"

Jazz crossed his arms. "Then we have to prove Rusty didn't take the money."

"If we can prove he wasn't involved," I said, "I'll gladly hand the diary over to the FBI and let them figure out who the embezzler is."

Lucy had been silently listening and sipping coffee. "And if it turns out Russell is the thief?"

I took a deep breath and exhaled loudly. "Then we have a whole new problem. We'll have to find out where he stashed the missing money and give it back so Birdie and Jazz don't lose everything they have."

Jazz spread his hands on the table in a helpless gesture. "How are we ever going to discover who the real crook is?"

A plan had already begun to form in my head. "I'm going to start with Nancy King. I want to find out the name of the bank employee who recommended she contact Five Star Packaging. I want to know exactly what he said. Then I'm going to look at the loan officers in all the branches of First Encino. At least one of those people—with or without Russell Watson's help—has been executing bogus loans and pocketing the money."

Lucy raised the orange arches of her eyebrows. "You mean there could be a whole ring of thieves working at the bank?"

I shrugged. "We have to consider every possibility."

We left a tip for the server and headed for the lobby. I turned to Lucy. "To change the subject, what does the Tony Hillerman room look like?"

"A lot like my living room. Heavy, handcrafted furniture, Navajo rugs, reed baskets, and Indian pottery. And a shelf filled with a whole lot of his paperbacks. What does the Faye Kellerman room look like?"

I thought about all the cheery, bright colors of Christmas and beautiful pastels of Easter versus the monochrome theme of all the Jewish festivals. Manufacturers of holiday decorations didn't seem to realize Jews enjoyed all the colors of the rainbow, too. "Predictable. All blue and white like the Hanukkah section at CVS. What about the Truman Capote room, Jazz?"

He held Zsa Zsa with one hand and waved extravagantly with the other. "It's all Southern. White walls, white iron bed with white linen, ecru carpeting, and two easy chairs slip-covered in blue chintz with white roses."

"Sounds pretty," said Lucy.

He put up his hand. "Not even. There's a ghastly painting of trees dripping moss in front of a plantation with a bunch of black slaves working in the fields. And next to Capote's books on the shelf is the *pièce de résistance*—a vintage woman-shaped bottle of Aunt Jemima pancake syrup. Zsa Zsa and I couldn't wait to close our eyes last night."

I was relieved to hear Lucy laughing again after so many days of anxiety and uncertainty. When we walked outside, the morning breeze had picked up a little. We settled in comfortable wooden rocking chairs in the shelter of the wide porch, and I looked at my watch. "We have an hour before my meeting with Rainbow and her CFO, Nancy King."

Lucy propped her long legs up on a wooden stool. "Don't forget about the fabric store, girlfriend. I feel the need for some major retail therapy."

Jazz stood. "Lucy, do you feel like going for a walk? There's a nice park down the street. We could treat the dogs to a little romp."

"Sure, hon. I'll wait right here while you go get the dogs."

Jazz and I returned to my blue and white room. After he and the animals left, I called the J.K. Rowling room. Rainbow wasn't answering the hotel phone, and I didn't have her mobile number. I'd just have to trust she'd show up with Nancy King at ten like she'd promised.

CHAPTER 30

At ten-fifteen, Rainbow walked rapidly across the front porch of the hotel, wearing a black pantsuit. "Sorry we're late." I recognized Nancy King immediately. Once again, her white hair was heavily gelled on top so it stood up in straight, hard spikes.

I had been sitting in a rocking chair slowly stitching around a blue circle in my Double Wedding Ring quilt. I put down my sewing and offered my hand to the other woman. "You must be Nancy."

She pumped my hand once and said in a booming voice, "Pleasure."

Rainbow appropriated the rocker with the footstool and gestured for Nancy to sit next to her. "We just came from McGinty's. Turns out the owner didn't want to sell the restaurant. It's a gold mine for him. He needs a loan to open a second restaurant in Portland. After he showed us his books, I decided to become a silent partner. Not only are his numbers good"—she winked—"I really liked that mushroom pâté last night."

Nancy briefly glanced at her boss. "Rainbow tells me you need my help?"

I liked the fact she came right to the point, even though her voice was loud enough for people to hear her all the way back in Cottage Grove. I put everything back in my sewing kit, folded my quilt, and removed my notepad from my purse. "I'm intrigued by the notion someone at First Encino made a large loan to a nonexistent company. I'd like to hear about your experience, beginning with the bank employee who recommended Five Star Packaging."

Nancy clasped her hands in her lap and settled back in her chair, ready to tell her story. "We were looking for a new co-packer." She jerked her thumb playfully toward Rainbow and grinned. "*The boss* suggested I call Russell to see if he knew anyone."

"What's a co-packer?" I wrote the word down.

"Co-packer is short for Contract Packer. They put the products their clients manufacture into the packages you see in the stores. Food co-packers often manufacture the food as well. We were looking for a company that does both."

"Please go on." I clicked the top of my pen a couple of times.

"I called the bank, but Russell wasn't in. One of his loan officers offered to take a message. Her name was Gail. When she heard what I wanted, she told me about Five Star Packaging."

"What exactly did she say?"

Nancy closed her eyes, etching thought ridges into her brow. "She told me about a company in our area. A new customer recently acquired by the loan department. Five Star Packaging. According to Gail, they were quite successful, because they were about to expand. From what she said, I concluded the bank had just given them a loan to do that."

"Do you remember Gail's last name?"

"Something Armenian." She shrugged.

I knew most Armenian names ended with "ian" or "yan," which meant "son of." I wrote *Gail (?)ian* on my notepad. "Okay, I can get the specifics later. Please continue."

"I was interested, so Gail got me their address and phone number. She wished me luck and that was that."

Gail with the Armenian last name recommended Five Star. I was pretty sure that meant we could rule her out as the embezzler. No criminal would deliberately send someone on a mission that might expose her scam. As soon as we returned to LA, I'd pay her a visit.

Rainbow had been texting but looked up from her cell phone. "Tell Martha about the phone messages."

"Right." Nancy nodded. "That same day, I tried phoning the number Gail gave me. Hiring a co-packer was a top priority. But nobody answered. Instead, I got a recorded message to leave my number. I must've called five times over the next two days, but nobody ever called back. You can't run a successful business like that. I sensed something wasn't kosher."

I had to agree. That was no way to treat a potential customer, especially one as large as Rainbow Enterprises. "Was it a man's voice or a woman's?"

"Man's. With an accent."

Every hair on my arms stood at attention. "French? Was it a French accent?"

Nancy exhaled sharply. "It might've been. I can't recall."

I scribbled furiously on my notepad. Was there a connection between Rene Levesque and Five Star Packaging? "What did you do next?"

Nancy shifted in her seat. "I realized the address of Five Star Packaging was near my regular route from home. So the next morning, I took a little detour on my drive in to the city. I expected to find Five Star in an industrial area. Instead, the address turned out to be a mailbox rental store next to a Laundromat. That's when I knew for sure something hinky was going on. I told Rainbow what I discovered and she called Russell."

I turned to the owner and CEO of Rainbow Enterprises. "Tell me what you said to him."

"I repeated what Nancy had told me and said I didn't want to do business with a company that wouldn't even return our calls. Given the treatment we'd received, I said he shouldn't be referring potential clients to Five Star."

"What was his reply?"

Rainbow opened her hands, palms up. "He seemed genuinely shocked. He said he'd never heard of Five Star Packaging but would look into it. I waited for a week, thinking I'd get an apologetic call from the CEO of Five Star. Or one from Russell with an explanation. But nobody ever contacted me. Finally, I got tired of waiting and phoned

Russell. He was curt and aloof. He insisted he couldn't discuss the incident with me because it was, and I quote, 'a confidential banking matter.'"

I stopped writing for a moment. "That sounds just like something Russell would say. He was strictly by the book, that one."

The corners of Rainbow's mouth turned down. "Yeah, but I was thoroughly pissed at being put off like that. Since I was the one who'd brought the problem to his attention, I deserved to know what was going on and told him so."

So far, of all the people I'd met in Russell's life, Rainbow was the most likely to approach him as a business equal and make demands. "What did he say?"

"He apologized but didn't budge. He said he couldn't comment on a confidential matter."

Nancy snorted and bellowed, "Wrong answer!"

Maybe she was hard of hearing. Sometimes the hearing impaired spoke extra loud.

"Nancy knows me so well." Rainbow smiled. "Russell's reaction only served to pique my curiosity, so I asked her to see what she could find out about Five Star Packaging." She gestured for Nancy to continue with the story.

"It was pretty easy to determine from public records that Five Star was incorporated as recently as December of last year," Nancy said.

I stopped writing and looked up. "Did those records reveal who the owner was?"

She shook her head and every hair in her Mohawk stayed as straight as a soldier. "Another shell corporation based in the Caymans. It'll take some digging to trace Five Star to individual names."

The FBI could probably uncover that information in a minute. Too bad we couldn't tell them yet what we knew. "Anything else you remember?"

The two women sat in silence for a moment.

Nancy bit her lip, took a deep breath, and spoke in a confidential voice—a normal tone for the rest of us. "I've known Russell Watson since I was a girl. He was the one who got me started. The man was as orthodox as they come. Strictly by the book, as you pointed out. I'm sorry, but I just can't imagine him stealing money from the bank."

Nancy King was a no-nonsense kind of person, loyal to her boss, Sandra Prescott, and to her mentor, Russell Watson. The more she talked, the more my gut told me to trust her. I decided it was safe to show them the diary.

I handed over the little red book. "Russell kept this diary hidden in his home safe. We believe the assassin, Levesque, was after this when he tried to break into the Watsons' house. Do any of these entries mean anything to you?"

Nancy put on a pair of black-rimmed reading glasses and pored over the record. "Aside from recognizing the entry for Five Star Packaging, this doesn't mean a thing to me."

Rainbow leaned over to read the diary. She ran her finger down the list of companies. "I haven't heard of any of these, either. What is it?"

"I think it's a record of bogus loans," I said.

Nancy pointed to the middle column. "That would explain these dates."

My ears pricked up, and I readied my pen to write.

She continued. "The entries are made just before the end of the fiscal year, December thirty-first, or before the half-year period ending June thirtieth. If an embezzler wanted to hide the loans, he could bury the information in the massive data generated by annual or quarterly fiscal reports. The specifics of those loans would get lost in the sheer volume of numbers."

"Could a loan officer do that?" I asked.

Nancy thought for a moment. "It depends on how the data was entered, but yes, I believe he could."

"Enough to hide it from Russell?"

"It's possible," she said.

"Except for the most recent entry," I continued, "each item has two dates approximately a year apart. Do you have any idea what that means?"

Nancy shrugged. "Not a clue, I'm afraid."

Rainbow leaned forward with a worried look on her face. "You should give this diary to the FBI."

"Not until I can prove Russell wasn't the embezzler. And if I'm right, I think I've just figured out how to do that."

Rainbow grabbed my hand. "That'll be great news for Birdie. How will you prove his innocence?"

I tapped my finger on the middle column in the diary. "It's all in the dates. If Russell was embezzling money from the bank and keeping a list of his crimes, the entries would be in a certain order. The first entry would be the first crime. So the dates would progress from the oldest year at the top to the newest at the bottom. And the entries would be written by different pens, using different inks."

"But this list is in the opposite order," said Rainbow. "The most recent date is the first entry, and the list goes down to the oldest year at the bottom."

I raised my thumb in approval. "Bingo! And it looks like the same pen was used, proving the entries were made pretty much at the same time. This tells me Russell wasn't recording his crimes, he was digging for evidence, beginning with the most recent fake loan. He must've gone back through time to see if there were any more of those transactions. As he discovered the others, he recorded them. We don't know who he talked to. But at some point, the real crook must've found out what he was doing and had him killed."

Rainbow narrowed her eyes and studied me. "Birdie was right about you, Martha. You're very good at solving crimes. Just be careful. Someone has killed twice to keep the secrets in this little book."

A half hour later, Lucy and Jazz climbed the front steps of the hotel with two panting dogs.

"Hey, girlfriend!" Lucy looked around the empty porch. "Where's Rainbow?"

"You just missed her. She and Nancy are on their way to the airport and a quick hop in her private jet back to San Francisco."

"Must be nice." Jazz smoothed his windblown

hair straight back off his forehead. "Sitting in luxury on your own airplane, sipping mimosas, and using cocktail napkins printed with your initials."

"More fun than taking a road trip with your friends?" I asked.

Jazz picked up Zsa Zsa, kissed the top of her head, and looked at us with brimming eyes. "Nothing could ever top this. I don't know what I would've done without your friendship and support this last week."

Lucy stepped over to Jazz and gave him a one-arm hug. She was just as tall as the six footer in her two-inch heels. "We're quilters, hon. That's what we do. Listen, I've got an idea. Let's settle the dogs in Martha's room, and the three of us go check out the fabric store. Maybe I'll find the polka dots I'm looking for and you can look for the iridescent fabric you need for Johnny's peacock outfit."

I had totally forgotten about the new wardrobe Jazz was creating for Johnny Depp. "I've admired some of your drawings in the car. Have you settled on a theme?"

Jazz tapped his lips with his fingertips. "Hmm. I'm still thinking Detective Debonair. *N'est-ce pas?* I can dress him from casual to business to formal with just a touch of noir and fantasy."

I pictured the actor in his most iconic roles as Edward Scissorhands, Jack Sparrow, and Willy Wonka. "Sounds just like him."

Lucy bobbed her head in agreement. "I think it's genius. So how'd your meeting go, Martha?"

I told them what I'd learned about Five Star

Packaging, Gail with the Armenian name, and the peculiar dates in the diary. I put my hand on Jazz's arm. "I think you're right about Russell being innocent. I suspect the list shows he was going back through time digging for evidence of more embezzlement."

Jazz exhaled sharply. "Then you'll give the diary to Agent Lancet?"

"There's just one thing I want to double-check first. I've got to talk to the loan officer who referred Nancy King to Five Star Packaging. If Russell questioned her, I'd like to know what he said. Her responses should settle once and for all that Russell was investigating, not covering up."

CHAPTER 31

Miller's fabric store took up a couple thousand square feet of commercial space on the corner of Third Street—twice as much if you counted the second floor. Windows all along the two outside walls provided an abundance of natural light, essential for gauging true colors. Pendant lamps made of ridged glass hung from a pressed tin ceiling. Wide pine planks, scuffed and darkened by age, creaked under our feet.

Jazz made a full 180 degree sweep of the store with his eyes. "I'm shocked. This store is fabulous!"

Acres of shelving held every kind of material from heavy upholstery brocades to delicate laces. Racks holding sewing notions from buttons to quilt batting lined the two inside walls. An arrow pointed upstairs, where sewing machines, irons, and other accessories were sold. Jazz drifted toward a rounder holding bolts of shiny lamé. Lucy and I followed a cheerful sign to the quilting section.

"Ohhh!" She grabbed a bolt of cream-colored fabric with tiny colorful polka dots. "This is exactly what I am looking for. I'm going to get the whole thing."

Bolts of quilting cotton typically held about twenty yards of fabric. Experienced quilters could estimate how much fabric was left on a bolt just by eyeballing it. I guessed at least ten yards of polka dots remained. "What are you going to do with all this yardage?"

Lucy gently fondled the material. "This particular fabric reminds me of the decorations my mother sprinkled on my birthday cakes. The dots make a wonderful background because they go with everything. And the tiny scale is perfect for backing small quilts."

Quilters often bought fabric they had an emotional reaction to. Either the colors or the print touched something inside that evoked a pleasant memory or feeling. For example, my own stash of fabrics had far more blues than any other color. Blue made me feel calm and happy.

Jazz hurried toward us with something exceedingly shiny. "I'm so excited. I found the shirt material for the peacock outfit. *C'est parfait!*" He clutched a bolt of Dupioni silk in iridescent teal. The shimmering effect came from weaving bright turquoise threads on the warp and dark green threads on the weft.

Lucy fingered the slubs in the fabric. "You're right, hon. This is perfect. The coarser texture of a dupioni is more masculine than a thin shantung."

Like a moth drawn to the light, I floated over to the shelves holding fabrics the color of sea glass and summer skies. I bought several cuts of floral prints and a yard of yellow and green plaid that reminded me of the field of mustard growing next to the Sepulveda Dam in Encino each spring.

We finished our shopping and loaded the trunk of Lucy's Caddy with bulging sacks when the sound of sirens pierced the air. Emergency vehicles whipped past us, speeding north. I counted three fire engines, a paramedic ambulance, and four state police cars.

Lucy slammed the lid of the trunk. "I wonder what that's all about?"

We watched the vehicles disappear down the road, and Jazz pointed to a huge column of smoke billowing in the sky. "Fire." Coming from Southern California, where brushfires could be devastating, we stared with alarm at the pink glow in the distance.

Lucy jiggled the car keys nervously. "Dang. July is a bad time of year for a forest fire. It's so hot and dry everywhere. To make things worse, there's a fair breeze blowing today."

A distinctive figure moved rapidly toward us. Phoebe Marple, Birdie's minister friend, wore her white caftan. She wrung her hands, muttered something under her breath, and stared down at the sidewalk as she walked.

Jazz whispered, "Isn't that the chief forest fairy?"

"Hello, Phoebe," I said as she came abreast of our little group.

She looked up, face wrinkled with anxiety. A flowered scarf wrapped around her forehead and held her long white hair in place. "You're Birdie's friends from LA."

"That's right." I smiled. "Is something wrong? You seem upset."

"The whole town of Lafayette is on fire, and I couldn't stop him."

I remembered the story about the curse of Anna Marple: *Lafayette will burn three times.* It had already burned twice before. "Stop who? Are you talking about the curse?"

She nodded vigorously. "My great-great-grandfather is Gus Marple. He was the one at Russell's funeral who played that trick with the birds."

Jazz rolled his eyes but said nothing.

I leaned in closer to the jittery woman. "Why did Gus choose this particular time to burn down the town?"

"He was furious that yet another Watson was buried in his cemetery. The judge who sentenced Gus to hang was Isaiah Watson, Russell's ancestor. I've tried to get the two of them to reconcile. A hundred and fifty years is a long time to hold a grudge. But so far, they've refused."

Jazz made little circles on his temple with his forefinger.

"As Gus and Anna's descendent, you weren't also angry at the Watsons?" I asked.

Phoebe pressed her palms together in the prayer positon. "In the name of all the goddesses, no! I'm a healer of souls." She shook her head sadly. "My great-great-grandfather has been my biggest challenge." She pursed her lips. "Now, if you'll excuse me, I've got to get to Pioneer Cemetery and have a serious talk with him." She walked across the street, got into her battered blue Taurus, and drove north.

Jazz shielded his mouth with the side of his hand and spoke confidentially. "Spook city! Do you think she set the fire?"

The same thing had occurred to me. "Good question. If all of Lafayette is ablaze, the first responders won't let her go anywhere near the cemetery. It's too close to the fire."

Lucy slung her purse over her shoulder. "Come on. Retail therapy always makes me hungry. Let's go get some lunch."

We found a little outdoor café down the street from Miller's and sat under an umbrella in the protection of a patio. The faint smell of smoke curled through the air.

"I guess we should talk about driving back to LA." I bit into my grilled eggplant and pesto panini.

"The sooner the better," said Jazz. "I've got a whole wardrobe to sew. If we leave early in the morning and take turns driving, we could be in LA by tomorrow night."

"Sounds good to me," said Lucy. "We need to tell Birdie to be ready by first light."

After witnessing Birdie's happiness earlier in the day, I wasn't so sure she'd return to Encino with us. I drew my cell phone from my purse. "Let's call her right now."

She answered on the third ring, and I laid down the phone in the middle of the table, with the speaker on. "Hi, Birdie. I'm here with Lucy and

Jazz, and we want to talk about driving back to Encino. We can all hear you."

She smiled right through the phone with her giggle. "Hello, everyone. Are you enjoying your rooms in the hotel?"

"Everything's great," said Lucy. "This is such a cute little town and so full of surprises. We just came from Miller's fabric store. I found yards of that polka dot fabric I've been looking for."

Jazz piped up. "And I found some fabulous couture material."

Birdie laughed. "What about you, Martha?"

"More blue fabric and a beautiful yellow plaid."

"Well," said Birdie, "Miller's has been around forever. It's the best fabric store this side of Portland."

I leaned toward the phone. "Did you hear about the fire in Lafayette?"

"Denny just told me. I understand it's a bad one."

"We ran into your friend Phoebe. She was very upset." I repeated her story about Gus and the Watsons.

"Poor Phoebe." Birdie clucked her tongue. "She's been living in fear of this event her whole life."

More sirens sped down the street. Lucy bent her head toward the middle of the table, raising her voice a little to be heard. "We're anxious to get back to Encino. Can you be ready in the morning?"

Birdie was silent for a few moments. "I have a big announcement. Denny proposed, and I accepted. You'll have to go back without me."

Jazz looked at me frantically and mouthed, *Say something!*

Lucy placed her hand over her heart as if she

were saluting the flag. "That's, uh, great news, hon. Congratulations."

Jazz frowned and poked Lucy's arm. "That's not what I had in mind," he hissed.

What could I say? After the talk with Rainbow and Nancy King this morning, I understood what Russell's diary was all about. I no longer believed Denver was a killer. I cleared my throat. "When do you plan to take the big step?"

"We haven't decided yet, but you'll be the first to know when it happens." Birdie's voice held all the excitement of a young bride. "After all these years, Denny and I are finally going to travel the country together. Only this time, we'll take his RV and go in comfort. We're heading for Encino first so I can pick up some things from the house. While I'm there, Lucy, I'll want to retrieve those items from your safe."

Lucy knitted her brows together. "Okay, hon, whatever you want."

Jazz blurted out, "I'm worried about you, Birdie. Anything could happen on such a long trip."

"She'll be fine!" a male voice came over the speaker. Apparently Denver had been listening to the whole conversation.

"She better be," Jazz's face hardened. "Or I'm coming after you, Watson."

Denver just laughed.

Jazz's nostrils flared, and he balled his fists. He opened his mouth to speak, but I put my hand on his arm and shook my head.

"Keep in touch, Birdie," I said. "We'll see you when you get back to Encino." I ended the call.

"*Je déteste* that man!" Jazz spat.

Lucy patted his hand. "I know, hon. But after all those years covering up for Russell, Birdie deserves to be happy. We have to respect her choice."

I pushed my chair back and stood. "Come on. I saw something in a store window this morning I want to buy. Then I have to get back to the hotel. Arthur needs a potty break."

When we returned to the Yamhill Country Inn, I phoned Agent Lancet. "I'm just checking in to tell you three of us are driving to LA tomorrow morning. Birdie is staying here with Denver Watson. They're going to get married."

"Good for her. It's nice to know something good has come out of this whole miserable case." She hesitated for a moment. "I've been in touch with Arlo every day, since he's been working with me."

"Oh?" Why was she telling me this?

"He's still interested."

"Well, Arlo can be persistent when he's got a crime to solve. He's very dedicated."

"I'm not talking about the murder. I'm talking about you. He's still interested in you."

How inappropriate was that—Arlo Beavers discussing me with his ex-wife? "I don't want to talk about him. What did he say?"

Kay B. Lancet laughed. "This feels like junior high school. He said he made a big mistake walking away from you, and he wants to get back together. He asked for my advice."

"Hah! He can forget that. It'll never happen. What did you say?"

"I told him I didn't think you were interested, and anyway, he should be talking to you not me. I said I didn't want to be his go-between."

Now it was my turn to laugh. "But you carried the message anyway."

"Hey. We exes have to stick together. Just remember, Martha, if you do decide to give him another chance, don't expect things to be fundamentally different. People don't really change all that much. Especially at this stage of life."

She was right. Arlo Beavers had a lot going for him. He was attractive, smart, owned the best dog on the planet, and smelled really good. But if he couldn't be in complete control of our relationship, who knew if he would cheat on me again? Did I want to live with that worry?

Agent Lancet's voice interrupted my thoughts. "I gotta go. My plane is boarding."

"Have a good flight, Kay. And thanks."

I felt guilty not telling her about Russell's diary, but I told myself I'd give her everything once I'd talked to Gail, the loan officer at First Encino Bank. I just wanted to be able to underscore Russell's innocence before I handed over evidence of bank fraud on a grand scale.

By Saturday evening, the conflagration in Lafayette had been all over the national news, including the legend of Anna's curse. Officials determined the blaze started in a mobile home park, where an outdoor barbecue loaded with burning coals and half-cooked hamburgers mysteriously tipped over, igniting dry weeds. The brushfire spread to a nearby trailer and surrounding pine trees. Burning embers traveled on the wind, igniting rooftops. The flames spread through surrounding neighborhoods clear into the center of the small town, destroying the city hall and several shops.

Gus Marple and his mother, Anna, were getting their final revenge.

CHAPTER 32

We left the Yamhill Country Inn at five Sunday morning. Lucy took the first shift driving. Jazz took Birdie's seat in front, where he had more leg room. Arthur and I had the whole backseat to ourselves. We ate our meals on the road and drove in shifts, managing to cover the 850 miles back to the San Fernando Valley. We arrived at Lucy's house before midnight.

An exhausted Jazz drove Zsa Zsa back to West Hollywood, and I took Arthur home. My orange cat, Bumper, greeted us at the door and gave me an earful for taking Arthur and leaving him behind. He refused to let the dog sniff his butt.

"So sorry for leaving you, my little fuzzball. But I'm home for good now."

After listening to my apology, Bumper allowed me to scratch him behind his jawbone.

A quick look around the house told me my neighbor Sonia had once again taken excellent care of him in my absence. I'd thank her with the pretty turquoise earrings I'd purchased at the Yamhill

County Art Association store. After a quick hot shower, I fell into bed, grateful to be horizontal.

Arthur woke me the next morning, desperately dancing in place. "Okay, boy, I get the message." I quickly unfolded my body from the bed and let him out into the backyard. I would miss my canine pal when he went home to his owner.

I telephoned Arlo Beavers and got his voice mail. "We're home in Encino, safe and sound. I guess you'll want your dog back—although I'm perfectly willing to adopt him permanently. Please call me."

The next item on my agenda was to locate the loan officer who referred Nancy King to Five Star Packaging, the nonexistent company. I hoped I could get her to talk to me. I called Russell's branch of First Encino bank and asked for Gail. "I'm sorry, I forgot her last name, but I know she's a loan officer."

A pleasant male voice responded. "Do you mean Gail Deukmejian? She no longer works here."

Deukmejian was a well-known Armenian name. George Deukmejian had been governor of California in the late eighties. Was Gail a relative? "Do you know how I can contact her?"

"No. But I can help you. Do you want to apply for a home mortgage, business loan, car loan, line of credit? We do it all."

"Uh, neither. This is actually a personal matter. Did she leave for another job? Do you know where she went?"

"I'm sorry, I couldn't say."

Couldn't or wouldn't? Time to think of something creative. "Please, I'm trying to notify her of the funeral of a mutual friend in two days. Can't you give me something to go on? A direction to search for her?"

"Well, I know she lives somewhere in the Valley near the Armenian school where her kids go. Maybe they can help you." I thanked him profusely for the lead and silently apologized for lying through my teeth.

An online search turned up two Armenian schools in an area of Hollywood called Little Armenia, and five schools in the San Fernando Valley. My search of the digital white pages yielded ten Deukmejians. I eliminated the ones not located in the Valley and hit pay dirt on the fourth number, which bore a Canoga Park address. "May I speak to Gail please?"

"Speaking."

"Are you the Gail Deukmejian who worked at First Encino Bank?"

She asked in a voice tight with caution, "Who's calling? What is this about?"

I decided to play it straight. Trying to remember lies took too much effort. "My name is Martha Rose. I'm calling on behalf of my friend Birdie Watson, Russell Watson's wife. I accompanied her to the bank two weeks ago when she came to pick up Russell's things. Maybe you remember?"

"Vaguely."

"I wonder if I could come over and ask you a couple of questions. Or we could meet somewhere for coffee if you're more comfortable with that."

"I've already told the FBI everything I know. And anyway, I heard on the news the robber was found dead last week. What does Mrs. Watson want with me?"

"Nothing negative, I promise you. She just wants to know about her husband's last weeks at the bank. You could be a big comfort to her."

Gail sighed. "Okay. I guess I can meet you somewhere. But it has to be before noon, because I'm picking up my youngest from school."

Yes! "Thank you so much. You pick the place."

An hour later, I sat at an outdoor table in front of Il Tramezzino, a trendy Italian restaurant in Tarzana. Gail said she'd be wearing a pink baseball cap so I'd recognize her. I spotted her crossing the street from the parking lot and waved. I vaguely remembered her face from the brief encounter we had in the bank the day Birdie emptied the safe deposit box.

Instead of a smart business suit, Gail Deukmejian trotted over wearing a tank top, workout pants, cross trainers, and no wedding ring. "Are you Martha?"

"That's me." I smiled and offered her my hand.

As soon as she sat, the waiter came over to take our order.

I looked at the menu. "Are you hungry? Their pastries are to die for."

"No thanks. Gotta watch my figure." She ordered a soy latte.

I noticed with some envy that Gail's thirty-something body didn't have an ounce of fat. Some people had all the luck. Even when I was her age and exercising, I tended to be zaftig.

I looked at the waiter. "I'll take a chocolate cannoli and a nonfat latte." You had to draw the calorie line somewhere.

She checked her watch. "I've got an hour before I have to leave. How can I help Mrs. Watson?"

"Do you remember Nancy King from Rainbow Enterprises?"

The waiter brought our order, and she took a sip from the oversized cup. "Sure. Rainbow Enterprises is an important client of First Encino. What does that have to do with Mrs. Watson?"

"Were you aware Sandra Prescott, also known as Rainbow, her CFO, Nancy King, Russell, and Birdie Watson were all old friends?"

She shook her head. "No, not really."

"Well, we think a referral you made to Nancy King started a cascade of events that led to Russell's death."

Gail stiffened. "Are you accusing me of something?"

I put up a calming hand. "No, no. Not at all. You did absolutely nothing wrong. Do you remember the referral I'm talking about? To Five Star Packaging?"

"Yeah, that whole thing was weird." She screwed up her mouth. "It turned out the company didn't exist, but they were definitely listed as a loan customer."

"Do you know how that might have happened?"

"All loans go through a review process before they're approved. Either the review process was skipped in this case, or someone made an error in data entry and listed them as a client when they weren't."

"Who does the reviewing, and who makes the final approval?" I asked.

"It's the loan officer's responsibility to gather all the pertinent documents into an application package. If the applicant meets all the criteria, then the package goes to the branch manager—in this case Russell Watson—who makes the final decision."

"Could anyone in the bank bypass this process?" I took a bite of my pastry and the chocolate filling melted in my mouth like butter and went straight to my thighs.

"I suppose a loan officer could forge everything, but he'd have to be able to hack into the computer system. I wouldn't know how, though. I'm no computer expert." First Nancy King, now Gail confirmed the possibility.

"What about the branch manager? Could he fabricate a package without anyone knowing?" I asked.

Gail nodded. "Absolutely. Any branch manager could fabricate a package, attribute it to an unsuspecting loan officer, and approve it." Her eyes widened. "Why? Do you think Mr. Watson perpetrated a fraud?"

"I'd like to know what you think," I said.

Gail turned up the palms of her hands and shrugged. "He was always a stickler for details. And rules. I really can't see him doing something like that."

"Do you know what Russell did after Rainbow Enterprises alerted him to the problem?"

"He spent a lot of time at the computer and

asked me to pull the actual paperwork for a few old loans made through several different branches of the bank, not just ours."

I put down my fork. "Gail, do you remember the company names on those old files?"

"Let me see." She scowled in concentration. "Mississippi Solar was one of them. There was also a nursery. I remember wondering why a plant nursery would need a half-million-dollar loan. Oh. And Wong Technologies. There were a couple more, but that's all I remember."

My pulse quickened. All those names were in Russell's diary. "Did he say anything to you about the files, or why he wanted to see them?"

"No, but the more files he looked at, the more upset he became." She sat back and tilted her head. "I did notice that all of those companies closed within a year of receiving their loan."

Now I knew what the dates in the middle column of Russell's diary meant. He was recording the creation and the demise of each company. No doubt Five Star Packaging was scheduled to close its proverbial doors this December, exactly twelve months after receiving the loan.

"Who pays back the loan when a company goes under?" I asked.

"Nobody. The bank has to absorb the loss as a bad investment."

So that was how it was done. The embezzler set up a bogus company, somehow arranged for a loan, and pocketed the money. After a year, he closed down the company so any future investigation would lead to a dead end.

"Wouldn't a string of bad investments raise a red flag on the profit and loss statements? Maybe call attention to an incompetent manager?"

Gail pushed her lips together. "Well, if the loans looked like they originated in different branches, there wouldn't be a pattern pointing to any one branch manager. I could see how bad loans could escape notice. During the recession, so many businesses went belly-up. That's why the government had to bail out the banks." She studied my face. "You think the bank robbery and shooting was tied to something Mr. Watson found in those files?"

"Yes." I finished my coffee.

"Are you saying he was deliberately killed?" She rubbed her hands on her bare arms and shivered, despite the July heat.

"Not only me. The FBI is also saying that. They just don't know why. But I think you and I have figured that out."

By now Gail Deukmejian was hugging herself. "Do you think I'm in danger for helping Mr. Watson?"

I didn't want to alarm her. "Probably not, but let's keep this conversation between us for now. It may not be safe to discuss what you know just yet. You never know who the real killer might be. If he thinks you have something incriminating to tell the authorities, you could be in danger. I have something I intend to hand over to the FBI. Once it's in their hands, the details would be common knowledge and you should be safe."

I scribbled my phone number on a napkin. "Here's how I can be contacted. Take this and call me if you think of anything else. I promise to let you know the minute I've given the evidence to the FBI."

"Evidence?"

"Russell kept a record of all the information you helped him uncover. The FBI will be able to use that record to track down his killer."

"But I thought the killer was already dead. That's what they said on the news."

"The man who pulled the trigger is dead, but the one who hired him is still out there."

CHAPTER 33

After I left Gail Deukmejian, I walked to the market down the street from the restaurant and picked up four bags of badly needed groceries. I had just unloaded the last of the organic veggies in my kitchen, when I remembered tomorrow was Quilty Tuesday and, for the first time in sixteen years, Birdie wouldn't be there. I made myself comfortable on the sofa and called Lucy at home.

"Hello, hon," she answered slightly out of breath. "You calling about tomorrow?"

"How'd you know?"

"You keep forgetting about my powerful sixth sense."

I laughed. "Or maybe you're just a good guesser. Where shall we meet? Your house or mine?"

"Jazz called this morning and says he wants to join us. He'd like to get started on a memory quilt, so I told him to bring all his fabrics and meet us at my house at ten. What're you up to today? I've got loads of laundry from the trip."

I told her about my meeting with Gail the loan officer and how Russell discovered the string of bad loans. "I'm ready to hand over his diary to Agent Lancet. From what Gail described, it seems pretty clear Russell was uncovering the embezzlement, not covering it up."

"Nice work, girlfriend. I'm sure both Birdie and Jazz will be sad but relieved to know Russell wasn't doing anything illegal."

My next call was to Agent Lancet's cell phone. "Hello, Kay. How was your flight back to LA?"

The phone beeped a couple of times and her voice faded back in. ". . . Virginia for a debriefing."

"Well, I have something that will break your investigation wide open."

She chuckled. "Come on, Martha. No disrespect, but what could you possibly have that we haven't already thought of?"

Well, that was a bit snarky. I told her about the diary.

"You held back evidence all this time?" Her voice turned from amused to angry.

"We had no idea what we had at first, so we didn't know how important it was. But after speaking to Gail Deukmejian this morning, I'm convinced I know *why* Russell was killed. I'm confident you'll find out who's responsible. It looks like it's someone within the bank."

"Are you accusing anyone specific?"

"According to Gail, it could be any of the other five branch managers. Even one of their loan officers, if he had access to the database and computer skills good enough to bypass the approval process. You probably know a lot more about how these things work than I do. Anyway, I'm more than happy to have you take this diary off my hands."

"You're damn right you're handing it over. I'll be back in LA early tomorrow morning. I expect to see you first thing."

"Wow, Kay. That wasn't the reaction I expected. I mean, how often does the FBI get such a big clue just dropped in their lap like this? Whatever happened to 'We exes have to stick together'?"

"That only applies to boyfriends and husbands. I mean it, Martha. Don't leave town."

Not more than five minutes later my phone rang. Arlo Beavers sounded really annoyed. "Why am I not surprised?"

"Did you not like my earlier message about adopting your German shepherd? It's just that Arthur is such a great dog, and I've grown so fond of him. But if you're going to get all sensitive on me, forget I ever asked."

"Kay just called. She told me about the diary you've been sitting on all this time. She wants me to take it from you before you do anything else stupid."

"I don't believe you," I huffed. "She wouldn't call me stupid. We've bonded."

"You and my ex-wife? God help me. I'm finishing something up here at the station. Don't leave the house. I'll be there in a half hour to retrieve the evidence and my dog."

The shepherd nuzzled my hand, asking for ear

scratches. "So you're definitely going to take Arthur back?"

The tone of his voice changed, and he spoke quietly. "Artie is part of a package. If you want to adopt the dog, you have to adopt me, too."

"I'll pack his things."

My body still ached from sitting in a confined space for eighteen hours the day before. I wanted to lie down, but a suitcase full of dirty clothes stared at me. And since my underwear drawer was almost empty, I had no choice but to start a load of laundry. I'd be able to relax once everything was clean and put away.

I'd just turned on the delicate cycle of the washing machine when someone knocked on my door. Beavers already? I looked through the peephole. Only one person I knew wore thick green eye makeup—my neighbor Sonia Spiegelman.

I opened the door and embraced her. "Sonia. Come in. Thank you so much for taking such good care of Bumper while I was gone."

"It was no problem. I really enjoyed spending time with him each day." The Indian bangle bracelets tinkled on her arm as she crossed the threshold and pointed to a pile of envelopes and catalogs on the hall table. "I brought in your mail each day and separated out the solicitations from the bills. No letters. People don't write letters anymore." She picked up one of the envelopes. "I noticed you've changed from cable to satellite. Do you like it better?"

Sonia was our resident yenta. Nothing, and I mean *nothing*, happened in the neighborhood without her knowledge. Her prying used to irritate me, but I gained a real affection for her when she helped save my life a year ago. Sonia was a lonely, middle-aged ex-groupie of Mick Jagger's. Her house was a shrine to the seventies, and she smoked medical marijuana for a condition I had yet to figure out. I guided her toward the living room and gestured for her to sit.

"How was your trip?" she asked.

"Exhausting. And my hip is really bothering me today. I brought something back for you."

Her face lit up. "You shouldn't have."

"Wait here." I retrieved a small cloth bag containing the handmade turquoise earrings. "When I saw these I thought of you. The tag that comes with them says turquoise has tremendous healing powers and protects the wearer."

Sonia's eyes sparkled. "I love handcrafted jewelry. I'm going to put them on right now." She walked over to the mirror above the hall table, removed the silver hoops she already wore, and threaded the new gold hooks through the holes in her earlobes. The turquoise stones swayed when she turned to face me. "How do I look?"

"Like a healthy, safe person."

"And I have something for you." Sonia reached into her pocket and pulled out a handmade cigarette. "I'm sorry you're feeling crummy."

"Weed?" I asked.

Sonia laughed. "Ganja. Boo. Paca lolo. Have you ever tried it for your fibromyalgia? I take a couple tokes of this special blend when I'm in pain." She thrust her fist forward and deposited the joint in my hand. "Just try it, but be careful. It's powerful. One or two hits should be enough." She kissed my cheek and turned toward the door. "Thanks again for the beautiful earrings."

With my mouth hanging open, I stared at her back as she walked out, leaving as abruptly as she came. I doubted Dr. Lim at UCLA would ever prescribe cannabis as an anti-inflammatory. But now that medical marijuana was legal in California, maybe I'd take her advice and give it a try. I put the cigarette on the hall table and headed for the kitchen, thinking what was the worst that could happen?

Beavers called again. "Sorry I'm late. Something came up. But I'll be there around six to pick up the diary and Arthur. Do you still have enough kibble to feed him dinner?"

What did that man have against saying a simple hello? "Sure. Everything's ready. See you later."

I ended the brief call and unloaded the bags from Miller's fabric store on my kitchen table. Most of my purchases were pieces of fabric cut into fat quarters. Cotton yardage was typically around forty inches wide. So a yard would measure forty inches wide and thirty-six inches long; a half yard 40"x18"; and a quarter yard 40"x9". A quarter yard cut that way was not a very useful strip of fabric. But if the half yard was divided vertically down the middle, the resulting piece was 20"x18", a much more useful size. Buying fat quarters was an economical way to build a stash of fabric, and quilt stores were happy to provide them for their customers.

I had a rule about new fabric. Every piece had to be washed and dried before it was allowed in my sewing room. For one thing, I wanted to get rid of all the chemicals from the manufacturing and dying process. For another, I wanted to preshrink the cotton fabric so the seams of the finished quilt wouldn't pull apart when washed later. I unfolded each of the fat quarters and sorted the lights and darks in preparation for washing after my clothes were done.

By early evening, the pain in my hip and lower back had reached a crescendo. I limped from the laundry room, where I was folding clothes, into the kitchen to take my pain meds. I reached for the bottle of Soma but stopped in midair. Maybe I should try that joint. What if smoking pot really could ease my chronic pain?

At least thirty-five years had passed since I'd experimented with marijuana in college, but I still remembered what to do. A small box of wooden matches hid out in the kitchen junk drawer. I pawed through expired coupons, rubber bands, odd plastic lids, and orphan screws to find them. Sitting at the kitchen table, I lit the cigarette, inhaled deeply, and held the hot smoke in my lungs. A cough exploded out of my chest.

What would Quincy think if she could see me now?

I inhaled a second time and pinched the flame off the end of the cigarette. As I held my breath, a gentle feeling of euphoria began to swirl around me in a soft cloud. *No wonder Sonia smokes this stuff.* I forgot all about my throbbing hip.

A sharp pang in my stomach reminded me it was dinnertime. I couldn't remember the last time I ate, and I was starved. I could make a salad with the organic veggies I had just purchased, but that would take too long. I rummaged through the freezer, looking for something already prepared that I could nuke.

Instead, I found something even better; a quart of Trader Joe's double creamy Coffee Bean Blast ice cream with a million calories per half cup, which came to eight million calories per quart. I took the unopened container straight to the table. Who needed to bother with a bowl when you could eat it right out of the carton? The coffee flavor burst on my tongue, and the cold silky texture cooled the inside of my mouth. My taste, my sight, all my senses seemed to be a thousand times more acute.

Twenty minutes later I was scraping the bottom of the carton when someone rang the doorbell. It had to be Beavers! Technically, he could cite me for possession since I didn't have a prescription for pot. I picked up the partially smoked joint and tossed it in the junk drawer. Then I reached under the sink for a can of air freshener and quickly sprayed the heck out of the air, hoping to mask any telltale smoke.

When I finally opened the door, he took one look at me and chuckled. He saw the puzzled look on my face so he pointed to my chest. "What have you been eating?"

I looked down at the girls. Big latte-colored drips

stained the front of my T-shirt, where my spoon had dripped on the way to my mouth. "Crap."

Arthur trotted over to greet his owner, who bent down to rough up the dog's fur.

"How's my buddy? Did you have fun in Oregon?"

Arthur responded with a bark and a wagging tail. Then Beavers stood and breezed past me into the house.

As he entered, I caught a whiff of his woodsy cologne. I had always found it sexy and compelling, but tonight the scent was so much sharper and complex. Mixed in with the musky, patchouli, lemony overtones, was the aroma of this man's body. Memories of our past intimacies flooded my senses like an aphrodisiac. I couldn't help myself. I was hot for Beavers.

He didn't waste any time. "Where's the diary?" I handed it to him and he looked inside. "Tell me what I'm looking at."

We moved to the living room, and he sat so close to me on the sofa, our thighs touched. At this proximity, his scent became even stronger. A warm flush started at the base of my spine and slowly crept all the way up to my chest. I leaned toward him and pointed to the diary lying open in his hands. I explained how Birdie had decoded the key phrase substitution code. "Russell made a list of loans awarded to bogus companies by someone in First Encino Bank. He uncovered evidence of systematic fraud. I believe he intended to report the embezzlement and that's what got him killed."

Can he feel the heat from my body?

I explained the meaning of each entry in the book. "When the FBI uncovers who owned these companies, they'll find the embezzler and the killer."

Beavers turned his head toward me. His face was inches from mine. I was so mesmerized by the movement of his soft lips beneath his white mustache, I barely heard what he said. "You're so damn smart, Martha."

I looked into his dark eyes and knew he was feeling the same urgency I was. All it took was a slight movement in his direction. With a little moan, he grabbed me and pulled me toward him. As his eager tongue probed my mouth, I knew "the worst thing" was about to happen, but I didn't care. I fell backward on the sofa, dragging him with me.

An hour later, Beavers and I lay both satisfied and spent in my bed. Our clothes were strewn around the room, and the sheets lay in a frenzied tangle. He kissed the tip of my nose and smiled. "Well. That was fun." He pulled me closer. "I've missed you, honey. We were always so good together."

Yes, until our breakup a year ago, we had been good together. That was, as long as he could be the boss. Beavers was an alpha male. Because of that, I found him both sexy and maddening at the same time.

I began to get an uneasy feeling in the pit of my stomach. Was I turning to Arlo Beavers merely out of loneliness? Did I really want him back in my life? I sat up in bed and regarded the man grinning beside me. What had Kay warned me? *People don't fundamentally change.*

I swallowed hard. "We have to talk."

"I thought that's what we were just doing." He ran his fingers up and down my arm.

"No. I mean about what just happened." I swept my hand around the bedroom. "This was fantastic, but I think it was a mistake."

He propped himself up on his elbow. "Look, I know you might be a little gun-shy, especially after what happened with Kerry and me. But that's completely over."

What happened was he cheated on me with Arthur's vet, Kerry Andreason, and I doubted I could ever trust him again. "I don't know what got into me tonight, Arlo." Well, I did know, actually. Sonia's giggle weed, but I wasn't going to tell him that. "Obviously I'm still attracted to you. Who wouldn't be? But we have serious issues."

He sat up and gently cupped my face in his hands. "I think we can make this work. If you're uncomfortable, I'm okay with taking it slow."

With tremendous relief, I watched him get dressed, gather Russell's diary and his dog, and head toward the front door. After I hugged the shepherd in an elaborate good-bye, Beavers kissed me and said, "I'll call you tomorrow."

CHAPTER 34

Beavers and Arthur left around nine. I stepped into the shower for a relaxing five minutes, toweled off, put on my cotton jammies, and tumbled into bed. Between the marijuana, the romp with Beavers, and the hot shower, I fell almost immediately into a deep sleep.

In the middle of the night, Bumper had a running fit and woke me. Cats could build up kinetic energy that normally got disbursed by outdoor exercise, like stalking birds, leaping toward grasshoppers, and climbing trees. But cats who lived primarily indoors didn't have the same opportunities for those behaviors. Being nocturnal creatures, the urge to release the buildup of stored energy often burst forth in the wee hours. Tonight was one of those nights.

His four feet thumped as he raced down the hallway toward my bedroom. He jumped up on my bed, landing with a thud.

I groaned and snuggled deeper under my Ohio Star quilt. "Go to sleep, Bumper!"

He leapt off the bed and thundered down the hallway toward the living room. Five seconds later, broken glass tinkled to the floor.

Crap! He must've jumped up on the kitchen counter and knocked a glass to the floor. Unfortunately, I couldn't wait until morning to clean the broken shards. That crazy cat might cut his paws.

Still groggy, I sat up and swung my bare feet to the cold floor. *Darn that cat!* In the dimness of the blue LED night-light plugged into the wall socket, I managed to locate a pair of Crocs with hard soles to protect my feet from the broken glass. I shuffled down the dark hallway toward the open-plan kitchen, dining, and living rooms. Soft moonlight illuminated the mullioned windows in the kitchen and adjacent dining area.

Something about the dining room window looked odd. One of the panes wasn't reflecting the moonlight in the same way as the others. Was it broken? How did Bumper manage to break a windowpane? I narrowed my eyes and peered harder. Something else was wrong. The window seemed to be open. I flipped the switch at the end of the hallway, and the overhead pot lights in the kitchen instantly sprang to life.

Out of the corner of my eye, I saw something move to my left. I turned to look. Ivo Van Otten, president of First Encino Bank and Russell Watson's protégé, stepped out of the shadows in the living room and pointed a gun straight at me. My heart stopped beating for a second then resumed at warp speed.

Van Otten was dressed for black ops. His hands

were covered with latex gloves, and his silver hair was encased in a black stocking cap. He intended to leave no trace evidence behind. And no witness. He had closed the living room drapes so nobody could see inside my house. If something happened to me, my neighbors would never know. It seemed like he had thought of everything.

Adrenaline coursed through my body like water through a fire hose. Every instinct screamed to run for my life, but my knees had turned to water, and my feet wouldn't move. Even if I could find the strength to run, a six-foot-tall man with a gun now stood between me and my front door.

My voice shook. "What do you want with me?"

His voice was silky as he spun a spider's web of false security. "Just give me the diary and I'll be on my way."

Panic squeezed my throat so I could barely breathe. "I don't know what you're talking about."

He took a menacing step toward me. "Let's not waste time. I know all about the diary, so hand it over."

I held up my hand to stop him. "Okay. Okay. How did you find out I had it?"

The corner of his mouth turned up. "Gail called me after your meeting."

Darn! I told her not to tell anyone. "Why did she call *you*?"

"Gail and I are . . . special friends. She was only too eager to tell me everything."

"You were having an affair? Was she in on this with you?"

"Obviously not, otherwise she wouldn't have

been stupid enough to refer anyone to Five Star Packaging."

"I don't have the diary," I said.

He opened and closed his fists. "We can do this the easy way or the hard way. Your choice."

I didn't even want to know what he meant by "the hard way." *How can I escape? Think. Delay.* I took a deep breath. "I'm surprised you're the one who embezzled four and a half million from your own bank. I must say, your scheme was very clever. You managed to go undetected for several years. Unfortunately for you, Russell was just as clever, because he figured out what you were doing."

"Actually it was five million. Russell missed one. It's too bad, really. Another couple mill and I would've been long gone."

I frowned. "Russell Watson was your mentor and your friend. How could you have had him killed?"

"Well, aren't you the curious cat." He sneered. "I gave him a chance. I even called him one night and offered to cut him in. But Watson was a stubborn old fool."

That must have been the phone call where Birdie overheard Russell say, "When hell freezes over." With those words, poor Russell had sealed his fate.

I took another shaky breath. "I gather assassinating people was Levesque's real specialty. Why go to all the trouble of staging a bank robbery?"

Van Otten's laugh was cold. "To obfuscate the real reason for Russell's death. Also, the robbery money provided Levesque with an easy bonus."

I'd never heard anyone use the word *obfuscate* in

a real sentence before. Clearly, Van Otten liked to show off. If I could keep him talking, maybe I could figure out how to stay alive. "What made you decide to kill Levesque?"

His eyes darkened. "What do you care? Just give me the diary. We both know how this is going to end."

I shivered. *Appeal to his ego.* "Your scheme was brilliant. You've completely stumped the FBI. I just want to know how you did it, that's all."

He smiled, visibly pleased with the flattery. "Okay, I'll indulge your interest. You'll never be able to repeat it to anyone else anyway."

Dear God, show me a way out of this!

"The FBI showed me the video of the robbery, hoping I might recognize the guy. I realized Levesque could be identified by the tattoo on his neck. I couldn't risk him talking if he were ever caught."

"How'd you get into the mortuary?"

"I never left. After the viewing, I slipped into an unused room and waited until the place was empty. Then I unlocked the back door, walked down the street to where I'd parked my car, and drove around to the back. I took Levesque's body out of the trunk and carried it inside. The rest was easy."

I recalled with sadness Birdie's lovely Baltimore Album quilt that had been removed from the casket to make room for the other body. "What did you do with the quilt?"

He gave me a puzzled look. "What?"

"The Baltimore Album quilt Russell was wrapped in. What did you do with it?"

"There was no quilt. Just his corpse."

For a moment my fear was replaced with outrage. "Towsley the mortician stole Russell's quilt? What is wrong with you people?"

Van Otten didn't reply. He looked at his watch and slowly closed the distance between us. "Time's up. I've got a plane to catch. The diary. Now."

If I told him the book was already in the hands of the authorities, he'd kill me on the spot. Then I got a blinding flash of insight. Something he said about never leaving the mortuary, being there all the time. Sitting on the hall table was the pile of mail Sonia had sorted for me, my purse, my cell phone, and a heavy brass dish where I tossed my house keys each day. *How can I get over there?*

I backed away from him and kept talking as I inched in the direction of the table. "I'll give it to you if you just let me live. Please. I don't want to die. I'll tell the authorities the diary was stolen in the middle of the night. I won't say a word about you to anyone. I promise."

His smile was cruel and insincere. "Of course. All I want is the book and then I'll leave. That is, if you really promise not to tell."

I knew he was just playing with me, but I went along with the charade. "I promise. Ask anyone who knows me. I never lie."

I managed to maneuver all the way over. Next, for my plan to work, I had to trick him into turning away long enough for me to make my move. I pointed to the bookcase on the other side of the

iving room. "It's over there. See the small book
with the blue cover on the top shelf? I've hidden it
up there. I had to use a stepladder, but you're tall
enough to reach it."

He pointed his gun at my head. I'd seen enough
cop shows to know the funny-looking thing on the
barrel was a silencer. "You better be telling me the
truth."

My heart was beating like a hummingbird and
my mouth felt like the Namibian desert. *Oh please,
God, don't let him shoot me.*

He backed up to the bookcase, training the gun
on my head the whole time. Finally, he lowered the
weapon, turned, and reached for the top shelf.

Now! I reached for my purse and groped inside
until I felt something cold and heavy. Lucy's Browning semiautomatic pistol. It had been sitting there
all this time. Thank God I'd forgotten to give it
back to her. With trembling hands, I removed the
gun and flipped the safety.

He opened the blue book and frowned. It was an
old edition of Dorothy Parker poems. Turning back
toward me with rage blazing in his eyes, he raised
his gun again.

I fired first.

Van Otten screamed in pain, grabbed his crotch,
and crumpled to the floor. His face had gone white,
and the floor beneath him turned red.

I stared in horror until I found my voice. "Oh my
God. I didn't mean to hit you *there*. But you're so tall
and I'm so short and my hands were shaking. . . ."

He groaned and turned his head away from me.
The gun with the silencer had fallen out of his

hand and skittered across the floor in my direction. I scooped it up and placed it on the hall table behind me.

Pulse pounding in my ears, I could hardly breathe. This man tried to kill me and now he lay bleeding on my living room floor. I couldn't think straight. What should I do next? I heard myself say, "I've just done the laundry. I'll go get you a clean towel."

Van Otten gritted his teeth and squeaked. "Ambulance."

"Oh. Right." I picked up the phone and dialed 9-1-1. Then I called Beavers.

CHAPTER 35

I wouldn't be able to occupy my house again until a cleanup crew removed Van Otten's blood from the living room floor. So, after giving my statement to the LAPD, I gathered Bumper and a suitcase full of clothes. Beavers promised to look into the theft of Birdie's quilt from Pearly Gates Mortuary. Then he asked me to stay at his place, but I politely declined. By seven that morning, Bumper and I had moved into Lucy and Ray Mondello's guest bedroom.

At nine, Lucy brewed a second pot of strong, French roast. "Jazz will be here at ten. He says he's got a lot of questions about last night. He's also bringing a bunch of Russell's old shirts to cut up for a memory quilt." My tall friend looked stylish in lemon yellow slacks, a white blouse, and green shoes. Thanks to Jazz's tutoring, gone forever were the days when everything she wore had to match.

I gulped the hot caffeine to combat the lack of sleep from the night before. "Did you call Birdie and let her know about Van Otten?"

"I did. She was shocked and sad to hear he was behind Russell's murder. There was a time, especially in the beginning, when Van Otten had been like a son to them."

"I hope you didn't tell her about her missing quilt, yet. If Towsley still has it, maybe the police can recover it for her."

"I didn't mention that part," Lucy said. "I didn't see any reason to add to her sorrow. She'll be disappointed when she finds out Russell went in the ground without it."

"Did she say anything more about her plans?"

Lucy added some cream and sugar to her coffee and stirred. "She and Denver are leaving tomorrow for LA. They're traveling in his motor home. She said if you want privacy, you can go across the street and stay at her place. They aren't scheduled to arrive for four days. But Ray and I really don't want you to go, hon. We want you to stay with us."

At exactly ten, Jazz knocked on Lucy's door. He carried the yellow tote with Zsa Zsa inside, a bag of apple fritters from Western Donuts, and several sacks of fabric. Once we got settled in the living room, I reached for a plate-sized fritter and repeated the story of last night's terrifying encounter with the man responsible for Russell's murder.

"You shot him where?" Jazz covered his mouth with his hand.

I closed my eyes and sank back into the blue wool upholstery of the easy chair. "I know, I know. Believe me, I didn't plan it that way. I just aimed in his direction and pulled the trigger." I opened my eyes and looked at Lucy. "By the way, the police said they'll eventually return your Browning."

She waved her hand. "You've used that gun before, remember? I think I'm going to just let you keep it. You know, girlfriend, I've heard from Richie. He said the news of your capturing Van Otten has already gone viral."

"How could it? Nobody was there to take a video."

"Remember when you caught that other killer seven months ago? Well, Richie used a picture of you with a gun from that video. He made a meme with a funny caption. It seems with this newest incident, you've developed a cult following."

"Thanks a lot."

Richie was Lucy's middle son, who worked in the tech industry. They spoke or texted every day. She must have told him about last night.

Zsa Zsa popped her head out of the yellow tote bag and yawned. She wore a red gingham sundress matching Jazz's shirt. He picked her up and set her on the floor. She sniffed the air and bolted off on her tiny Maltese legs straight for the guest room, where Bumper rested on the bed, still exhausted from all the nocturnal drama. We heard a lot of yipping and hissing.

Lucy pointed to the bulging bags Jazz had brought with him. "Let's see what you've got."

He removed dozens of colorful shirts. "I sewed all these for Rusty. Some of them go back twenty years. Not all of them are cotton. Can I still use them together in a quilt?"

"The great thing about quilting," said Lucy, "is that there are no rules. You can do whatever you want. You just have to be aware that different kinds of materials will react differently to the process. Cotton and linen will be easier to cut and quilt, but silk will be tricky. As you already know, it's more slippery and unravels easier."

She handed Jazz a thick encyclopedia of quilt block patterns. "Before we cut into those shirts, you need to decide what pattern you want to use. Then we'll draft the design. Take some time to look through these."

I finished my apple fritter at the same time FBI Agent Kay Lancet showed up at Lucy's front door. She breezed into the living room and sat in a chair facing me. "Well, Martha. Seems as if you managed to deliver not just the proof of his crimes, but the archcriminal himself. I've gotta say, nicely done."

"How is he?"

"Van Otten's out of surgery. Don't worry, he'll live. But he'll never be a father. He confessed to everything." Her voice softened. "Are you okay? You've been through a lot lately."

Tears stung my eyes as I recalled for the millionth time how I almost died last night. "I'm still as shaky as heck and really tired. But I guess I'll live too."

She stood. "Can I borrow you for a little bit outside?"

"Sure." I mouthed an apology at Lucy and Jazz and followed her out the front door.

She turned to face me and placed her hand softly on my shoulder. "You should've handed over that diary as soon as you and Mrs. Watson found it,

Martha. We have people and software that could've decoded it and traced those accounts in an hour. Your decision to hide the evidence almost cost you your life."

I shifted on my feet. "We really didn't know what we had at first. And then when I deciphered the code and realized what it was, I just had to make sure Russell wasn't guilty before I handed over the diary."

"What difference would that have made? He was already dead."

I looked at the agent and sighed. "If Russell had stolen the money, there would've been dire consequences for Birdie and Jazz. The bank could've sued his estate to recover the missing funds. The two of them could've lost everything. I thought if Russell was guilty and I found the money and returned it, Birdie and Jazz would be safe. But after talking to Gail Deukmejian, I was convinced Russell was innocent. That's when I called you." I lowered my eyes and stared at the ground.

Lancet gave my shoulder a reassuring squeeze. "You're lucky everything worked out the way it did." Her next words took me totally by surprise. "So you slept with him again?"

I jerked my head up and stared at her. "How'd you know?"

"I didn't know for sure." The corner of her mouth turned up. "It was something in the way Arlo told me about being with you until nine last night that led me to suspect as much. You're confident enough to try a relationship with him again?"

I sighed. "He's attractive. I had a vulnerable moment. It just happened."

"Well, you know Arlo. He doesn't do well with indecision. He'll want to wrap you up and stake a claim as soon as possible."

I shifted uncomfortably. "He's going to be disappointed then. I'm certainly not ready to admit that what happened between us last night was anything more than a moment of weakness."

She raised an eyebrow. "Let me know how long that lasts."

I hugged Agent Lancet good-bye and went back inside Lucy's house. We sorted Russell's old shirts into lights and darks while Jazz chose a pattern.

He held up the book and pointed to an eight-pointed Lemoyne Star. "I'm crazy about this pattern. It's *très jolie.*"

"Mazel Tov," said my orange-haired Catholic friend. "This block is usually not for beginners, because it requires sewing set-in seams. But since you're already a pro, you shouldn't have any problem with it."

I held up a pile of Russell's shirts. "You can use different fabrics for each ray of the star. And if you use a dark fabric for the background, the finished quilt will look like a colorful constellation."

"*Parfait!*" Jazz clasped his hands. "What do we do next?"

Lucy printed pattern pieces for ten-inch blocks using Quilt Block software and cut templates for each piece from a sheet of Mylar plastic. We spent the rest of the day cutting Russell's shirts into diamond shapes that would become individual rays in the Lemoyne Stars. Jazz finally left at three and air kissed us on both cheeks in the European style. "I'll be back next week. *Au revoir.*"

Lucy closed the door behind him and said, "I think we've just gained a new member for our group."

CHAPTER 36

At four, Lucy's phone rang just as she put a meat loaf in the oven. She wiped her hands on her apron and answered. Then she put her hand over the mouthpiece. "It's Arlo," she whispered. "He wants to talk to you."

I shook my head vigorously and whispered back, "He's been texting me all day, but I'm ignoring him. Tell him I'm asleep."

Lucy removed her hand from the mouthpiece. "I'm sorry, Arlo, but she's sleeping right now. I'll give her the message you called." After she ended the call, she asked, "Why is he so anxious to speak to you?"

"I slept with him last night."

Lucy's mouth fell open. "Are you sure that was a good idea?"

I shook my head. "No! But I was feeling needy."

A minute later, my cell phone rang. "Crap. That better not be Arlo again." I looked at the caller ID. I recognized the number. The caller wasn't Arlo Beavers, it was my missing boyfriend Crusher!

My hands began to shake. "Lucy! Yossi's on the phone. What do I do?"

"Answer it."

The phone kept ringing. "But I don't know what to say. I'm really pissed he hasn't called since he left town five months ago."

"Did you ever try calling him?"

"At first. I also sent a couple of texts. But when he didn't respond, I figured he didn't love me anymore and had moved on."

The phone stopped ringing.

Lucy began slicing a tomato. "Okay, I get why you don't want to encourage Arlo. But don't you at least want to hear what Yossi has to say for himself?"

"I don't know what I want. I'm pissed off at him but, to be honest, I've missed him terribly. I was really sad when he didn't call or return my texts."

She put down the knife and turned to face me. "Well, girlfriend, you asked for my advice, so here it is. If you miss him, talk to him. Find out why he disappeared. Maybe there's a good reason. And for pity's sake, don't tell him about Arlo!"

"But what if he was just being a jerk?"

Lucy resumed cutting vegetables. "Then you'll know what to do."

I looked at my cell phone and saw a text from Crusher. Pls. call me.

I took a deep breath and pressed the call button.

He answered on the second ring. "Babe."

A shiver ran up my spine at the sound of his deep voice. "Yossi! Where have you been all this time? Why didn't you ever call me or return my texts?"

"I couldn't contact anyone. The minute I left LA

I was under deep cover. But my assignment's over, and I'm coming home."

My heart sped up a little. "By 'home' you mean . . ."

He chuckled. "I'll see you tonight."

Well, that was presumptuous. Did he think he could just waltz in and out of my life without explanation and I'd be waiting for him? "There's something you need to know before you get here. I'm not exactly home right now."

"What is it? Are you okay?" He sounded deeply concerned.

"I'm fine, but I'm staying at Lucy and Ray's for the next couple of days. I'll explain when you get here."

I could scarcely eat dinner, I was so nervous. On the one hand, I was relieved and elated to see Crusher again. He hadn't moved on and he wanted to come back home to me. On the other hand, I had just cheated on him in a moment of weakness. I tried to rationalize my romp with Beavers by telling myself it was Crusher's fault for not contacting me in five whole months.

For the next two hours I checked my watch a hundred times. At eight, the doorbell rang and my stomach lurched.

Ray opened the door and my pulse fluttered in my throat. A bearded, six-foot-six Crusher walked through the front door, wearing a black T-shirt and blue jeans and a blue bandana over his red hair. He shook hands with Ray, clapped him on the back, and stepped into the living room. Ray and Crusher had become pals while Crusher recovered at my house from a gunshot wound.

Crusher greeted Lucy warmly, but his blue gaze never left my face. After some small talk, Lucy and Ray excused themselves and left us alone in the living room. As Lucy walked past, she handed me the key to Birdie's house.

In one long stride, Crusher closed the distance between us and wrapped me in his arms. It felt like home. I put my arms around his neck and he lifted me up for a long, tender kiss.

He smelled like gasoline and lemons. "Babe, I've missed you so much."

My feet dangled about ten inches above the floor.

"I've missed you, too, Yossi. I was so sad. I didn't know if I'd ever see you again. But I'm also upset you never once contacted me in five whole months!"

He lowered me gently to the ground. "I'm sorry I had to put you through that, Martha. But that's the nature of my job. I would've called if I could. I kept hoping you'd wait for me. Please tell me you haven't moved on."

Lucy was right. Best not to mention my night with Arlo Beavers. I led him to the kitchen table and took the foil off a dinner plate I'd saved for him. "Eat!" I ordered. I poured us each a glass of wine from an open bottle of Chianti and watched him cut into a thick slice of meat loaf with his fork.

"Why are you staying here? Did the water pipes at your house break, or something?"

I took a deep breath. "Not exactly. It all started when Russell Watson was killed."

He put his fork down and frowned. "At your house?"

"No. He was shot during a robbery at his bank. So Lucy, Birdie, Russell's gay lover, Jazz, and I followed his hearse to Oregon to bury him in the family plot. Along the way, I ended up driving his body until a crazy Swedish rapper forced me off the highway and I totaled the hearse. The coffin flew out the back and that's when we discovered the body of Russell's assassin stuffed inside with him."

Crusher put down his fork and his shoulders began to shake. "Babe."

"I'm serious! We finally managed to get him buried, but the ghost of Gus Marple got so angry he burned down Lafayette for the *third time*. Then Birdie got engaged to Denver so the three of us came home without her."

Now he laughed out loud. "What about your house?"

"I'm getting there. Russell kept a secret diary. Birdie cracked the code and I deciphered the entries. It was a record of embezzlement. Last night the embezzler broke into my house demanding I hand over the diary. He would've killed me with his silencer, but I tricked him into looking away and shot him with Lucy's Browning instead. That's why I can't go back inside my house just yet."

His raised his eyebrows. "Did you kill him?"

"No. I shot him in the crotch. I didn't mean to,

exactly. This morning Richie posted a meme of me on the Internet. He's calling me *Dead Eye Dick.*"

Crusher threw back his head and laughed so hard, tears rolled out of the corners of his eyes. I was not amused. When he saw the expression on my face he suddenly became sober.

"You don't still have the gun, do you?"

Please turn the page for a quilting tip
from Mary Marks!

CARING FOR YOUR QUILTS

Quilts have two basic purposes: to provide warmth and comfort, and to decorate. Either way, they're meant to be used and enjoyed. So whether your quilt is going on a bed or hanging on a wall, you'll want to take these simple steps to preserve your work of art.

With the exception of baby and children's quilts, *don't wash*. At least don't do it often. Exposure to harsh detergents and chemicals can weaken the fibers and dull the colors. If you must wash a quilt, use only a mild soap like Ivory or Orvus, and cool water. Always lay your quilt flat to dry. The heat and agitation of the clothes dryer will weaken and break the fibers. And for heaven's sake NEVER send your quilts to the dry cleaners! Remember, chemicals are bad for quilts.

I made a lovely, hand-stitched Grandmother's Fan quilt for my daughter when she went away to college. She laundered that quilt right along with her sheets every week. At the end of four years, her poor Grandmother's Fan was in shreds, too damaged to repair. The combination of heat and chemicals destroyed the cotton fibers and thread.

Don't sit on your quilt. If the quilt is on your bed, keep your bottom away from it. The weight of your body will put a strain on the stitching and break the threads—especially if the quilting has been done by hand. Quilts are meant to cover your body, not the other way around.

Keep your quilt out of the harsh light. That means natural sunlight as well as indoor lighting. Wall hangings are especially vulnerable to fading from light exposure. If you've hung a quilt on the wall, chances are you've done so because you love it and want to show it off. Resist the temptation to shine a spotlight on it. If you do, the colors may not only fade, but a strong light may also weaken the fibers.

Today, a copy of the Declaration of Independence, a document precious to our national heritage, is barely readable because the ink faded due to decades of exposure to direct sunlight. The same damage can happen to the dyes in your quilt.

If you want to store your quilt, be sure to let the organic fibers breathe. *Don't store it in plastic.* Don't let it come in contact with untreated wood or ordinary cardboard since the former contains oils that may stain the fibers, and the latter contains acid that can also stain and damage fibers.

The best place to store your quilt is somewhere flat, like on an unused bed. If you have to fold your quilt, be aware that the fibers can weaken along a fold, resulting in fraying and fading. The best way to prevent this from happening is to *change the way the quilt is folded* every six months. If you fold it in halves one time, fold it in thirds the next. If you fold it right side out, reverse the next time and fold inside out. Varying the way you fold a quilt allows the fibers to rest.

With just a little thought and effort, your quilts can last for generations.

Please turn the page
for an exciting sneak peek of
Mary Marks's next Quilting Mystery

KNOT WHAT YOU THINK

coming soon from Kensington Publishing!

CHAPTER 1

I hefted my red tote bag stuffed with sewing supplies, and made my way across my best friend Lucy's newly landscaped front yard. Today was Tuesday, the day we always got together to quilt.

Peeking through a thick layer of redwood mulch were clumps of blues: pungent rosemary, English lavender, and cobalt salvia. Rows of giant white African Lilies on long stalks flanked the wide brick walkway. Dots of yellow kangaroo paws and red flax added more color, while pepper trees provided lacy shade. The water shortage in California was worsening, and homeowners in Los Angeles County were being encouraged to replace their thirsty lawns with drought tolerant plants. Lucy had opted for Mediterranean rather than Mojave Desert as a theme for her new garden. I pushed my way through the front door into the colorful interior of her living room.

"Hey, Martha." My orange-haired friend Lucy waved me over to a blue easy chair. She wore pink linen trousers and a white cotton blouse. On her feet were blue espadrilles with three-inch wedge heels that boosted her height to over six feet. Even though she was in her sixties, Lucy carried herself like a runway model. This morning, she held a pencil and note pad instead of needle and thread. "It's time to plan Birdie's wedding."

Our seventy-seven year old friend Birdie Watson wore her signature denim overalls, white T-shirt and Birkenstock sandals—a style acquired during her hippie days living on a commune. She looked up from her appliqué project and blushed. "At least I won't have to change my last name."

Birdie's longtime husband Russell had been killed during a bank robbery last year. His death brought her back together with Russell's younger brother Denver, the man who had always been her one true love. Lately, the reunited couple divided their time between Birdie's house in Encino, and the Watson ancestral homestead in McMinnville, Oregon, where she was about to become a bride for the second time.

"Have the two of you picked a date yet?" I asked her. "How much time do we have to plan this thing?" I unloaded scraps of fabric from my red tote bag onto a coffee table made of burled tree roots. A black and white cowhide rug lay beneath the table. The décor of Lucy's house screamed Wyoming, where she and her husband Ray had grown up.

Birdie twisted the end of her long white braid. "Denny and I don't want a big fuss, Martha dear. We prefer a simple ceremony with all our family and friends. At our age, we don't have many of those left. So the sooner, the better."

Just then the front door opened, and the newest member of our regular Tuesday morning quilting group breezed into the room. "*Bonjour,*" Jazz Fletcher sang in a very bad French accent. The six foot tall, fifty-something fashion designer crossed the room and claimed an empty space on the sofa beside Birdie, carefully placing his yellow tote bag on the floor next to his feet.

As usual, his chestnut brown hair was perfectly coiffed. My gray curls, on the other hand, were always a little chaotic. Even though Jazz was close to my age of 57, I'd never detected a single silver strand on his head. Apparently he had a close relationship with L'Oréal or Revlon.

Today he wore a yellow silk shirt with a banded collar tucked into ivory twill cargo pants with extra pockets at the calves and ankles. His sole accessories were small diamond studs in his ears, a thin gold watch and a gold wedding band encrusted with diamond baguettes. The wedding ring had come from his longtime lover, Russell Watson.

When Russell died, Birdie was finally free to reveal her husband's deepest secret. Russell was gay, and for the past twenty-five years he'd led a double life posing as a straight banker with Birdie as his wife, while also living with his much younger lover, Jazz Fletcher. When Jazz turned up after the murder, tenderhearted Birdie embraced him and invited him to join our group.

"Sorry we're late." He reached inside the yellow canvas bag and removed his little white Maltese dog—Zsa Zsa Galore. She wore a yellow pinafore sewn with the same silk as his shirt and a rhinestone clip in her topknot. "I had a delivery to make this morning, but it turns out my client wasn't at home." Zsa Zsa jumped off his lap and made the rounds, greeting each of us with a wagging tail.

"You left a message you were bringing a surprise. Do you have it with you?" asked Lucy.

Jazz bent down and extracted a sketch pad from a pocket in the dog carrier and grinned at Birdie. "I wanted to design the perfect wedding dress for you. *Et voila!*" He flourished a drawing of a white lace shift with bell-bottom sleeves and a skirt that ended mid thigh. He passed the image to Birdie. "I remembered seeing a 1960s photo of you in a dress like this. You had fabulous legs, so I thought, why not show them off again? It's very Mary Quant." A satisfied smile split his face. "What do you think?"

Birdie's mouth fell open. She struggled to find the right words. "You've, um, done a beautiful job, Jazz." Long pause. "But it's a little too, ah, youthful for me. My legs don't look like that anymore. I have terrible arthritis in my knees. I'm sorry dear, but there's just no way I'd ever wear a mini dress again. I prefer to cover my legs now."

The more she spoke, the more Jazz's face fell. He slumped his broad shoulders and shrank back into the cushion of the caramel leather sofa, arms crossed and knees pressed together. When Birdie saw his reaction she added, "But you're such a talented designer, I'm sure this dress would be perfect for a younger person."

As we worked on our individual quilts, Lucy served each of us coffee and thick slices of zucchini bread with walnuts and cinnamon courtesy of Birdie's excellent baking. This morning I sorted through the pile of random cotton prints I intended to cut into rectangles for my newest quilt. I chose a design called Prairie Braid which consisted of pieces sewn together in a herringbone pattern. This would become a true "charm quilt."

Charm quilts were a special kind of scrap quilt— where no fabric was repeated. They were first popular during the nineteenth century when cotton calico became affordable and abundant. According to quilting lore, unmarried girls traded scraps of material in order to collect 999 different pieces. The thousandth scrap was supposed to come from the shirt of the young woman's future husband.

Shortly after he joined our group, Jazz had the brilliant idea of opening a business selling custom-made clothing and quilted bedding for dogs. His expert fingers busily sewed the finishing touches on an Irish Chain quilt that was much larger than usual.

"Who are you making that for?" I pointed to the green and white quilt cascading over his long legs. "Isn't it a little big for a dog's bed?"

He ended off his thread and cut a new length from a spool of green. "I've got a customer in Beverly Hills with an Irish Wolfhound. When the dog stands on his hind legs, he's nearly as tall as me."

"Beverly Hills? So business must be good," Birdie said.

Jazz threw his hands in the air and arched his eyebrows. "I can hardly keep up with the demand.

I just finished an order for my manscaper, Dolleen Doyle."

"Man what?" Birdie's eyes widened.

Jazz cleared his throat. "Manscaper. That's someone who specializes in male waxing. Dolleen's the best. She has a salon on Rodeo Drive in Beverly Hills. I always see at least one movie star when I'm there."

Birdie seemed mesmerized. "You get waxed?"

Jazz's cheeks colored. "After Rusty died, I sort of let myself go. But I started working out again and visiting her salon. One day, while she gave me a Brazilian, she ordered an extensive wardrobe for her Chihuahua, Patti. She also commissioned three coordinating dog carriers."

"I didn't know you had expanded your line to include carriers," said Lucy.

He shrugged. "Dolleen's just like me. She takes that dog everywhere with her. Even to work."

Birdie laughed. "I'm surprised she didn't want quilts, too."

Jazz wagged a forefinger. "*Au contraire.* Not only did she order quilts, she wanted four whole bedding ensembles. She asked me to rush the order. I agreed to deliver everything last night, but that didn't work out. Actually, I'm really annoyed." He closed his eyes halfway and sniffed. "I drove all the way to the Valley from my boutique in West Hollywood to deliver everything at the time we agreed. But when I got there, she was gone. I could hear Patti barking inside, but Dolleen never answered the door. Frankly, I was surprised. I've never known her to be flaky. Just the opposite. She's a sharp businesswoman. Anyway, I ended up taking the entire delivery back home with me."

"Why didn't you just leave the package on her doorstep?" asked Lucy.

"Oh no!" Jazz gasped. "You can't leave stuff on the porch anymore. Package pirates come by and steal everything. Don't you watch the news? Anyway, I thought I'd try again this morning. She lives in Tarzana, not that far from here, but she still wasn't home. I hung around for several minutes and tried calling and texting, but she wouldn't answer her phone. That's why I was late."

The hairs on the back of my neck tingled. "You said she never goes anywhere without her dog?"

Jazz nodded.

"Yet she left the Chihuahua alone in the house last night? Even though she knew you were on your way over? And then again this morning?"

Jazz nodded again, this time more slowly.

I immediately thought of the time Lucy, Birdie, and I discovered the body of another quilter in her house, and—more than a year ago—how the body of yet another friend had lain undiscovered in her bedroom closet for ten months. I didn't want to alarm him, but a bad feeling gathered in the pit of my stomach. "Jazz, maybe you should try calling her again. Just to make sure she's not sick or something." My bad feeling grew at the possibility of the woman lying helpless on the floor after a stroke, or worse.

His face turned pale and he stared at me. "Now you're beginning to scare me, Martha Rose."

Lucy's head snapped up sharply and said just one

word. "Martha!" But the tone of her voice spoke volumes. I clearly heard the caution and the *Oh no, not again.*

Birdie spoke quietly and twisted the end of her long, white braid. "Well, you have to admit, it does sound suspicious."

Jazz punched his cell phone and waited. After a minute he ended the call and looked at me. "Nothing."

I took a deep breath. "Since she's close by, maybe we should go over to her house and peek in the windows or something. If she's incapacitated, she'll need help."

Lucy scowled. "Or maybe we ought to call the police instead, and have *them* check on her. After all, it's their job."

I understood what she left unsaid. If we happened to stumble on yet another suspicious death, her husband Ray would *plotz.* The way he saw it, I'd put Lucy's life in jeopardy before, and I wasn't sure he had any room left to forgive me if it happened again.

Jazz put down the quilt and jumped off the sofa. "I'm going over there right now! I'll break down the door if I have to."

At the sound of his outburst, Zsa Zsa trotted over to him and barked once. Jazz picked her up.

Birdie began putting her sewing things away. "I think we should go with Jazz. We'd never forgive ourselves if we knew this woman was in trouble and did nothing to help."

Lucy sighed and slowly pushed up from her chair. "Okay, okay. But only to investigate from *outside* the house. If we discover something bad, we're calling the police. Agreed?"

"Agreed," Birdie and I responded together. Jazz merely pursed his lips.

The four of us piled into Lucy's vintage black Cadillac with the shark fins in back. Jazz leaned forward in the backseat and tapped Lucy's shoulder. "Take Ventura to Lindley and turn left." Five minutes later we pulled into the driveway of a one story mid-century house just south of Ventura Boulevard. "This is it!" Jazz unbuckled his seatbelt even before Lucy turned off the engine.

We followed as he hugged Zsa Zsa to his chest and marched rapidly to the woman's front porch. Jazz pounded on the door and rang the bell. All we heard were the frantic yelps of one very small, very agitated dog. He turned to us with deep concern etched between his eyebrows.

We stepped sideways to a large picture window on the front of the house. A red sofa was pushed in front of the glass. A buff-colored Chihuahua stood on the back of the sofa and yipped at us. Then she raised her head, curled her lips, and began to howl. Zsa Zsa tensed, barked back, and looked at Jazz as if to say, *What are you going to do about this?*

Jazz at six feet and Lucy even taller with those wedge heels had the best view of the home's interior. "Can you see anything?" I asked.

Lucy stepped back from the window and shook her head.

I pointed to the driveway. "Let's keep going."

We hurried around to the side of the house and

peered through a dining room window. Nothing. Farther down the wall we spied a kitchen window. It was too high for Birdie and me, but Jazz and Lucy could peek inside if they stood on their toes.

"Oh my God!" said Lucy. "She's on the floor."

We ran around the corner to the back of the house looking for a door into the kitchen. Jazz didn't need to break it down. When he tried the handle it easily swung open. We rushed inside behind him, forgetting about our promise to call the police first. We stopped when we saw the blood.

Jazz rocked back on his heels and grabbed the granite counter for support. Zsa Zsa shook violently and whined so pitifully, he carried her outside, using the walls to steady himself. Birdie turned green and followed him into the fresh air. Lucy and I grasped each other for support. Patti looked at us from ten feet away and whined.

Dolleen Doyle's arms stretched away from her body, and her legs twisted to the side where she fell. Strands of blond hair lay across her face as if blown there by a hostile breeze. The top of her pink robe hung open to reveal abnormally large breasts barely contained in an expensive black lace bra. I estimated her age to be in her thirties, judging by the fine wrinkles just beginning to show at the corners of her unseeing eyes. Who did she remind me of?

Frantic Chihuahua tracks dotted the floor in all directions, from the puddle under her head into the living room and back again. The blood had turned dark brown where it had dried, indicating she'd been lying there since the day before. Clearly, Dolleen Doyle would never get up again.

Lucy closed her eyes and shook her head. "Dang it. I can't believe we found another dead body. Please don't say anything to Ray. I'm sure this was just an accident. She must have just slipped and fell."

I scanned the room to see if I could determine what she could have fallen against. A thready trail of blood on the floor led away from her body to where an aluminum trash can stood. I pulled it away from the wall.

A two pound metal hand weight had rolled behind the can from where it had been dropped. Blood and strands of blond hair covered one end. The room spun when I stood, so I grabbed Lucy's arm for support.

"This was no accident, Lucy. This was murder."